BLOOD TROUBLE

GOD WARS SERIES, BOOK TWO

CONNIE SUTTLE

Print Second Edition (2018)
Print ISBN: 1-63478-056-6
Print ISBN-13: 978-1-63478-056-8
eBook ISBN: 1-93975-902-1
eBook ISBN-13: 978-1-93975-902-3

Published by:
SubtleDemon Publishing, LLC
PO Box 95696
Oklahoma City, OK 73143

Cover art by Renée Barratt @ The Cover Counts

To Walter, Joe, Larry, Lee, Dianne, Sarah and Mark.
Thank you.

And for Brandy, Lisa, Dolly, Susan and Sharyn—you keep me going.
Thanks!

ACKNOWLEDGMENTS

As always, this book is the result of collaboration. If it weren't for the support of my editor, my cover artist and my beta readers, it would be less than it is. All mistakes, as usual, are mine and no other's.

About the Author:
Connie Suttle lives in Oklahoma with her husband and a conglomerate of cats. They have finally banded together to make their demands, which has proven disconcerting to all humans involved.

You may find Connie in the following ways:
Facebook: Connie Suttle Author
Twitter: @subtledemon
Website and Blog: subtledemon.com

~

R-D Series:

Cloud Dust

Cloud Invasion

Cloud Rebel

~

Latter Day Demons Series:

Hot Demon in the City

A Demon's Work is Never Done

A Demon's Due

~

Seattle Elementals Series:

Your Money's Worth

Worth Your While*

~

BlackWing Pirates Series

MindSighted

MindMage

MindRogue

MindMaster*

~

Black Rose Sorceress Series

The Rose Mark

Rose and Thorn

Black Rose Queen

Queen of Thorns and Roses

Future Wars Series

Buffer Zone

Black Zone*

Other Titles from SubtleDemon Publishing:

Malefactor

Transgressor

Underhanded*

by Joe Scholes

*Forthcoming

PROLOGUE

"There is one last thing you must do," a shining one informed Li'Neruh Rath.

"What is that?" Li'Neruh Rath, *Darkest Star* in the High Demon language, bowed respectfully to the one before him.

"You must explore humanoid sexuality. All facets of it."

"Is that necessary?"

"Yes. If you are to walk among them, you must act as they do. All of them. Not just those accepted as the norm, but those who may not be so readily accepted. You must understand all of it—their motivations, desires, passions, urges—everything."

"But I have already done so many things. I have studied criminal behavior on countless worlds. Have engaged in wars, from the lowest to highest-ranking soldiers. Worked as a healer for those not only sick in body, but also in mind. What more do you want of me?"

Li'Neruh wanted to shudder. Coming from the light as he had, and accepting the assignment to watch over the Dark Realm and its god had been a sacrifice. A very great sacrifice—for him. Before, he had no contact with the created races. After accepting the position, he'd been thrust among them without knowing them. He knew them now, from the best to the worst.

"Li'Neruh, were you not promised a reward, should you accomplish this work?" The shining one shook his head—a very human gesture.

"I was, but I took the assignment because I was asked and not for any reward you might offer."

"Then it is my hope that your duty and obligation will be greatly rewarded, and that it will exceed your desires and expectations."

"Where should I go, then, to experience these things?" Li'Neruh blinked as information filtered into his mind.

Breanne's Journal

I always wanted to see San Francisco. Had never had an opportunity to go there—too many things stood in my way, least of all my appearance and disabilities. Today, I was seeing it from a distance on a cool, foggy morning in early August. The top of the Golden Gate Bridge was the only thing visible as I stood at a lookout in the Marin Headlands, on the other side of San Francisco Bay.

I'd come to Earth in the past, hoping to get to my own past and *Change What Was*. Something prevented me from getting any closer than I had. Two years had passed since then. At the present, Lissa had been gone from the planet for two years—I'd arrived shortly after she was taken away by our shared sperm donor, and after discovering that I couldn't travel farther backward than that, I'd chosen San Francisco as my new home. Did the two events coincide, somehow—that she'd be gone almost the moment I showed up? I had no idea.

Even after learning that I couldn't get to my past to change important parts of it, I'd decided to stay. Lissa had returned to Le-Ath Veronis; therefore, there was no need for me to remain. Gavin, I'm sure, was delighted to be without a vampire child, and there was little chance that any of them might come looking for me.

I'd been a convenience—somebody to fill a void left by the Vampire Queen. If I'd stayed, even with the power and abilities I held, I'd likely be stuck in a tiny office again, transferring funds for this group or that individual until somebody ordered me to go do something they couldn't accomplish on their own. My personal purgatory, after becoming vampire that is, seemed to be eternal life as a lowly public servant. I'm sure there was a joke there, I just wasn't in any mood to solve the punchline.

In the two years I'd been on Earth, I'd accomplished many things, but the first of those things had been using power to create an identity so I'd fit in again. I now had a Social Security number, an address, and anything else I might need to survive as a human. I just wasn't human. Not anymore. Well, that wasn't completely true. I'd always been a quarter Karathian witch, an eighth Elemaiyan, half human and another eighth I didn't want to guess at.

The second thing I'd done was buy a lottery ticket with a dollar I found on the street near Fisherman's Wharf. It had been soggy and ragged, that dollar, but it had been accepted after I'd filled out the numbers for the next lottery drawing.

Yes, it was probably cheating, but I figured cosmic karma ought to kick in somewhere. I'd won four hundred million and took the cash option, netting nearly two hundred million after taxes. I'd also done something I always wanted to do after renting an apartment with my newfound wealth—I hired an attorney and set up an anonymous charitable foundation, placing a priority on helping children.

The next thing I'd done (so as not to be completely bored), was to volunteer for Mercy Crossings, a charity that arranged for health professionals and volunteers to help wherever needed, and usually it was in the poorest and most vulnerable places on Earth.

The Director of Mercy Crossings had been skeptical at first, when I walked into his office in Los Angeles nearly two years before, asking to volunteer. I had no medical career and absolutely no credentials. What I did have was an understanding of and the ability to speak any language on the globe. I also had compulsion and employed it on several occasions to deal with this despot or that warlord, in order to clear a path for the needed personnel and supplies. Mercy Crossings had certainly benefited from my volunteering.

The last thing I'd done, and this I'd done for my own peace of mind, was to promise myself not to read anyone unless there was no other choice. I'd be happier and it would give anyone I encountered an even playing field—they'd be judged as everyone else saw them and not by their past, which only I might see. Things were so much better that way.

Sighing and hunching my shoulders against the early morning cold, I misted back to San Francisco and stood in line at my favorite coffee shop to get a latte. While I was walking back to my one-bedroom apartment, which lay on the second floor above an empty storefront, I saw Hank Bell for the first time.

He drove a green Chevy truck that shuddered as it died when he parked it on the street in front of my apartment. I'll admit I blinked at him when he exited the truck, before deciding that it was rude to gape.

Was he handsome? Handsome couldn't come close to Hank Bell. Handsome would have to take the very back seat on a very long train to Hank Bell's strikingly beautiful features. Without glancing in my direction even once, he strode purposely toward the rather large crate a delivery crew had left in front of the empty shop's door.

I'd slowed my steps so I could watch him for a few seconds longer before searching for the key to unlock the door leading to my upstairs apartment, and noticed that he was checking his watch. Then, I listened as he cursed under his breath.

"Fuck, shit and damn," he muttered. I shouldn't have heard. With a vampire's sharp hearing, I heard every word.

"Need help?" I asked, pulling the apartment key from my purse.

Jerking his head up in a startled fashion, he blinked as if noticing me for the first time.

"Where did you come from?" he asked.

"Texas."

"After that," he grumped sarcastically.

"From the coffee shop." I held up my latte cup.

"I'd kill for coffee, right now. And then I'd kill my partner, for not being here to help with this fucking safe."

"Do you think that safe is going anywhere?" I lifted an eyebrow. "It probably weighs a ton. Literally."

"At least a thousand pounds," he agreed, raking fingers through dark-as-sin hair.

"You can leave it there and I'll buy you coffee. I doubt wandering gangs or packs of criminals will come by and haul it away while you're gone. They'll get a hernia."

"I really want to get it inside, then I need to make a list of supplies to fix the place up. The goal is to open in three months." Dark eyes blinked in my direction.

"This place has been empty the whole time I've lived over it," I pointed out. "And that's nearly two years. I doubt it's going anywhere, either."

"I got a really good deal on it, because it's been available so long," he said, drumming his fingers on the crate's top.

"I can help you get the safe inside, I think," I offered. Yes, all this was so out of character for me, but something drew me to this man, and I sure couldn't explain any of it. I was tempted to read him, too, but squashed that thought quickly.

"You think you can?" He was finally giving me his full attention, but as it was cold out, I'd dressed in a bulky sweater and jacket and he probably thought I was a short, humanoid roly-poly.

"Yeah. I think I can," I nodded before setting my latte beside the stairwell door. I felt bad that I couldn't tell him I was vampire and could haul the stupid safe inside his new store without batting an eye.

"Well," he sounded indecisive.

"Give it a try," I said. "Who knows? Stranger things have probably happened."

"Probably," he raked long, well-shaped fingers through his hair again. Honestly, he needed to stop that. I was watching those fingers much too closely as it was.

"Let me unlock the door." He pushed back the metal security gate first, then squeezed into the narrow space left between the door and the crated safe before putting a key in the lock and opening the door with a wooden scrape. Looked like the door would have to be replaced, along with a lot of other things.

Holding back the majority of my strength, I worked with him as we scooted the heavy crate first this way and then that, to shove it through the door. Once it was inside far enough, he studied it with a critical eye before hauling out a cellphone and punching in a number. It rang three times before someone picked up.

"Paul?" he said when someone—a sleepy someone—answered.

"Yeah? Hank?"

"Yes, it's Hank. Where the fuck are you?"

"Late night, man. Look, I'll be there in an hour." The call ended.

"Well, I'll just go, then." I edged toward the door as Hank looked ready to explode. Anger frightened me. Had, for a very long time.

"You're not buying coffee?" Hank asked.

"What? Oh, yeah. Coffee. The Lean Bean is a block down." I pointed vaguely in the proper direction.

"Come on. I'll be mad later."

"You can do that? Be mad later? Dang, why didn't I think of that?" I said before I thought. He grinned. I wanted to gape. If I'd thought he looked good before, it just got ramped up a few thousand notches.

"Hank Bell," he stuck out a hand and officially introduced himself.

"Breanne Hayworth." My hand was engulfed in his as we shook. Yes, I'd taken my old last name. I'd just never had proper ID before. I wasn't supposed to be on anybody's radar in the past—by design.

"This is good coffee," Hank said later, after we'd chosen a tiny table at The Lean Bean. The fog was lifting outside, with occasional patches of sunlight shining through. We were just outside the Castro District in San Francisco, and if you were curious—or even if you weren't—you might see just about anything there. "I wasn't sure we were going to get that safe moved, but you're tougher than I thought." Hank broke into my thoughts.

"You know, I get that a lot," I agreed, shucking my jacket. It was warmer inside the coffee shop, and I sure didn't want to start sweating while staring at Hank. More than I already was, anyway.

"Paul and I decided last year we wanted to open our own club, but it took a while to put the financing together," Hank said, sipping more coffee. He'd asked for a caramel mocha, and it smelled almost as good as he did.

"What did you do before?" I asked. He didn't wear a ring and only wore a plain white T under a leather jacket.

"Paramedic. Quit last week after I signed the paperwork. Paul is supposed to pay for the renovations on the bar, so I made the down payment and signed my name on the papers."

"Was Paul a paramedic, too?"

"Yeah. He's still working, but he's supposed to turn in his notice today so we can get started on the building this weekend." It was Friday, so they'd be working on it pretty quick. "What do you do?" he asked, sipping more of his drink.

"I'm in between assignments. I volunteer for Mercy Crossings."

"You don't hold an eight-to-five?"

"No. At the moment, I can afford not to." I studied my paper cup, which was nearly empty, instead of meeting his gaze.

"What do you do in between, then?"

"I run most mornings. I read a lot. Do a little traveling." I did, I just didn't use conventional methods to do it. I'd been in places I'd never thought I'd go, because I could fold there and back.

"How far? Running, that is?"

"Usually five miles or so. It lets me clear my head."

"Your head needs clearing?"

"Yeah. It's more cluttered than the warehouse in *Raiders of the Lost Ark*."

"How cluttered was that?" he chewed a plastic stir-stick he'd grabbed from the condiment bar and grinned.

"Dang, don't you ever go to movies? You could fit Pluto inside that warehouse. Not the dog, the planet."

"I heard Pluto wasn't a planet anymore."

"It's a dwarf planet. Are you a planet racist? You don't consider dwarf planets to be real planets?"

"I didn't say that. I'm sure Pluto is still a card-carrying celestial body in the solar system, but it can't get on some of the rides at theme parks because it's not tall enough."

"Are you saying that Pluto can't get into R-rated movies unless it's accompanied by Jupiter or Saturn? Is that what you're saying?"

"I'm saying it can order off the dwarf planet menu at any restaurant. That's all I'm saying." His grin had widened, and dark eyes gleamed wickedly at me. Any other woman would probably have swooned where she sat. Me? I wanted to turn into a puddle of helpless goo. I think he could have asked for the Moon right then, and I would have handed it and all the other moons and planets (including the dwarf one) right over.

His cellphone rang, breaking the moment and the mood. His partner, Paul was on the phone. "Look, Hank," he began, "I'm having second thoughts. Jorge wants to move in with me and well, I don't think I can do this. Sorry." Paul hung up while Hank stood and cursed.

"How much?" I asked. Yeah, I was probably setting myself up for real trouble, but Hank had been silent after his initial bout of quiet cursing, and we now made the short walk back to the shop and my apartment over it without speaking. Until I'd broken the silence, anyway.

"What?" It took a few seconds for him to turn toward me.

"How much? To renovate the shop?"

"Probably fifty grand, with us—me—doing all the labor." Dark eyes raked my face, as if he were attempting to determine my reason for asking.

"I have a lawyer. How much of an interest in the business will I have if I put up that money? I can do minor stuff, too, to help out."

Hank blinked for a moment before replying. "Paul was getting a third," he sighed. "Look, you don't have to worry about me. I'm a stranger, and most people don't have that kind of money lying around."

"I can do it," I shrugged. After all, if this turned sour, there was always compulsion. I was hoping things would work out, although I'd only just met him.

"How about this—you take a fourth interest, and I pay half back," Hank countered my offer.

"Is that what you want?" I looked up at him—he was more than a foot taller than I was.

"I don't have a choice. I put everything I had into the down payment, and there'll be no business if I can't renovate."

"Then I'll have my lawyer draw up a contract."

We spent most of the afternoon in Terry Johnston's office, hammering out a simple contract with a payment schedule after the business—a nightclub—opened.

I wrote a check from my personal account for fifty thousand and handed it to Hank.

"Thanks. What are you doing tomorrow morning—around seven?" Hank stuffed the check in his wallet as he asked the question.

"Getting back from a run, usually."

"Meet me downstairs afterward, and we can make a list of what we need."

"All right. I've never really renovated anything, so this will be a learning experience."

"Exactly."

∼

"The power signature was detected in two different time periods, and neither registered long enough to track it properly." The lieutenant reported the findings to his superior.

"Meaning this one hasn't stayed long enough to draw our attention again in any particular period," came the reply.

"Or that the Mighty has ceased expending energy in that timeframe. I have several searching in both, but nothing has been reported."

"Keep searching. I have planted many throughout time, and each has been instructed to perform specific tasks, designed to draw one out. I find it amusing that they weren't to know what they were after their birth—that it would be discovered by accident, for the most part. A very great flaw, wouldn't you say, that it would be easy to discover them? They find their power and before they learn to hide it, they use it indiscriminately?"

"I find it humorous that they don't know one another," the lieutenant's face held a grimace—he wasn't used to smiling and that was as close as he might get.

"You should work on your humanoid expressions, they are lacking."

"Of course."

~

"Trajan."

"I heard."

"Traje, I'm not sure what to say."

"Then don't talk." Trajan clipped off another limb—he'd gone to help Bear Wright trim trees between fruit bearing seasons.

"Will it help to tell you that she seems to be powerful? Renegar says she's the Vhanaraszh."

"I don't know what that means." Trajan jerked on the pruning saw, allowing the cut branch to drop away.

"It means Restorer, in Larentii."

"What does that mean?"

"It means she can do alone what all five of the Larentii Wise Ones can do together."

"You should have let her look at Kay, then. I knew she could read anybody. She could tell you immediately what's wrong with Kay."

"What?" Ashe stared at Trajan in shock before cursing and tugging at his hair.

"I'm telling you, you screwed up. Breanne could read almost anybody, and tell you everything about them. Kevis can't get Kay to talk, and he says she's an unreadable. I don't think that would stop Breanne. Go ahead, ask Gavin or Queen Lissa. I heard she saved Grey

House's bacon, too, but I couldn't get the full story on that one. She's been gone three weeks, Ashe, and nobody knows where she is. Nobody knows where to look, either. She's gone, plain and simple."

"Traje, I didn't mean to take her away from you. You know that. I was terrified Kalia—Kay—would be upset. I know you wanted to bring Breanne here—I could see it easily. You wanted to get her away from Le-Ath Veronis—admit it."

"Because she was being mistreated."

"I know. I didn't wait for you to explain anything, I just lost my temper. Look, if she shows up again, I'll do my best to get her here to take a look at Kay. I'll grovel if that's what it takes."

"I'll have to grovel first, and that probably won't work. You say she's powerful? What can I do against that?"

"Traje, I've given you a lot. You don't use half what I gave you."

"I usually don't need it. You don't use a jackhammer to hang a picture."

"I understand that." The corner of Ashe's mouth curved slightly.

~

Lissa's Journal

"Are you kidding?" I stared at the report on a comp-vid—Grant had shoved it into my hands and showed me what only a few months of collecting taxes had accomplished toward paying the crown's expenses. Breanne had done that for me, while I'd been gone.

She'd done so many things to benefit Le-Ath Veronis in my absence, and Gavin and Cheedas had given her nothing but grief the whole time. Cheedas, too, had been manipulated in some way—Belen informed me of that. I'd also learned that he and Gavin had suffered from a mind cloud. If Gavin had done the mistreatment on his own, he'd still be locked out of the bedroom.

Cheedas still wouldn't talk to me and disappeared if I came anywhere near—he was deeply ashamed, although his actions had been coerced. Yes, I recalled my death, as did he. I think, at times, he felt a hundred times worse about it than I did.

The mind cloud had been removed at least—Belen saw to that. He told me he'd removed it from Gavril, anyway, so it was likely he'd done the same for Gavin and Cheedas. We were still no closer to locating Breanne, though. Belen didn't seem to think it a bad thing—he worried that she might be a target if she stayed in one place for long.

"Mom?" I jerked around to see Gavril standing at the door to my study, as if I'd called him.

"Gav?" I sighed when I looked at his face. Something was wrong. Would he tell me what that was? Probably not. He and Gavin wore the same look on most days—as if they'd done something horrible and weren't ready to own up to it yet.

"Dad and I have talked. Several times."

"I know." I did. My son just hadn't bothered to talk to me. Until now.

"I didn't know, Mom. How was I to know she was related? Nobody knew that, except you."

"If you'd been a little nicer, she could have told you herself," I snapped.

"She knew?"

"The whole time. She saw it in your face. Saw it in my face, whenever she looked at a photograph. Nothing like getting mistreated by family, huh?" I lowered my eyes and pretended to scroll through figures on the comp-vid. "You had that asshole hit her in the face and break bones."

"That'll follow me until the end of time," Gavril muttered, ducking his head.

"Probably just like the fact that your father sired a vampire, and then did absolutely nothing in the sire department. He didn't teach her a single thing, starved her and worked her—with your help—day and night. I've been advised, you see." I still didn't look up from the comp-vid.

"Your assistants hired that dickhead Rathik Erwin, who stole from her and got her attacked by the other dickhead, Skel Hawer," Gavril attempted to deflect my wrath onto new targets.

"I've already had that discussion—with my assistants and with Norian," I snapped. "You, on the other hand, see fit to speak with your father several times, while I, having been gone for months, see you three weeks after I return—temporary death notwithstanding."

"Yeah. That's just, well, Mom, I'm sorry."

"If your aunt hadn't been here and decided, even after you and your father did your best to kill her, to save my ass anyway, where would we be right now? Answer that, will you?"

"Mom, you know I don't have any excuse. Sometimes I wish you'd just punch me and get it over with."

"Gavril Tybus Montegue, that's pure stupidity, so stop it now. You don't know what it's like to get punched in the face by someone who's supposed to be your parent. I do. Take your lumps. You fucked up. Admit it." I threw the comp-vid in my hand at the wall so hard it shattered. "Grant will just have to use the crown's funds to buy another one," I growled. "Gavril, go home. Come back when you're more sorry and I'm less pissed." He disappeared and I wiped away stubborn tears.

"We have another aunt," Kyler rubbed her forehead. "Why couldn't we see it?"

"I get the idea that not many can," Cleo sighed. Kyler had come to visit Grey House when Cleo sent mindspeech. "I healed her headache and still didn't know I was putting my hands on a relative."

"Lissa's really upset, according to Flavio. She barely talks to Gavin, and threw Norian out of the palace. Flavio says she used power and sent all of Norian's stuff to Ildevar's palace on Wyyld."

"What would you do? He almost let an attempted murderer go."

"He would have, but Ildevar told him to put Hawer in jail."

"At least Ildevar remembers the law. Norian doesn't seem to."

"Daddy still wants to reward Breanne somehow, but how can you do that if nobody can find her?"

"At least we're not being bled dry by Bexari anymore and the wizards are getting more days off. Nissa, Toff, Yoff and Trik have been to Le-Ath Veronis four times since Lissa got back."

"That's probably a relief to all of them," Kyler observed, brushing back long, auburn hair. "Daddy says that Toff and Trik will make First Level soon."

"That'll make Nissa happy. Since she made Master Wizard level, she's felt a little guilty."

"Any idea where Breanne might go? I'd really like to talk to her. Nobody knows what her background is or anything. All we know is she's from Texas, and that's because Erland and Rylend treated her well."

"Both of them are so good," Cleo sighed. "Ry was the best choice for the throne. Wyatt wanted to be a healer so badly."

"Have you seen him lately? Garwin Wyatt?"

"No. Still at that prep school on Wyyld."

"Doesn't appear to be interested in healing, this time."

"Yeah. Too bad. I hope he learns more from Lissa than he does from his father."

"Teeg is too heavy-handed. I wonder if he knows people say that about him?"

"Would it matter? He's got Gavin in him. Goes and does what he thinks ought to be done, and be damned with everybody else."

"Yeah."

CHAPTER 1

"I found an antique bar on the Internet and ordered it last night. Three thousand, but it'll be more than worth it after it's refinished." Hank grabbed two paint cans from the back of his truck and walked toward the door of his soon-to-be nightclub.

We'd spent the morning buying supplies at a local home improvement warehouse after putting an extensive list together. We had paint, tape, paintbrushes, boxes of wood flooring, sinks for the bathrooms and bar, light fixtures—his truck was completely filled and we hadn't gotten a fourth of what the list contained.

"We'll have to clear it out, first," I gazed about me after we'd piled supplies in a corner near the window.

"Yeah. I have one of those construction containers rented for trash and debris; they're supposed to drop it off this afternoon in the alley behind us." Hank stood roughly four feet away from me, surveying the space just as I was. Three ancient display cases stood against a wall, and they were in such bad shape we couldn't even give them away. Trash, dust and debris littered every available surface, including the ancient, vinyl tile floor.

"I can see why you wanted wood flooring," I muttered, toeing a cracked tile, which lifted and scooted away. "At least it looks like it'll come up easy."

"I hope so. We've got a ton of stuff to do before we can even start painting and laying the new floor."

"Lovely," I muttered.

"Afraid of hard work?" He turned to me and grinned. Well, he might have to stop smiling—in any form. I never wanted to lean against anyone so much in my life. Could I explain that? *Nope.*

"I know hard work. Hard work knows me. We're like this," I held up two fingers twined together. Hank chuckled. It was a heavenly sound.

"Well, shall we?"

"Yeah." I pulled on work gloves, grabbed a box of industrial strength trash bags and started clearing away the clutter.

"I still don't understand how you can do this—the side of this trash container is almost as tall as you are," Hank said later.

"Are you saying I'm short?" I said, attempting to pull him away from any evidence of my unnatural strength. We'd just lifted the third rickety display case over the edge of the metal receptacle and dropped it in with a crash.

"Undertall? Vertically challenged?" He was grinning again. Both of us were covered in dust and grime; I hadn't bothered to look at my face in a mirror—the tiny facility at the back of the shop was nothing more than a cube with a broken toilet, a stained sink and no mirror. We'd already swept up shards of the mirror that had previously hung over the sink.

The sad thing? Hank looked good, even covered in dust and grime. I probably looked like an ostrich after a dust bath. An undersized ostrich, anyway.

"Dinner?" Hank sighed after we'd mutually agreed to stop working at nine that evening. At least the place looked minutely better when we stopped.

"I can't go like this," I held out the hem of my gray T-shirt—it was filthy.

"Meet me at Bogey's in an hour, then. That'll give us both time to go home and clean up." Hank's grin was tired, this time. I didn't grin, but I felt exhausted. Hungry, too. We'd ordered pizza for lunch, and the delivery boy had stared at our mess as Hank handed over a wrinkled twenty as payment.

"Bogey's?" I blinked at Hank.

"A bar two blocks south. They have a decent menu, and they stay open late."

"Because it's a bar," I nodded.

"Yeah. You may even find something for your awkward, inconvenient vegetarian preferences."

"Hey," I frowned at him. "I don't eat animals. They don't eat me. It's a good system."

"What if you're attacked in the woods by a hungry wolf? Or a bear?"

"I don't go into the woods," I pretended offense.

"A rabid seal or sea lion, then?"

"If I knew you better, I'd just shake my head and call you hopeless," I said. "Besides, if I'm eaten or attacked by evil, mutant sea lions, then it's probably karma or something."

"Come on, short karma woman, I'm starved. Go clean up. I'll lock up, drive home, shower and still get to Bogey's ahead of you."

"Are we issuing a challenge?" My fists automatically went to my hips in mock indignation.

"Women always take forever," Hank rolled his eyes and drew out the word forever.

"If Paul were here, would you be insulting him like this?" I lifted an eyebrow while my fists remained firmly planted on my hips.

"I'd be calling him prick or asshole, but he can drag his heels, too." Hank was enjoying himself, I could tell.

"Unbelievable," I muttered, shaking my head. "Look, you do all those testosterone-inducing things you mentioned earlier, and I'll go upstairs, get a shower and show up at Bogey's when I feel like it. Don't wait on me to order or stuff your face." I turned and stalked toward the door.

"Hey, now, I'm teasing," he called softly behind me.

"I know. I am, too." I kept walking.

~

"What's this?" A flat-screen television hung over the bar to the left of Hank's booth, and the news was on. I settled on the opposite side and wriggled out of my jacket—the fog and mist had drifted in again and the temperature had dropped outside.

"Missing college students," Hank muttered, emptying a mixed drink.

"When?"

"Earlier tonight. At least that's when they were reported. Two freshmen girls."

"Not good," I sighed. "Did you order?"

"Nah. Waited on you."

"I told you not to."

"I know. It didn't seem right. Besides, I needed a drink to unwind."

"What's that?" I nodded to his glass.

"Old fashioned. They make good ones, here. Not everybody does."

"Care for a drink?" A waiter sidled up to our table.

"Glass of wine? Soda?" Hank lifted an eyebrow in my direction.

"White wine," I nodded. "Not too dry. And some water."

"I'll get that and come back for your order, Mr. Bell." The waiter turned and walked toward the bar.

"You a regular, here?"

"Yeah. My apartment is nearby."

"Ah."

"And they're open late. Works out well if you're assigned to swing shift," he added, chewing on two slender, red drink straws that came with his old fashioned.

"Glad to leave that behind?" I asked, meaning his work as a paramedic.

"Yeah. It was taxing, to say the least. Not that I didn't mind saving lives; it was the ones I couldn't help."

"Understood," I nodded as glasses of white wine and ice water were set on bar napkins in front of me.

"Know what you want?" Hank grinned before going back to chewing his red straws.

"I haven't even looked at the menu," I muttered, opening the item in question and staring at the plastic-covered sheets inside. "Grilled cheese sandwich?" I looked up at our waiter, "with fries and a side salad?"

"Dressing?" He wasn't writing anything down. I always admired waitstaff who could do that—keep everything in their head.

"Red wine vinaigrette?"

"Sure. The usual, Mr. Bell?"

"Yeah."

Hank's usual turned out to be a roast beef and Swiss sandwich, toasted, with fries and a half-order of onion rings.

"They let you order a half-order of rings?" It hadn't been listed on the menu.

"Tommy will bring me anything I want," he said.

"Because you're a regular."

"Yeah."

I wanted to tell him that he cleaned up nice. I didn't. He was clean, smelled really good and wore a yellow polo over dark jeans and boots. His leather jacket lay on the seat beside him. Dark eyes caught me staring at him. I dropped my gaze.

"So, Texas, huh?"

"Yeah. The hot-as-hell-in-August part."

"That describes most of Texas."

"It does," I agreed.

"You don't have much of an accent."

"I can do the accent." My "I" came out "ah."

"I can see that. Hear it, too." Another old fashioned was set at his elbow, and he hadn't even ordered the thing. He really was a regular. Our food came shortly after that, so we didn't talk for a while.

"Want me to drive you home?" Hank asked as he shrugged into his jacket after paying the bill. I'd offered to cover mine and he'd declined, handing Tommy a credit-card.

"It's only two blocks. I can walk." I buttoned up my jacket against the mist and chill outside.

"You sure?"

"I'm sure."

"Be downstairs at seven-thirty tomorrow morning?" he asked.

"I'll be there. I'll try to get up and run first, though."

"Suit yourself." I walked away after flinging a half-wave behind me. Hank didn't even say good-bye.

CHAPTER 2

I did go for a run the following morning, but I ran three miles instead of five, and went early enough so I could run near the wharf before the tourists started showing up in droves. It still meant I had to hurry through a shower to get to the shop downstairs at the designated time. I was on time, though.

"Punctual," Hank nodded as he unlocked the metal gate and slid it aside before putting his shoulder to the stubborn, ill-fitting door and pushing his way inside.

"Well, the cleaning elves didn't show up during the night," I said, surveying the main room while chewing my lower lip.

"Or the painting elves or the tile elves," Hank agreed. "Would you rather clean walls before we spackle and prime, or scrape up old tiles?"

"What do you want to do?" I asked. "I can do the other. It doesn't matter to me."

"I'll scrape tile."

"Then I'll clean walls."

"Sore shoulders?" Hank asked when we broke for lunch. I did have sore shoulders from reaching high and low to clean walls. I'd have to get a short ladder and go around the main space a second time, to get what I couldn't reach on the first pass. "We need to replace about half the baseboards, too," I sighed. "I think they had some kind of water damage in the past. The bottom is rotted out on some of the wood."

"Damn," Hank swore softly.

"I'll get it. It can't be much, can it? Do you have a table saw?"

"I can borrow one," he said. "I know somebody who lives across the bay who has a lot of power tools."

"Then you handle the borrowing and I'll see about getting baseboards."

"After we eat," he said, pointing a finger in my direction.

"Sure. What are we eating, again?"

"Sub sandwiches?"

"Yeah. The sub shop makes a good veggie sub," I nodded. "I want extra olives and cheddar and Swiss."

"Okay. If I get the subs, you want to order baseboards while I'm gone?"

"Yeah."

I ended up ordering a synthetic version that couldn't be damaged by water, and arranged to have it delivered before Hank got back.

"That's more expensive," Hank said when I told him what I'd bought.

"I don't care. It'll last longer and you won't have to worry about water damage again."

"Look, you've already invested more than either of us expected. Let's keep this as inexpensive as possible."

"Fine."

"Fine."

"Fine."

Hank grinned. I was coming to love that smile, and I had no right to. And, for probably the hundredth time, I wondered at my willingness to just jump in and help him. It didn't make sense and most other women, even if they'd fallen for the face and physique, would have approached such an investment warily.

I watched Hank take off his shirt to work that afternoon; he was lifting a section of stubborn tiles. Ashamed of myself, I watched as muscles rippled and averted my eyes from abs that any bodybuilder would be proud of.

"Dinner?" Hank asked when we stopped working at nine.

"I have something to do," I sighed, attempting to work the kinks out of my shoulders.

"What's that?"

"Personal stuff."

"All right, but you have to come to dinner tomorrow night. It's fajita Monday at Bogey's."

"Can they do veggie fajitas?"

"I believe one of the options is Portobello fajitas."

"That sounds really good," I said. It did. I almost wished it were Monday instead of Sunday.

"Okay. See you in the morning at seven-thirty?"

"Yeah."

Lissa's Journal

"Where do you think she might be?" I said.

"My love, I wish you'd stop worrying," Rigo murmured. "It is my hope she'll show up—I have left instructions with trusted spies in both Alliances."

"But what if she doesn't show up or come back? Granted, Belen was able to clear Gavin, Gavril and Cheedas of the mind cloud, but she may never forgive them." I held my head in my hands as I huddled against my Hraedan vampire mate. "What if she's terrified that we'll force her to spend the rest of those five years with Gavin? I sure wouldn't want to come back to that."

"Can Adam Chessman not locate her as well? He is her half-sire, and should there be any lessons left, he can perform that duty."

"I'd like to work with her, Rigo—as the Vhanaraszh, she could help me figure out what's causing these freak sandstorms on the Dark Worlds we're trying to repopulate." I didn't add that what else she was might ensure that she'd be able to help. That secret needed to stay with me as long as possible.

"Tiessa, I realize you wish to get to know her, too. You don't say it to spare Gavin's feelings in this but in truth, he, his son and Cheedas have managed to rob you of something precious. Even if they are not fully to blame."

"Rigo." I pressed against his side and brushed tears away.

"Hush. All shall go as it will. We cannot change these things, my love."

"I know." I sniffled, despite my best efforts.

Ashe's Journal

Trajan often seems distant, since Breanne disappeared from Le-Ath Veronis. Somehow, she'd managed to save Lissa when she was stabbed by one of her comesuli, and Renegar and I are still discussing that. Information on the incident is very sketchy, and I hesitate to ask Gavin about it, as he has become nearly unapproachable since learning he'd been infected by a mind cloud. I am at a loss, too, as to how Belen was able to clear it from him, his son and another vampire, but I have not studied it thoroughly—I'm just glad it was possible to destroy it. Kay still wanders around as if she's in a daze, eats only because Bill coaxes her and shies away from my (or anyone else's) touch.

Rabis and I have discussed this, but he has seen no possible way to repair the damage done, and the information escapes me as well. Regardless, Bill has placed secure locks on all knife drawers and anything else in the house that might tempt Kay to take her life.

Kay hasn't shown further indications of suicide, but Kevis can't get through to her, either. She resides somewhere in the recesses of her mind and none of us have been able to draw her back. It is more than frustrating; my love is with me but abhors my touch, and walks away whenever anyone attempts to speak with her.

Breanne's Journal

I walked a community college campus, where two freshmen girls had disappeared the day before. Lissa's nose was better than mine, but any vampire's nose is pretty good. Did I mention that crime rates have declined in the area since I took up residence? They have. I didn't bother to investigate burglaries or the occasional, random murder, but two missing girls sort of riled me up, as they say in Texas.

Campus security had been increased and I saw several guards patrolling the grounds, but I was shielding myself and they never knew I was there. It didn't matter—I found no evidence of those girls where a witness claimed he'd seen them last, so I misted back to my apartment, scrambled two eggs with shredded cheese, ate, brushed my teeth and went to bed.

I decided not to run Monday morning, since opening my eyes turned out to be harder than expected. I slept the extra hour instead, before hauling my aching shoulders out of bed, downing a protein shake for breakfast and wandering downstairs to meet Hank at seven-thirty. Spackling and sanding were on my agenda for the day, while Hank scraped up tile in the back room and bathroom.

He intended to knock out the bathroom wall, too, enlarge it, put in three stalls and make it a unisex bathroom. I just shook my head when he'd said it would be unisex. Even though I never needed a bathroom for the usual purposes, I sure didn't want to be looking at my hair in the mirror while some guy did his business in a stall nearby. Hank laughed at me when I said that to him, too. I didn't bring it up again.

"Shoulders sore?" I attempted to rub the ache away while he unlocked the outside door and walked into the building.

"A little." I dropped my hand.

"You're not used to this much physical labor," he pointed out.

"Tell me something I haven't already discovered for myself," I huffed and followed him inside.

"I'm in a redundant sort of mood, today," he smirked.

"Redundant? Wow, fancy word," I muttered before searching out the tub of spackle and a putty knife.

After cleaning up at the end of a seemingly endless day filled with white, pasty spackle, intermingled with wiping off the excess goo with a rag so it wouldn't dry on the putty knife, I had all the holes and gouges filled. I got no sanding done—I'd found too many spots that needed spackling. Sanding would have to wait until the next day. My shoulders were screaming by the time I showered and walked toward Bogey's for the promised Portobello fajitas.

"Damn," I muttered, my fork halfway to my mouth when the nightly news announced that another girl—a college sophomore, this time, had gone missing from a nearby college. A different campus had been hit this time, and there were no witnesses to the abduction—only the girl's roommate, who said the victim left their shared dorm room around four to study at the library. Somewhere between the dorm room and library, the girl had disappeared.

"Another one?" Hank looked up from his plate of beef and chicken fajitas.

"Yeah. Nobody seems to know anything," I added.

"Not good," Hank stabbed a strip of beef with his fork, lifted it to his mouth and chewed.

"Yeah."

"Nothing we can do," he mumbled around his food.

"Yeah."

A week later, we were deep into painting and working on the ceiling, which had cracks. Two more college girls had disappeared and the local news stations pointed out that all the victims were from different campuses. Nobody ever saw anything, which worried and aggravated me.

My shoulder aches were improving, but I was still tired at the end of every day. Hank didn't seem to understand the concept of a day off —he was like a machine when he worked. The inadvertent break in the disappearing college girls mystery and an earthquake happened two weeks later, but that was after a total of nine girls had gone missing.

Hank was taking down an old light fixture, intending to cover up the hole for the wiring before placing several discreet pendant lights over the bar area instead, when the earthquake hit. The quake was reported to be a six-point-two later and caused several problems, including cracking the foundation beneath our feet. It also damaged a city sewer. That's where city maintenance workers found the decomposing bodies of nine girls, whose throats had been cut.

"Hank, calm down," I soothed as best I could. He was cursing when the building inspector left, after telling us the cracks would have to be repaired before we could open Hank's nightclub for business.

"How much?" I asked, when Hank muttered a few more expletives before falling silent.

"At least forty grand," he sighed, raking fingers through dark hair. The cracks ran from one end of the space to the other, and were spread out. Unsurprisingly, the businesses on either side had cracks, too.

That was the day I learned, too, that Hank was my landlord. He owned the space for the club and what was above it—which turned out to be my apartment and the apartments on either side of mine. As an investor, I suppose I owned a portion of my apartment as well— twenty-five percent, according to the contract. I'd paid my rent for a year in advance, and a rental company handled all that. It made sense, I just hadn't thought about it before.

Hank argued with me at first, but after making calls and working on getting estimates, he finally breathed a sigh, accepted my personal check for forty thousand and asked my attorney to revise our agreement, giving me half the club. Terry said he'd have the papers ready the following afternoon, which worked out great—I had things to do during my night hours, and part of that included a misting trip through a broken sewer to see if I could determine who'd killed nine young women.

$\sim$

"Bree, you need to eat," Hank said later as he locked the gate outside the bar.

"I'll eat. I have eggs and cheese, bagels, canned vegetable soup—I won't starve," I said. "I just have a couple of personal matters to take care of."

Hank wanted to argue or say something else; I watched his jaw work for a few seconds before he shrugged. "Okay. But dinner tomorrow night is on me—at Bogey's."

"That's fine," I agreed, hauling the apartment key from a pocket of my jeans and offering a forced smile. Working with Hank was great in some ways and horrible in others. I watched him paint, stain, lay flooring and a multitude of other tasks, continuously wondering what made him tick and (if I were honest) inwardly weeping because he'd shown absolutely no interest in me. No, he wasn't gay—his eyes would occasionally follow an attractive woman as she walked past, but he never glanced at a male more than once, unless it was our waiter at Bogey's. Even then, it was only polite not to ignore your server.

Hank waited until I'd shut the lower door and walked up the steps to my apartment before he left, hands in pockets, for dinner at his favorite restaurant and bar. Once I was inside my apartment, I spent ten minutes wiping off most of the grime from working, changed clothes and misted toward the broken sewer.

~

Kay's Journal

I was beginning to work through the fear, but Kalia's terror was so overwhelming that it was much like attempting to swim through thick mud to get to the surface of consciousness. I'd be there for perhaps a few hours, until someone reached out toward me, attempted to touch or said something that frightened Kalia so badly that I'd be thrown right back to the mud pit's bottom again. At times, the struggle wasn't worth the effort, and I allowed her fears to dictate everything. Only time might tell if we'd ever reach any sort of equilibrium again.

~

Breanne's Journal

Vampire. Even with the stench around me, I could smell the vampire and the lingering scents of nine bodies. The smell of blood, too, rose around me. Most of the victims' blood had washed away, but the vampire drank from all of them—I was certain of that—before slitting their throats. I wondered, too, how he'd dealt with the stench in the sewer—most vampires wouldn't have chosen that as a location to drink from and then dispose of victim's bodies.

More than thankful that most vampires slept through the day, I waited after hearing the noise down the way—the sewer was taller than I was where I stood and the vampire's scent reached me before he did. Turning to mist, I waited for him to arrive.

He did, carrying another girl in his arms. She was already dead, unfortunately, from a snapped neck. She'd struggled, at least, before she'd died, but she'd died all the same—no human could fight off a vampire's strength.

I didn't see it, either, until he came closer, but it was there and unmistakable. He carried an obsession, along with his latest victim. Granted it was an old obsession, but an obsession just the same. A Sirenali had visited Earth. I had no idea whether the Sirenali remained on the planet, but one had come. That in itself was frightening.

I waited, hovering as mist while the vampire lowered his victim to the rounded floor of the sewer. Blinking at his surroundings for a moment, he worked to puzzle out the differences in his location. Yes, he'd finally figured out that his other victims were missing.

Police had the aboveground entrances watched—they'd searched the sewer earlier in the day and found nothing besides the bodies. The vampire had his own secret entrance, apparently, but that was about to be a moot point. Before he could register his surprise at my sudden appearance, I materialized before him and relieved him of his head.

"Investigators still have no leads on how the killer managed to get the latest victim past local police, but another body was discovered in the sewer early this morning," the news anchor announced as Hank and I ate at Bogey's the following evening. Hank was working on his third old fashioned while I sipped a second glass of white wine. Both of us turned to the television hanging over the bar.

"That bastard needs to be stopped," Hank muttered, chewing on his drink straws.

"Well, nothing we can do about it, huh?" I shrugged and dropped my gaze to the remains of my meal.

"Yeah. Bree, will you answer a question for me?" Hank changed the subject. I looked up from my plate to find him staring at me.

"I guess," I hedged. What was he about to ask? I hadn't read him. Thought about it several times, especially when he never treated our relationship as anything other than friends or worse—a business partnership.

"Who was your best lover?" A glint appeared in Hank's eyes and he grinned at me from across the table. He chewed on the short straws from his old fashioned as he asked the question. I stared—this was certainly a change in verbal scenery, and a fast one at that.

"What?" I sputtered. The conversation had suddenly turned very personal and it threw me.

"Come on, somebody musta stood out. Man, I remember my best one. I was half drunk and got propositioned by an Asian girl in a Singapore bar. She let me do things to her that nobody has offered since."

"Damn, your eyes just glazed over," I said, hoping he'd laugh and go past the question. He did laugh. He didn't let go of the question, though.

"Come on, Bree. Fess up. Who was your best fuck?"

I continued to stare at him. Likely, my mouth worked silently while my brain struggled vainly to find an appropriate gear. I still have no idea why I blurted the truth. No idea at all. "I've never fucked anybody," I said. Yeah, it should have been a snappy comeback. It wasn't. It sounded much more like a strangled, helpless whisper.

"No way you're a virgin," he accused, staring at me.

"The hymen's gone, a doctor saw to that when I was fourteen," I stared at my hands, ashamed of the way my face heated. "He wanted to know why I hadn't had a period. He just stuck a speculum right in with no warning. It hurt like hell, I screamed, his assistant came running and I was sent home. I've never had a period, before or since, so no kids for me." My face was still hot as I looked up at him again.

"Damn, baby. You're virgin in the way that counts. And trust me, he was a prick to do that to you. Sex is a good thing. Maybe the best thing. You really never tried it?" Hank studied my face, attempting, perhaps, to read an answer there.

"I've thought about it now and then, but the ones I considered, well, they sort of got removed from the short list." I blew out a sigh and turned my head to stare at the bar. As usual, Hank and I were closing down the place. The bar was empty, except for one old drunk sitting at the end.

"Have you ever thought about a fuck buddy?" I turned back to Hank as he asked the question. His dark eyes were serious as he searched my face for an answer. I had a difficult time keeping my shield up and a shiver from becoming obvious. I'd promised myself that I wouldn't do any readings, but this was trying my resolve.

"What's a fuck buddy?" I had to say the words slowly to keep my tongue from tripping over them.

"Like friends or exes with benefits. You know, when you have a good friend or an ex who really knows how to fuck, you keep that part of the relationship open. If you need a good fuck with no strings, you call them up. Next day, you're back to being friends or exes. They need a fuck, they call you up. It's a pretty reliable system, as long as you establish the ground rules going in. No serious entanglements. Sex only. No kissing or intimate embraces. And if anybody finds another partner for a permanent relationship, it ends. That's how it works."

"Are you serious? You've done this before?" I was shocked by the casual way he'd described it.

"Not for a couple of years—too busy working, getting the bar funding together and going to business school in my spare time." He shrugged and dropped the thin, red straws into his empty drink. The ends he'd chewed were almost worn through.

"Uh-huh." I nodded, not understanding in the least.

"Bree, you don't have any experience with sex. Not any good experience, anyway. I need a fuck. I think you do, too. A really good fuck. I've been told I'm good at fucking. Why don't we solve both problems at once? We can be fuck buddies when it's needed, and still be friends the rest of the time."

"But—what?" I only thought I was shocked before. I was well and truly shocked, now.

"Come on, baby. It's just fucking." He tapped the straws into his empty drink, rattling ice cubes. "I'm wound up after the earthquake and expensive cracks in the bar's foundation. You're wound up because helping me out wasn't in your plans. Sex is a great way to calm things down. I give you a climax or two and we'll both relax."

"But," my mouth was working like that of a landed fish. No coherent sentences passed my lips, I know that much. Was he right?

Was it just sex—or, as he put it, fucking? Could you do such an intimate thing with another person and not be (or get) involved?

"Come on." Hank tossed money on the table and lifted his jacket from the seat beside him. When I failed to stand up, he gently grasped my arm and practically lifted me from my seat. He explained the rules as he herded me outside and into a foggy, San Francisco night.

"No kissing, that implies intimacy," he shrugged into his jacket and grabbed my arm again. Perhaps he was worried I'd run away. I thought about it, but my legs were too rubbery to comply with my addled brain. "No expecting flowers or dinner or anything that implies a relationship. This is sex only, and mutually provided. One partner is within his or her rights to point out that they've gotten multiple calls from the other party without making any of their own. Compensation may be made to the party owed, in the form of their choosing."

"This is too complicated," I muttered.

"Then you should make sure that you ask as often as I do," he said simply. "Bree, it's not brain surgery."

"I think I need a lobotomy, then," I mumbled. The alcohol was wearing thin and I really hadn't agreed to this.

"Here." He steered me into an alcove and pulled a key from his pocket. "I like Bogey's because it's close to home," he said. I smelled the bourbon from his drink as he spoke. It wasn't unpleasant, it just was.

His third-story apartment was clean, if a bit Spartan. Consisting of a kitchen, sitting room and bedroom, I saw that the sitting room doubled as Hank's office. A desk took up a corner next to a bay window, and papers and file folders lay in stacks upon it. I briefly imagined that he'd sat at that desk, frantically working figures, trying to find a way to finance the bar and then fix cracks in the foundation on his own. Then I'd made my offer, he'd accepted, and now he was making another offer.

Was sex really that good? It must have something to recommend it or people wouldn't be doing it all the time.

"What if it hurts?" I turned to ask. He'd gone to the kitchen, and I heard ice cubes hitting the bottom of a glass. "I don't do pain, if I can avoid it."

"Bree, if there's pain, then we need to get you to a doctor. Our parts are supposed to fit together. Pain can be added into the mix, for those who want it. Straight sex shouldn't hurt." He walked the short distance from the kitchen to the sitting room, sipping his bourbon.

"Well, keep it pain-free, then." I turned to stare out his window. He didn't have much of a view—only the building across the street. More bay windows—the kind San Francisco was famous for, stared back. I shivered. I was about to have sex for the first time and it had turned into a business arrangement.

"Baby, we'll get undressed, and then I'll tell you what to do," he said.

"Is it always this clinical?" I rubbed my arms as goose bumps dotted my flesh.

"Usually the participants already know each other in the biblical sense," he replied, emptying his drink and setting the glass on the corner of a tiny, scarred coffee table. I stared at the nicks and scores in the wood, recalling similar marks on my skin in the past. I shivered again. "Fucking is fucking, and the participants usually can't get to it fast enough. I'll take it slow and explain everything. If you like what you get, we'll go on from here. If you don't, we'll let it go like it never happened. Deal?"

"I don't know," I moaned, rubbing my forehead. Of all the possible endings for the day, this was one I'd never imagined.

"Baby, look at me." Hank took my wrists in his hands, forcing me to focus on his face. "You've never had sex, let alone good sex. Let me do this, so you'll at least have the benefit of somebody who knows what he's doing."

"It won't hurt?"

"If it does, we'll go to the ER. I'm a paramedic, remember?" he let go of my left wrist and tapped his chest. "I can do basic first-aid." He offered a crooked grin.

"We undress together?"

"I can undress first and then stroke my cock while you undress," he said.

"You know, I never thought I'd hear those words come out of your mouth," I muttered.

"Don't be shocked, Bree. When sex is in the offing, I've been known to say much, much worse. Now, will you undress with me, or wait for me to watch?"

"I'll undress." My hands shook as they lifted the hem of my tee. Holding my breath, I pulled it over my head. The bra I'd slipped into after a quick cleanup earlier was pale pink with only a touch of lace across the top. It was serviceable and built to keep my breasts covered. That's it. One of Hank's eyebrows lifted as he studied my exposed flesh.

"God, Bree," he whispered, "please take your bra off next."

"We aim to please," I muttered, my voice cracking as I reached behind me to undo the hooks.

"I'll take that," he pulled the bra down my arms. "Bree, that's just, that's—damn." He shook his head. I flushed.

"Are you undressing?" I croaked. My bra dangled from his fingers as he stared at my chest. Embarrassingly enough, the cold air made my nipples harden. Hank drew in a breath. I unsnapped my jeans. As if he'd awakened from a deep sleep, he dropped my bra on the floor, jerked his T-shirt from the waistband of his jeans and pulled it over his head in one fluid move.

I unzipped my jeans and moved to slide them down my legs. Hank was watching again. I'd already seen his upper torso. Yes, he had abs that most men could only dream of. He'd worked often enough in the bar without his shirt, so I was used to that. He didn't take his eyes off me as he unbuckled his belt.

Feeling embarrassed, I slipped off my athletic shoes and stepped out of my jeans. Hank's jeans dropped to the floor, wallet and keys still in his pockets. He hadn't taken his eyes off me. Stepping on the left toe of my white athletic sock with my right foot, I slipped out of it, then did the same with the right sock.

Had he planned this? Hank's underwear was black and tiny, barely covering a sizable bulge. I'd never seen a real erection. I found myself wishing this one wasn't as close as it was. He appeared shaven too—

there was no visible pubic hair on his skin. At least my panties covered what I had. They were French-cut and a darker pink to match the bra.

"Underwear, baby," Hank jerked his chin toward the only piece of clothing I had left. "Turn around," he ordered. "Take them off slow, and bend down to slip them off your feet."

Silently I turned to do as he asked. With my vampire hearing, I didn't fail to hear the indrawn breath. "Now, turn around. Watch me." I turned and watched him do the same—he turned his back and bent down to remove the scrap of underwear he wore. I got the full, up-close and personal view of a very tight ass. Then he turned.

"Holy shit." I backed away.

"None of that, now," Hank grabbed my hand and pulled me toward his bedroom. I thought about misting away and destroying the only friendship I'd ever really had.

"This is important to you?" I wobbled out as he pulled me to a stop inside his small bedroom.

"Baby, I need a fuck in the worst way. Don't distract me or you won't get my best. Okay?"

I blinked at him. What the hell was he talking about?

"Come on. Climb on the bed about halfway down and kneel there. I'll be right back." He walked toward one of two closets inside his bedroom. I went to kneel on the bed, halfway down, like he said. I watched as he pulled a large, wedge-like vinyl pillow from the closet, then stopped by his bedside table to pull a small bottle and a condom from the drawer.

I didn't tell him the condom wasn't needed. Let him keep thinking I was human. If he ever learned the truth about me, he'd likely be scared witless.

"Here." The vinyl pillow was shoved in front of me. I turned to stare at him. "Lean over it. I want your little ass in the air," he directed.

"What?"

"Bree, this is my fuck. I'll make sure you enjoy it, too. Lean over the pillow. You can pull one of the regular pillows down to lay your head on. Come on, baby."

Praying that he really did know what he was doing, I leaned over the pillow and then pulled one of his pillows from the top of the bed toward me. I'd barely laid it beneath my cheek when his hand touched my thigh. I jerked.

"Bree, I'm not gonna hurt you." His hand moved to cup my left cheek. "Hug your pillow, baby." I shifted the pillow beneath my head as his fingers moved between my legs. Except for the asshole doctor, nobody had touched me there.

"Gonna touch you, baby. Ever pleasure yourself?" When he pinched that part of me, I almost came off the bed. Hank hauled me back. "Guess not," he rumbled. "Come on, I'll be touching that part. A lot. Just relax."

"Easy for you to say," I hissed. He was squeezing the sensitive spot again, and my insides tightened. He took his hand away.

"This is lube, just to make things slide a little better." The hand was back, rubbing a slick substance over my sensitive spot. His fingers began a steady rhythm. My body tightened again. "Feel that, don't you?" he said. The rhythm increased. I whimpered. This was something I'd never felt before. A need I'd never experienced. Was this what everybody felt? This desire for something more? A thumb slipped inside me. I jerked forward, attempting to shy away from the intrusion. Hank wasn't having any of it.

"Oh, baby, you're gonna come for me. So hard," he whispered. His fingers were moving faster, my body wound tighter and my breaths were loud gasps. In my addled state, I knew something was about to happen, I just didn't know what that was. Was he waiting for some sort of response from my body, or was he gauging the sounds of my breaths or the flush of my skin? I didn't know, but suddenly his fingers stilled. I bit back a cry of frustration.

"Calm before the storm, baby Bree," he said softly. "Condom going on, now." The foil packet tore. "You're wet, now, but we'll still use more lube. Just in case." I heard the sound of liquid rubbed between his palms, and then rubbed elsewhere.

"Here we go," he positioned himself. I felt pressure and I moaned. His hands gripped my waist as he pushed inside. I briefly wondered how he managed to fit what he had inside me. It didn't hurt, and I experienced a fleeting moment of gratitude for that. And then he moved. Pulled himself out and then shoved in again. Yes, I understood the dynamics of sex, but that doesn't prepare you for the reality. My body tightened again when he touched me with his fingers once more.

"Feel that, baby?" I felt it, all right. In a place I'd never felt anything like it before. I felt flushed. Hot. "Ready, baby?" he swatted my buttocks and slammed into me. I screamed as wave after wave of pleasure hit me. By the time it was over—for both of us—I was sprawled helplessly across the vinyl pillow, with no thought in my head and no strength in my body.

So, *that* was what sex was all about.

CHAPTER 3

$\mathcal{H}$ank wasn't kidding about the rules. The next morning, he was all business as we screwed panels of plywood to the frame we'd built the night before, to create the locker room he'd insisted on building. The plywood would be covered with sheet rock and painted chocolate-brown later, to match the other walls.

I was sore from the night before—he'd gotten three fucks, but he'd brought me to climax every time. I now understood things better—sex was pleasurable if you did it right—and it could become addicting, I think.

I followed Hank's lead and never mentioned the sex we'd had the night before. All three times, he'd bent me over the vinyl pillow. All the movies I'd seen had depicted sex face-to-face. Maybe this was his way of keeping it impersonal. How was I to know? I was inexperienced and I knew it.

"Want dinner?" he asked the usual question as we closed the metal gate across the bar front at nine that night.

"I just want to soak in a hot tub of water." I did. My abdominal muscles ached and I was hoping ibuprofen and a tub of really hot water would help.

"Baby, why didn't you tell me you were hurting?" my arm was

grasped in his fingers as I turned toward the stairs leading to my apartment.

"Because that would violate the agreement. There wasn't anything in the rules about whining." I pulled my arm from his grasp. "I'll see you in the morning." I walked up the stairs to my apartment. He didn't try to stop me.

~

It was early and the heavy fog bitterly cold when I clambered down the stairs for my morning run the following day. The ache had subsided somewhat, and I'd missed my run the day before because of it. Maybe running would help. I pulled the collar of my jacket up and zipped it as high as it would go—it would take a few minutes of running to dispel the chill.

My feet hit the pavement lightly and in a regular rhythm as I made my way down the street. Five miles—that's what I set for myself. I could always mist back if I couldn't go the distance. I increased my pace. I had to force myself to ignore the thought of Hank's hands on my body.

Yeah, I always thought I'd get kisses and caresses when I had sex the first time. Maybe even love. Just as things usually happened for me, those things weren't in the cards. Could I have said no to him? Absolutely not. I was putty in his hands and he probably knew it. It didn't keep me from feeling embarrassed by my wantonness, though.

By the time I made it back from my run, Hank had arrived and set about unloading cans of wood varnish; he was ready to sand and varnish the antique wood bar. Without saying anything, I lifted a can of varnish in each hand and carried them inside as soon as Hank shoved the metal grill back and unlocked the door.

"Want to do some sanding today?" he offered a wry smile. I didn't return it.

"Sure. Let me clean up and I'll be right down." I walked toward the door.

"Eat breakfast, first," he called after me. I gave a noncommittal wave as I left the bar.

≈

"I got shot in Afghanistan," he said conversationally two hours later. I hadn't said anything when I returned, settling for grabbing a hand sander and going to work on the massive bar instead.

"You don't say," I kept my head down and my eyes on my work. "I can't imagine why anyone would go to all the trouble of shooting you," I added.

"That's what this scar is," he pointed to a pale indentation beneath his right arm. He was working shirtless, again.

"Is that your opening line for all the women who walk into this place? Here's my scar?" I asked, raising my head to look at him.

"And I was afraid my friend Bree was gone," he grinned.

"Your friend Bree was sore and grumpy. End of statement," I grumped, going back to my sanding. "Did you want me to swoon because you didn't jump out of the way when they shot at you?"

"Maybe I expect women to ooh and ahh because I have a Purple Heart and a Silver Star."

"Women will be positively dripping off you," I nodded. "Maybe you should tattoo that stuff on your chest. That way you'll only attract the ones who can read. It could be a big time saver," I waved my sander at him.

He laughed. "Bree, where were you when I was getting my ass shot at? Letters from you would have helped a lot."

"Probably a few light-years away," I replied. He'd never know I wasn't joking. "And that scar isn't on your ass, dude."

"Too bad. I could show 'em that right off." He grinned.

"You'd have to fight off all the men the women came in with, because the women can't resist your ass, with or without scars."

"So, you think wearing a thong while tending bar will bring in the women?" He snickered at the look on my face.

"They'll be on you like June bugs on a screen door," I nodded and went back to sanding.

"Is that what they say in Texas?"

"If they have June bugs stuck on their screen door," I agreed.

Hank stretched as we stopped for the night. "Clean up and dinner?" he asked. "Or clean up, fuck, clean up and dinner, or clean up, dinner and then fuck?"

"You've had three fucks already," I pointed out.

"Nah, that only counts as one. The requests count, not the number of fucks after each request."

"Now see, you didn't mention that in the rules," I shook a finger at him.

"I was half drunk and it slipped my mind. I'm telling you now. This is my second request."

"What happens if your fuck buddy turns you down?" I asked. "For future reference, of course." Yes the thought of another climax made my body tighten in a way it wouldn't have only two days before. I wasn't about to tell him that, though.

"The fuck buddy needs a legitimate excuse," he replied and shoved me through the door. "Do you have a legitimate excuse?"

"No idea," I mumbled.

"That's definitely not a legitimate excuse. Therefore," he pulled the grill shut and locked it, "I get to choose. I choose clean up, fuck, dinner and more fuck."

"Who made these rules?" I frowned at him. He grinned.

"I made most of them," he replied.

I got to shower first, and to calm my nerves, I poured a glass of wine for myself and sat by my bedroom window, drinking it while I waited for Hank to finish cleaning up. My robe was wrapped tightly around me while butterflies chased through my insides.

Hank walked into my bedroom naked, his hair damp and ruffled.

He'd pushed me up the stairs earlier, pointing out the obvious—that my apartment was closer.

"We're not staying in here," he informed me. "And take off that robe. My fuck buddy has to be naked if I'm naked."

"Another rule?" my eyebrows rose at his statement.

"Yeah. FBs have to be concurrently naked."

"Damn, you do know a four-syllable word," I sighed. "I may swoon."

"Don't swoon unless you want me to carry you to the kitchen."

"The kitchen?" What the hell did he want in the kitchen?

"Come with me, FB. Damn, that rhymes." He grinned, the white flash of his teeth a contrast to the dim light in my bedroom.

"Uh-huh. The President will call any day and make you poet laureate," I huffed. He was still grinning as he herded me into the kitchen.

"Now, this is for making you sore," he lifted me onto the bar. Since I hadn't removed my robe, he slipped it off my shoulders, allowing it to drop to the counter behind me. "Spread your legs, baby. I'm about to put my mouth on you."

"What? No." I kept my knees tight together.

"This is my fuck," he reminded me. "Spread your legs."

I wanted to argue and resist, but his eyes hardened, so I didn't. He pushed my knees apart and stared at my privates for several seconds before dipping his head. The moment he sucked the tender part of me into his mouth, I moaned. If I thought his hands were good, his mouth was better. I think plenty of *oh my gods* came out of my mouth while he sucked and stroked and licked.

"My turn." He hadn't let me come—he backed off every time I was on the edge of it. He lifted my boneless body off the bar and settled me on the end of the kitchen table. "See—just the right height." I stared at his erection.

"On the table?" I squeaked.

"Yeah. Lie back, I've got this." He pushed me back gently until I was spread out on the table. The foil packet of a fresh condom was ripped open. "Wrap your legs around me, baby, and hold onto the edge of the table," he instructed. My fingers gripped both sides of my small table. Hank lifted my legs and pulled them around his waist before sliding into me. I was coming and screaming as he pounded into me only a few minutes later. Surprisingly enough, the table didn't collapse when he lowered his weight onto me when he finished.

"Those pea pods are swimming with that shrimp. I will not eat them." I pointed my chopsticks at Hank an hour later. He'd called for Chinese takeout, after deciding that I didn't need to dress to go out. He'd answered the door wearing only his jeans, while I waited in the kitchen, wrapped in my robe. The moment the delivery boy left, he shucked his jeans and forced me to pull off my robe. I couldn't recall ever eating naked before.

He'd ordered Kung Pao Shrimp, but shoved the pea pods aside, devoured the shrimp, rice and other vegetables, then offered the pea pods to me.

"Baby, you don't eat enough," he rose to dump his container in the trash. "You weigh five pounds."

"I weighed a hundred and two pounds," I corrected him. "This morning."

"Are you fucking kidding?"

"No." Actually, that was an improvement. I'd dropped to ninety-two after leaving Le-Ath Veronis behind. My weight had gradually built up over the months.

"How the hell are you so strong?" he muttered, shaking his head. I could have told him. I didn't.

"I'll buy a vinyl pillow to bring here," he told me later, after he'd stuffed every pillow he could find beneath me and having me that way. "They're built for that, and they clean up easy."

I didn't argue with him; I was too tired. In fact, I wanted to curl up and sleep.

"Bye, baby." Hank pulled the pillows from beneath me, covered me with the comforter on my bed and let himself out of my apartment. It made me wonder if any chance I ever had at romance had died without me knowing it.

~

For the next three days, we made a lot of progress on the club. We finished sanding the antique bar and Hank applied two coats of varnish, painstakingly painting the oak stain onto the wood with loving strokes. I envied the wood, it received so much care from his hands.

Just as always, it was business in the bar. We didn't talk about sex or anything truly personal as we worked. All three nights, though, he was ready to fuck as soon as we locked the door. I wasn't sure why I'd ever allowed him to talk me into this arrangement. I wanted intimacy; he wanted sex.

We were laying the hardwood floor on the fourth day when my cellphone rang. It was Mercy Crossings.

Hank stopped what he was doing and stood up as I spoke with Barry Stokes, the Director of the charity.

"Breanne, we're heading into Somalia," he informed me. "We need your language skills." He likely needed my negotiating skills, too, but I didn't point that out.

"How soon?" I asked.

"I've got a ticket waiting at the airport. Departure time is seven tonight. Can you make that?"

"Yeah." Barry gave me the airline and flight number, then hung up.

"I have to go," I shoved the phone in my pocket.

"Baby, you can't go." Hank called me baby for the first time while we worked together.

"I have to. They don't have anybody else who can speak the language." I watched as his jaw tightened—a rare display of emotion from Hank Bell.

"Where?" his words were terse.

"Somalia."

"Fuck me running," he growled.

"Interesting visual. I have to go." Somalia wasn't high on my list of places to visit, but the time away from Hank would give me breathing space to decide about my role as his fuck buddy. Outside of work, that's all I was—something to fuck and nothing else. Sure the sex was good, but I wanted to be held and kissed. Henry Hank Bell didn't want those things.

"Bree, see that you come back," he growled deeper as I turned away. I didn't reply, I just walked out the door.

Somalia was in its secondary rainy season, usually lasting from September through November. We landed during the first week of October, to warm temperatures and no rain. I had no idea why they bothered to call it a rainy season—Somalia received an average yearly rainfall of eleven inches.

Mogadishu, the largest city, was also Somalia's capital, and since many of the charitable organizations that wished to come had been banned from the country, Barry Stokes had achieved the near-impossible by getting us into the country to begin with. Once we arrived, we were searched, the equipment inspected, and then inspected again every time we moved from one place to another.

Our destination was Beledweyne, to provide medical care after several attacks had occurred in the city and medical assistance was sorely needed. As we drove through devastated neighborhoods, I saw concrete walls riddled with bullet holes. What remained standing, anyway.

Buildings had been destroyed, with only rough skeletons left behind. Most of the roads were pockmarked and difficult to navigate, and I wondered if I could get close to anyone important enough to allow food, water and other assistance to come in.

I did speak with several minor officials with the African military— primarily forces from Djibouti, who, with Somali assistance, were busy working their way through the city, searching for those responsible for the attacks. Even with compulsion, nobody seemed to know much of anything. Our tents went up and children were brought in, often on stretchers, many of them unconscious.

"Breanne," Ray Knowles, our chief of operations, whispered next to my ear as I worked to get food and supplies through the country and into needy hands. My efforts were futile—nobody there had enough power or clout to bring anything in through Mogadishu and Ethiopia, which borders Somalia, certainly wasn't prepared to allow anything through.

"Ray?" Ray took my elbow and led me away from the two men in charge of the Djibouti forces—they'd been offended to be approached by a woman to begin with, and after I laid compulsion and they became more compliant, I learned there wasn't anything they could do to help the situation.

"We're getting additional help," Ray muttered as he led me away. "Special help."

Special help could mean several things, but Ray's reading told me that people from Special Ops were coming in, disguised as volunteers for Mercy Crossings. I sighed.

"All right," I nodded. Ray didn't know the reason they were coming, and that didn't surprise me. I'd find out eventually, when I read the new arrivals.

"Look, you've been working since you got here," Ray said. "Take a break. Our help should be here in a couple of hours. They'll need your language skills when they arrive."

"Okay." I walked toward the tent I shared with two doctors, both of them women. I thought about calling Hank on my cellphone, but reception was spotty at best and usually the calls would be dropped. Breathing a sigh, I pushed past the tent entrance and flopped onto my tiny sleeping cot.

Jayson Rome, Second Vice-President of Rome Publications, with offices in Los Angeles and San Francisco, was responsible for the magazine publishing portion of his father's publishing empire.

Jayson's older brother, James, Jr., was First Vice-President and his offices were in Los Angeles, where the main body of the corporation was housed.

"Why do you think the abductions stopped?" Jayson glanced up at Ross Gideon, who normally wrote articles for the Los Angeles newspaper his father owned instead of magazine articles for Jayson's publishing branch.

"I think the killer was killed. Possibly by a vigilante, who doesn't want to be discovered."

"Ross, that's pure speculation and you know it. What evidence do you have?" Jayson slid the offered thumb drive back toward Ross, who sat on the other side of Jayson's desk. "Look, I know your name carries a lot of clout, but this—I can't publish anything like this without at least some verifiable truth in it."

Ross Gideon was practically a household name—if that household read political nonfiction and biographies of politicians. Ross was currently writing a biography commissioned by James Rome, Jayson's father. He'd stopped briefly to write a piece on the co-ed murders in San Francisco.

"Most of that article is fact—the dead girls, their parents, the investigation, all of that is covered factually," Ross insisted.

"But it doesn't have much of a resolution, and the fact that you added wild speculation into the mix leaves us nowhere. If you want to rewrite it, leave out the speculation and focus on the families left behind. That'll be a decent article and I'll publish that."

Jayson Rome, six-three in his socks with blond hair, brown eyes and regular workouts scheduled five days a week in the gym downstairs, drew many a debutant's eye. He had no interest in any of them. Most nights he drove from the office to his spacious home in San Rafael, which overlooked San Rafael Bay. He worked at home, often late into the night, before going to bed, rising early and starting the same routine again the next day.

"I don't have time for revisions. Let one of your hacks do it, give me credit and a paycheck and we'll call it even," Ross rose from his chair and nodded to Jayson. "I need to get back to that biography your dad asked me to write."

"I'll see what I can do," Jayson said as he watched Ross stalk out of his office. It was never a good idea to get on Ross Gideon's bad side. He sighed and turned to gaze out the window of his penthouse office. He'd see which of his in-house writers was available, hand the thumb drive to them and see if they couldn't make something decent out of what Ross had provided.

~

Breanne's Journal

I blinked when he stepped out of the van. Sure, he was dressed like the rest of us—in camo fatigues and a green T-shirt with the Mercy Crossings logo embroidered on the shirt pocket. Bill Jennings—*the* Bill Jennings—who was still Director of the Joint NSA and Homeland Security Department, walked toward Ray and me, followed by five Special Ops agents.

Bill had been nice to me, the brief time I'd met him at SouthStar. He wouldn't know me from any other interpreter now, though. I waited for him to get close enough so I could read the purpose for placing himself in such a delicate position.

Undercover operatives—gone missing. That was easy enough for me to see as Bill and the others shook hands with Ray. I was just the interpreter, not chief of operations, but Bill smiled and took my hand anyway.

"I hear you can understand and speak just about anything," he said.

"I can, sir." I nodded.

"Even the dialects?"

"Yes."

"Wonderful. We're here to find some of our own, and we need all the help we can get."

"I can give that help," I nodded. Bill's reading had given me information on the two missing men—one of them had two young children at home. If he were still alive, I'd go hunting for that reason alone.

"We just need to keep things quiet, if you know what I mean," Bill leaned in to whisper.

"Of course I do, sir," I nodded.

That night, it rained just a little. Not even a quarter of an inch, but it was rain. Ray was closeted with Director Bill and the Special Ops guys, and since they didn't need an interpreter for that, I was left out of the meeting.

I was called into a surgery tent instead, to calm a frightened mother while a bullet was pulled from an infected wound in her son's shoulder. I wanted to sigh—she'd dithered about bringing her child to the doctors in the first place, allowing the wound to grow even more infected. I hoped the physicians we had could ultimately save the arm.

The mother was even more surprised when she learned how well I could speak and understand the Somali dialect she used. Some spoke Arabic, as it was listed as a national language just as Somali was, but there were three main dialects to the Somali language. It didn't matter —if I had any difficulty with the spoken words, all I had to do was read the speaker. It even told me when they were lying, and that was just a bonus.

Lissa's Journal

"Norian, we're not speaking. Remember?"

"Lissa, I don't forget things like that," Norian muttered.

He'd appeared unannounced inside my private study and sat uncomfortably on one of my guest chairs. He hadn't been a victim of the mind cloud affecting Gavin and the others; he'd done what he had deliberately. If Ildevar hadn't stepped in, Skel Hawer would likely have gone free and the King of Serendaan would be dead, most likely, along with three of his wives.

Belen had given me that information, which was unusual. Belen seldom offered sensitive information. He wouldn't tell me why, either, and my curiosity rose. I didn't ask, though. Belen can be more inscrutable than any Larentii.

"Lissa, we have trouble. Big trouble," Norian said, raking fingers through thick, brown hair. "We've had a prison break. Every prisoner inside Yigga Prison has escaped. Information is sketchy since all the guards died, in addition to anyone within three miles of the prison. A witness from farther away than that says he saw a huge dust storm in the distance, heading toward the prison. After that, bodies were left behind and none of them were prisoners."

"What?" I was standing and blinking at Norian in alarm. "Oh, no. No, no, no," I sat again, my mind and body in shock. "Norian," I whispered, feeling numb. "Norian, oh, God."

～

Breanne's Journal

Bill Jennings spent the morning with his operatives while I translated for local parents and the wounded who could speak. We were treating adults, now, when our excuse for being in Somalia in the beginning was injured children.

I watched dispassionately when a man came in, held up by two friends. He had a chest wound, which was bleeding profusely. The injury was fresh. The doctors knew it, as did I, and he was immediately placed on a table, his shirt cut away and two physicians and three nurses gathered around him. If they didn't move swiftly, he'd die. Actually, with the severity of the wound, the chances of his survival under such primitive conditions were very small.

"How did this happen?" I turned to the injured man's companions. I'd only spoken aloud to give the medical personnel present a plausible reason for what I already knew—they had the operatives Bill was searching for, and the injured man had accidentally been shot when one of the prisoners wrestled a gun away. That prisoner now suffered from a head wound, inflicted by the two I spoke with after he was overpowered.

Chest wound's companions gabbled some excuse—that their

injured friend had been cleaning his gun. The excuse might have been a good one, except the man couldn't have shot himself with the rifle used. I think everybody in Somalia owned at least one gun, which was frightening enough in itself. Both of these had rifles slung over their shoulders.

"Leave now," I commanded softly, compulsion thick in my voice. Without a word, both turned and left the surgery tent.

"Let me know if you need me again," I patted the walkie-talkie clipped to my fatigues. The doctors and nurses barely gave me a glance—they were too busy attempting to save one of those who'd captured and tortured Bill's agents.

~

Compulsion had to be used—twice—before I was able to get in to see Bill. He was sequestered in a tent not far away, but his five Special Ops agents didn't want me near Bill. I disabused them of that notion. Ray was with Bill, going over a map and what little he knew of the area when I walked into Bill's tent.

"Ray, get out," I said as pleasantly as I could, employing compulsion. "You won't remember I said that," I whispered as he passed me on his way out of the tent.

"Young woman," Bill began, practicing as much patience as he could. He could call me young woman if he wanted—he was in his forties and I looked half his age.

"Bill, someday you won't call me that. You'll know better. Now, if you want your two spies back before one of them dies of a head wound, then I suggest you gather those grumpy agents outside and come with me."

~

Lissa's Journal

I recognized what lay before me, only it was worse than I'd seen before. I was used to seeing the flayed bodies of Centaurs, Manticores and other creatures many thought were myth. These were humanoids, and all of them resembled raw meat. The children, however, if their bodies were large enough to survive the scouring sands, were so insubstantial it made me ill.

"Norian," I whispered, "How could this happen?" I wanted to weep and there were no tears. I was drained. Empty. Somehow, those who'd attacked the Dark side were now attacking the worlds of Light.

"Lissa, beloved, come walk with me." Belen appeared beside me while Norian continued his examination of bodies. Six of his agents and ten of Gavril's searched nearby, all of them looking for something they wouldn't find—evidence. The small community, located near Yigga Prison, housed many of the guards who worked at the maximum security facility. At least it had. All were dead, now, their homes blasted down by the fiercest winds, allowing the terrible sand and grit to destroy the lives inside.

"Belen?" I blinked up at him. As usual, he was shining brightly, although he'd dampened it so I might look at him.

"Lissa, this is certainly the beginning." He gazed around us. At leveled homes and devastated bodies.

I understood what he said. All too clearly. It had been my suspicion, but I was too afraid to voice it aloud, as if saying it might make it real. It didn't need my words to make it real. It had already become real. The God Wars were upon us. "It'll only get worse, won't it?" I whispered.

"If this is not stopped," Belen lowered his head as if in thought. "Either the opposing forces know something we don't, or evidence we do not have indicates that the three are now revealed."

"You don't know who all three are, do you?" I shivered.

"We know of the Mighty Hand—he has revealed himself to us, but he has placed himself behind a shield only the strongest might breach, and to my knowledge only the One might get past Strength's barrier. One other we have both felt," he nodded slightly to me. Neither of us was willing to speak Breanne's name aloud. She was in enough danger, I think, and I didn't want to add to that.

"The other I cannot say, although we have seen evidence," Belen sighed. He hesitated for a moment, as if he wanted to say something else and then thought better of it.

"I am afraid to say what I might think about this," Belen murmured instead. "It worries me that even the quietest voice might be heard if I speak my suspicions about this. Lissa, there's something you do not know," Belen continued.

"What's that?"

"I only removed the mind cloud from your son. The others—it had already been removed when I arrived to do it."

"What?" I stared at Belen.

"Someone quite powerful arrived before I did. I believe Gavin and Cheedas benefited from a visit from one of the others. At this time, I cannot say—am afraid to say—which it might have been."

"I don't understand this," I rubbed my forehead.

"Lissa, do not make yourself ill, I beg," Belen knelt next to me. "We must be strong and vigilant in the coming days. It is up to us to do what we can to protect innocents during these times. As much as we can, for as long as we can. We cannot say if our enemies are destroying these lives, attempting to draw one or more of the Three out. After all, if one of them falls or turns to the other side, all will be lost. More than one destroyed will only hasten our demise."

"This is the flaw, isn't it?" I sighed.

"Yes. This is the flaw," he agreed.

Breanne's Journal

One of Bill's agents drove the medi-van. Bill sat in the passenger seat up front while I knelt in the empty space behind him, hoping we wouldn't be shot at while I gave instructions on how to get to the building where two prisoners were being held. The roads were filled with potholes and gaps where rockets or grenades had detonated. I wanted to shake my head, too—what good did it do to create anything if someone intended to come along and destroy it anyway?

"Young woman, if you are misleading us," Bill turned in his seat to look into my eyes.

"I'm not wrong," I said as the van shuddered—we'd driven over another huge crater in the road. What might I do to get Bill out of this if everything went sour? His life was safe in my hands—I'd protect him with everything I had. I still wasn't sure about the other five—they'd been giving me foul glances since they'd arrived. At least they were focused on their job and loyal to Bill.

"This is it," I said, pointing to the partially destroyed two-story building to our left. It had been my idea to haul the (now dead) captor with the chest wound in the back of the van, as if we were returning his body to his companions. I hoped in the ensuing confusion over how that might happen, we'd be able to overpower those who came to investigate our arrival. I didn't want to tip my hand (any more than necessary) on what I might be able to do.

Six men carrying rifles surrounded the medi-van immediately, like cockroaches pouring from the walls, ready to devour whatever they might find. At least we were all dressed in Mercy Crossings uniforms —green shirts and camo fatigues with boots. Bill, in his wisdom, had seen to that.

All of us scooted out of the van, our hands in the air. Our captors spoke Arabic, so I translated as Bill spoke, saying we'd brought the body back—our doctors hadn't been able to save him.

The back door of the van was flung open and sure enough—the sheet covering the body was flung back and the dead man was examined.

"Come—you will carry the dead inside," one of our captors ordered in Arabic. I translated for Bill, who nodded. He knew, just as I did, that we were about to be added to the two prisoners they already held.

"Let's go," Bill ordered quietly.

Two of Bill's agents carried the stretcher inside behind two rifle-toting renegades while Bill, the three remaining agents and I were waved inside behind them. We were led straight into the room where the two captive agents were. One of them was unconscious, his head bloody where he'd been hit with the butt of a rifle.

They intended to do the same to me, too—they thought I was more than offensive, walking about with my head and face uncovered. When the butt of the gun was aimed at my head, I snatched it from my assailant's hands faster than he could see.

After treating him to the same fate he'd intended for me, our other captors were handled exactly the same way. Except for one, that is. I was breathing hard, my claws at his throat faster than he could blink. Yes, he wet himself. Likely he'd never come as close to a vampire as he was now. That's when the shrieking winds hit.

"What the hell?" Six agents' gazes swiveled from me to the windowless walls—if my guess was correct, we'd just been hit by a horrific sandstorm.

I was forced to think faster than I'd ever been forced to think before. Gathering Bill, his agents and the two captives inside my mist, I raced toward the tents of Mercy Crossings. Those tents were never meant to survive any sandstorm, and would be torn apart by what screamed around us as I sped toward them.

CHAPTER 4

I never wanted to place compulsion on so many people again in my life. I was wrapped in a blanket, as were the others, while we stood inside a meeting room on a U.S. Naval destroyer. That Destroyer currently floated in international waters off the coast of Somalia. Everybody involved now believed we'd been rescued by helicopters and delivered to the ship while the city of Beledweyne was wiped away by a vicious sandstorm.

"Breanne, may I speak with you in private?" Bill Jennings stood beside me and leaned in to whisper in my ear.

"Sure." I nodded. He took my elbow, the ship's captain nodded at Bill and we were led away to a private room. The captain left us alone after getting us seated comfortably inside.

"Breanne, what was that I saw earlier?" Bill lifted an eyebrow at me. We sat on opposite sides of a small, metal table.

"Which time?" I asked.

"I didn't even see you pull the gun away and hit that man," he sighed.

"Someday, Bill," I reached across the table and smoothed a straying lock of hair off his forehead, "I'll let you remember that. For now, you have to forget. I'm sorry." His eyes went blank before he nodded.

"You're interpreting skills are exceptional," Bill sighed when his eyes focused again. "Might it be possible for you to work with us again, sometime? When you're not busy with Mercy Crossings, that is?"

"If you want," I agreed. "I'd be happy to work with you anytime, Director Jennings."

"That would be wonderful," Bill sighed. "Want to come with me? I understand they have coffee and food for us in the galley."

"Do they make anything vegetarian?"

"If they don't, I'll order that they make something," Bill grinned for the first time. "I understand from spotty communications," he held a hand at my back while he ushered me out of the small meeting room, "that Beledweyne was razed behind us. If what the satellites are showing is correct, everybody in the city is dead, now."

My shoulders drooped. I'd brought the sick and injured children with me, but there'd been no time to gather parents. All the children on board the ship were now orphans.

"Breanne, we couldn't have saved them. There wasn't enough room on the helicopters."

Bill only understood what my compulsion allowed him to understand. "Yeah," I placed an arm about his waist. He smiled—he didn't mind that one bit. "You're right, of course."

"I am," he raised his hand from my back and dropped it on my shoulder. "Don't let this upset you. There's no way we might control a sandstorm."

"Yeah," I repeated. Only I suspected this was no ordinary sandstorm. I just hadn't had time to attempt to analyze any of it—I'd been hard-pressed to save the lives I had. There was no other time available, unless I wanted to bend time. Somehow, I imagined that expending that much energy might be a mistake. Bill patted my shoulder, allowed his hand to drop and led me to the ship's galley.

I spent two weeks aboard the ship, translating ill and injured children's words for Mercy Crossings. Bill and his agents (including the one with a head wound) were transported away by helicopter the day after I'd dropped them onto the ship. Eventually, we were transferred to another ship, which carried us to Egypt. From there, we were flown to London and then sent back to the U.S.

I stayed two nights in New York, courtesy of the Joint NSA and Homeland Security Department. I was escorted to meetings, where they spoke every language to me that they had in their arsenal. I could always answer.

Bill, who now had my private cellphone number, called me three times, explaining the tests they were putting me through. He was always nice to me, letting me know that he was clearing the way for me to work with him and his agents again. I told him I understood.

Obviously, they were more than happy with me when they put me on a plane to San Francisco on the third day—the agency didn't have anyone else who could speak as many languages as I could. They didn't even dig too deeply into how that might be possible. I believe Bill had something to do with that, and I was glad. Mostly, I was glad to get away from such a bad experience in Somalia, and while I wasn't allowed to discuss what had happened there, I didn't really want to talk about it anyway.

"The signature disappeared from Le-Ath Veronis," his lieutenant bowed before him. "We have not been able to trace it since then, and it is our supposition that it has fled. Perhaps time has been altered to protect it."

"I have already taken this into consideration." He allowed a small amount of violet light to escape his disguise. "I have already planted servants and traps throughout likely periods and places in the timeline—should anything appear, I will be informed."

"Shall I continue my search, then?"

"Of course. We must consider every possibility, and those possibilities include travel from here to there. We cannot guess at these reasons, yet. We only have supposition."

"Then it will be as you command." The lieutenant nodded and disappeared.

~

Breanne's Journal

Although it had been nearly a month since Beledweyne had been wiped off the map by the strangest of events, some news programs were still showing images of the devastation afterward. Only a few images of bodies were shown, and those were the least affected. Most of the bodies, I knew from reading some of Bill's highly placed agents, had the skin and much of the underlying muscle scoured away by a sandstorm like no other.

Needless to say, I was looking forward to seeing Hank again. After arriving in New York, several undelivered messages appeared on my cellphone. The most recent text from Hank said he'd gotten the club open. Well, good for him. He'd opened ahead of schedule, and that was almost a miracle, considering he'd had to get the foundation cracks fixed in my absence.

The trip from New York to San Francisco was tiring, with two stops and a layover in between. It was late when we landed, and I was nearly too tired to mist to the bottom door leading to my apartment. Wearily, I dropped my duffle and stared at the sign over the bar.

No, we'd never talked about the name of the club, and heavy-metal music thumped inside as I blinked in exhausted confusion. *Dom Bell's* was spelled out in green neon above the door. As tired as I was, I only wanted a shower and sleep, but figured the music from the club would be vibrating my apartment. Lifting my duffle, I climbed the steps and unlocked the door.

The floor between the club and my apartment turned out to be less substantial than I thought. There wasn't any way I could sleep like that; my bed was just about to vibrate across the room. I also had endless nights to look forward to the same thing. Had Hank known that, too, and conveniently forgotten to tell me?

Well, there was one way to find out. I left my apartment, marched downstairs and stalked through the door of the club. I figured he was having a theme night—Goth seemed to be the order of the day with dyed-dark hair, heavy eyeliner, chains and collars everywhere. Hank wasn't behind the bar—someone I didn't recognize was. Just my luck to show up on Hank's night off.

The bartender was short, with a round face and a shaved head. My anger rising as the song changed to something that sounded very close to the wailing of giant porcupines mating, I marched to the bar. The bartender offered a scathing glance and kept washing glasses.

"Is Hank here?" I almost had to shout to make myself heard.

"Who's asking?" His voice was gruffer than his expression.

"Breanne Hayworth. You know, the one who owns half the place," I snapped. Well, I did. I didn't want to play that card, but it was either that or let the claws and fangs slide out. Discretion is always the better part of valor.

"Oh. Master Bell said to watch for you. Didn't know when you might be back. He's in the back, presiding over a public flogging. Go on through." The bartender jerked his head toward the back room. Deciding that he was daft or I hadn't heard correctly because the pounding music was giving me a headache, I walked through the back door and straight into a medieval dungeon.

I might have only felt ill if it hadn't been for the whip and handcuffs. Now I understood the club's name. A young woman was handcuffed to a thick, wooden post while a short, stocky male in black leather flogged her with a whip. I was horrified—she appeared to be enjoying herself. And there was Hank, standing to the side and dressed in black leather pants only, his well-muscled arms crossed over his chest as he watched the naked girl being smacked.

I can't begin to describe the memories that flooded through me at the sight, and I almost vomited on the spot. Hank looked up, then, and saw me. Snapping his fingers, someone peeled away from the crowd and took his place as he stalked toward me. I turned and ran.

I don't know how long I walked the streets of San Francisco that night. Dawn was close when I finally wandered into a hotel near the wharf. I'd turned my cellphone off after Hank's third attempt to call me. I had nothing to say to him.

Over and over, I berated myself for not reading him. For believing that everybody deserved a chance without me knowing their entire history and having that prejudice stand against them. I was all kinds of a fool and I knew it.

After I slept—if that were possible—I intended to find a real-estate agent and get another place to live. I was sick with the thought that I'd allowed Hank Bell access to me in the most intimate way possible. At least he'd only swatted me once. If he'd tried to hit me, he might have died.

~

"Terry, I need to buy a house. In a quiet neighborhood," I muttered as I dropped my gaze. I was more than tired, hadn't slept more than half an hour in an expensive hotel room, misted to my old apartment, cleaned up and dressed there and then went to my attorney's office.

Terrence "Terry" Johnston looked as he always did, dressed in a white dress shirt, his tie loosened, and wearing nicely creased dress pants. His suit coat was draped over a coat rack in the corner of his office. Terry's dark-skinned fingers held a nice pen, which he tapped against the blotter on his walnut desk while deep-brown eyes studied me. Then he nodded. "I can see that you do," he agreed. "I've driven past the club a few times. Always seems to be crowded in the two weeks it's been open. I was worried you didn't know about it."

"I didn't."

"Want me to ask for your money back? In a nice way, of course."

"Terry, I'm walking away. If you want to draw up papers telling Hank it's all his, then do it. I don't want anything to do with that." I shuddered at the images from the night before—it had been impossible to remove them from my memory.

"Look, I'll keep that option open, in case you change your mind."

"Terry, I trust you, but in this case," I shivered again. "I really don't want any part of that. Consider it a lesson learned."

"A ninety-thousand-dollar lesson," Terry muttered.

"Back to the house," I said.

"How much do you want to spend?"

"Not more than five or six million, but I want it private." At that moment, I almost didn't care how much it cost, I just wanted privacy, somewhere far away from Hank Bell.

"My sister works for a real estate firm in San Rafael," Terry ventured.

"Consider her hired. I want this done as soon as possible."

That afternoon, I was shown three houses, all of them located in the hills above San Rafael. The third one overlooked the waters of San Rafael Bay.

"This one," I nodded, as Davonna Johnston-Little showed me through it. It had everything I wanted and was very quiet. It stood on a hill, and the two closest homes were a quarter of a mile away.

Davonna blinked at me, her dark eyes lighting up. "Really? Terry said you were anxious to buy, but this is six-point-two million."

"I'll take it. How soon can we close?"

"Well, there is one problem," she sighed. Digging through her purse, Davonna pulled out her cellphone. "The owner has to approve the buyer," she muttered. I didn't bother reading her—my shields were firmly in place as she spoke to her manager at the realty firm, who said he'd contact the owner.

"The abstract is up to date and everything is ready to go, but he has final approval. His family owned the entire hill in the beginning, and I get the idea that the last tenant had too many loud parties. The original owner purchased the home back and is looking for more suitable neighbors this time."

"I don't throw parties," I said. "And this will be a cash sale."

Davonna and I ended up in her boss's office that evening, while information I'd been asked to provide was spoken to the owner over the phone. I could hear his responses easily as he spoke on the other end of the call.

"She volunteers for Mercy Crossings?" Suddenly, his voice betrayed excitement.

"Yes. I have information here, listing her as an interpreter for the organization," Davonna's boss replied smoothly. He did have documentation—Terry had faxed it to his sister at my request. Terry had all my information in a file. As much information as I was willing to allow anyone to have, anyway. And he handled the checks for all my charitable foundation's gifts. That was also registered with the IRS and anybody else who needed to know.

"What languages does she speak?" the owner asked.

"What languages do you speak?" Davonna's boss covered the mouthpiece and asked.

"Just about everything," I said.

"She says just about everything," was relayed to the owner, whose name I still didn't know.

"Hand the phone to her," he instructed. I took the phone when it was offered to me. The scent of Davonna's boss's aftershave tickled my nose as I said hello. My greeting was acknowledged by a spate of Italian, demanding to know why I wanted to purchase the house in question.

"For peace and quiet," I returned in the same language. "I can make the same reply in French, Spanish, Arabic and Setswana," I added.

"How quickly would you like the deal to go through?" He asked in English.

"Yesterday," I said. "I just got back from a trip with Mercy Crossings, and discovered that a very loud bar had opened beneath my apartment in the city. Loud music doesn't allow much sleep."

"Understood. How long will it take to put your funding together?"

"I can write a check tonight. Or get certified funds from my bank tomorrow."

"You don't want to get an appraisal?"

"That's not necessary. Right now, I just need a place to stay that isn't over a bar."

"Do you want the furnishings to stay?"

"For now. I can replace anything I don't want later."

"Have a cashier's check to your agent tomorrow afternoon. I'll see she has the keys. You can move in whenever you like after that, I'll have my attorney go through the rest of the paperwork and finish up the sale. When he's done, he'll send copies."

"Thank you. That would be wonderful."

"You're welcome."

I handed the phone back to Davonna's boss, who waved us out of the room. "Congratulations, you're a homeowner," Davonna smiled brightly. She should, she'd just earned a huge commission.

"Tell Terry thanks for recommending you—I found the perfect house," I replied, taking Davonna's offered hand and shaking. "I'll find a hotel room for tonight. I'm excited to be able to move in tomorrow."

"It's a lovely home, and it was inspected last week before it was offered for sale. Everything works."

"Great."

I'd spent the night at a hotel in San Rafael, then spent my morning at a TinyCar dealership, purchasing a new car. Yes, just as advertised, the car was tiny. I now owned a three-car garage and my new vehicle would take up half of one of those spaces. It didn't matter—if I replaced any of the furniture, the old stuff could go in the garage while I waited for a local charity to pick it up.

I'll admit I felt almost giddy—I'd never owned a house before. At one time, I'd never believed anything like that might be possible. Now, it was. This house, too, was no starter home. It was eight thousand square feet of pure bliss overlooking the waters of San Rafael Bay. On a clear day, I might even be able to see the Richmond-San Rafael Bridge from the spacious patio. My cellphone rang as I climbed into my newly-purchased TinyCar to drive it off the lot. It was Hank.

"What do you want?" I asked, my voice turning sour as I answered the call.

"Baby, come home and let me explain," he said.

"No chance. I just bought a house. I won't be coming back. I told

Terry to rip up our agreement and send the pieces to you, but good lawyer that he is, he refused. I don't want anything from you, Hank. Not now and not ever."

"Bree, what are you so afraid of? This is me. You know me. I'd never hurt you. You said you don't do pain. I understand that."

"Hank, you understand nothing," I said. "And it's obvious I don't know you, isn't it? If I did, I'd never have offered to invest."

"Baby, just agree to meet with me. I'll pay you back. I'm good for the loan. The club's been busy since it opened."

"Yeah. I saw what kind of business you do, Hank. Sorry. Gotta go." I hung up, my hands shaking. A dealership salesman began walking toward me as I dropped my head in my hands and moaned. Before he could come close enough to tap on my window, I put the car in gear and drove away.

"Something wrong?" Davonna asked kindly as I handed her the cashier's check with shaking fingers.

"No. I just need that peace and quiet in my new house, that's all." I did need it. The sound of leather slapping against human skin invaded my dreams, now, and woke me with a panic attack in my hotel room. Intending to mist back to my old apartment to gather clothes and personal items, I accepted the house keys from a concerned Davonna.

"Look, it's personal and not your problem," I sighed. "And don't ask your brother. He doesn't know, either." I waved as I walked away.

After buying groceries and several bottles of wine, I drank my third glass while staring at my new kitchen. The counters were covered with expensive granite that gleamed in the light cast by pendant lamps overhead. The stove might be any cook's dream, with six gas burners and a grill in between. My shoulders ached and I had a headache from stress. I was putting off going after my clothes, too. I hadn't realized I was crying until a tear dropped onto my hand.

"Fuck," I muttered, wiping my face. The first man I'd ever had sex with had turned out to be this. Did I care about Hank? I'd loved him. Probably still did, but that was agony in its infancy. When was he planning to tell me? Or had he just expected to string me along until a long line of submissive women started coming to his bar? He'd asked to be my fuck buddy, nothing more. Well, it was all coming clear to me now.

"Just get your stuff and go," I muttered to myself. Squaring my shoulders and ignoring my headache, I misted to my old apartment.

Hank apparently had the landlord's set of keys to my apartment. I found six notes from him scattered about as I gathered up my clothes and other belongings into a pile on the floor. I'd mist them to the new house.

Call me was written tersely on the note beside the bed. I ripped it into shreds before dropping pieces on the floor. *Bree, trust me. It's not what you think*, was written on the note taped to the refrigerator door.

"Then what the hell is it?" I wept as I tore that one up, too. I couldn't take any more—I misted what I'd gathered to the house in San Rafael, dropped to the floor in a corner of my new bedroom and cried my eyes out.

Three weeks passed. I was grateful that Mercy Crossings and Bill Jennings hadn't contacted me during that time. It gave me space to put myself back together, without Hank's image and that of a flogging invading my thoughts and dreams. For the most part, anyway. I'd made a trip to the nearest grocery store to stock my pantry when I met Trina for the first time, early one Saturday morning.

"Having problems?" I slowed to ask. The tall, curvaceous black woman had the hood up on an ancient Honda, staring as smoke poured from the radiator.

"I have the car filled with groceries, Mr. Rome will be furious if I don't have lunch waiting when he gets back and this piece of crap decides to die on me now." She kicked the car's bumper while I watched.

Lowering my shield, I read her long enough to see that her employer, Jayson Rome, had also been the one who'd sold the house to me.

"How much do you have to carry? I only have part of the back filled up," I raised my shield again and offered Trina James a smile. "I can drive you up the hill, if you want."

"You're the one who bought the house," she said.

"Yes."

"That car don't look big enough to carry both of us, let alone the groceries."

"Well, we'll just make it fit," I said. "We'll make it, even if I have to get out and push."

"All right," Trina muttered, hands still on her hips. She and I unloaded the back seat of her car, and shockingly enough, we did make everything fit into my tiny vehicle. The bag containing the eggs and bread she held on her lap as I drove her to the extremely large house sitting at the top of the hill.

"You keep this behemoth cleaned?" I stared around me at a house nearly twice as big as the one I'd just bought.

"And cook," Trina nodded. "Trina," she held out her hand. "Trina James. Anything you need, all you have to do is ask."

"Do you need help getting your car to a shop?" I asked.

"Nah, I got Triple-A," she said. "It's cheaper than a new car."

"Then maybe your boss doesn't pay you enough," I said, heading for the door.

"I tell him that all the time," she said. I laughed. "Don't forget," she reminded me, "if you need anything, just let me know."

"Don't worry about it," I waved off her offer. "If you need something else, don't hesitate to call me."

"I don't have your number," she pointed out.

"Okay." I walked toward her and pulled out my cellphone. "Here's my number. What's yours?"

Trina ended up putting my number on her cellphone, then entering her number on my phone, as well as the main number at Jayson Rome's house. "It's not his business line, and he never answers it anyway. You'll get me, either way."

"Sounds good," I nodded. "Have fun." I walked toward the door a second time, and this time I managed to get through it.

~

"Breanne Hayworth?" A woman's voice asked when I answered my cellphone on the third ring after carrying the last bag of groceries inside the house.

"Yes?" I replied cautiously.

"Hold for Director Jennings, please," she said. Well, there it was. Bill needed my help. Honestly, I was happy to hear from him. At least I trusted Bill. More than I'd ever trusted anyone else, I think.

"Breanne?" Bill's voice was clear and confident.

"Hey, Director Bill," I said.

"Can you meet me at my office? I'll have a ticket ready for you if you can get to the airport tomorrow morning."

"I can do that," I said. "Should I pack, or is this just a meeting?"

"Go ahead and pack for a few days, and bring a nice dress or two. The President is entertaining foreign dignitaries, and while they have interpreters, I want to hear what you have to say."

"I can do that," I agreed. "Let me know which airline and when, and I'll be at the airport, packed and on time."

"You're the best," I heard the grin in his voice. "Thanks, Breanne."

"No problem." He hung up.

~

Hank sat at his favorite table in Bogey's, an old fashioned sitting in front of him. He couldn't fathom how Breanne had managed to clear out most of her belongings without his knowing—he'd asked for help to have her apartment watched. Somehow, she'd gotten in and out without being seen. She'd ripped up two of his notes, too.

"What are you doing, baby?" Hank murmured in a language none around him might recognize. "Why can't I find you?" He emptied his glass and tossed money on the table before rising and stalking away.

"This is my interpreter, Breanne Hayworth," Bill introduced me to the President and First Lady. I nodded respectfully to each of them. "She'll be my date for the evening," Bill added. I watched as a corner of his mouth curled into an almost-smile.

I wore the only nice dress I owned—a black silk, calf-length sheath, coupled with the only nice dress heels I owned, which were also black. If Director Bill wanted to take me to another event, I'd be forced to go shopping. I had no need for dresses, actually, and only had this one because I wanted to get through the door of an upscale San Francisco restaurant to try their vegetarian lasagna.

The President was entertaining OPEC at a luncheon. Sheiks and oil company executives filled the room, and most enjoyed the food served by the White House staff. I heard the President speaking with this one or that, as hors d'oeuvres and drinks were served. Bill leaned down a time or two as I interpreted what this one or that said, and then Bill listened while interpreters did their jobs. Only one took his employer's instructions exactly, telling the President that he would never hire terrorists and that all his employees were carefully screened.

Bill, I sent mindspeech while he barely turned a hair, *that one definitely has terrorists on the payroll, and is aware of them.*

"Breanne, I've only met one other person who could do what you just did," Bill's lips grazed my ear as he spoke. "Mindspeech is very rare, I understand."

"I'm special," I mumbled back. "And not in a good way."

"It's all right, we've suspected him for a while," Bill said as I sat with him after the luncheon was over. "Now, you should know that mindspeech makes you an even more valuable commodity."

"I was afraid of that," I said, dropping my gaze to my hands.

"You don't like it?"

"It's uncomfortable at times. All of it." I didn't go into detail on what "all of it" actually entailed. I sat across from Bill, with only a fragile, antique table between us in one of the many rooms inside the White House. The President, the First Lady and their bevy of Secret Service agents had already disappeared inside the residence.

"But it can prove more than useful to me and to the Department," he said. "I want to pay for your work. Sign you on as a special agent and compensate you for your time."

"I have no idea what that might do to my status as a volunteer with Mercy Crossings. I'd never have been allowed in Somalia if anybody knew about that kind of connection."

"I've already contacted Barry Stokes. Your connection to my Department will never be revealed officially to the charity. Only Barry will know, and he's trustworthy. You see how my team was allowed in Somalia, don't you?" Bill smiled.

"I saw that," I nodded. "I was surprised," I added.

"Don't be the next time," Bill chuckled. He had a nice laugh. "Now, I saw that you didn't eat much—we forgot to mention to the White House chef that you're vegetarian. Why don't you let me take you to lunch?"

I was given a driver and a car for the afternoon, when I informed Bill that I only had one dress with me, and it was the one I'd worn to the luncheon. He offered to pay for my clothing purchases, too, but I refused, telling him I could buy for myself. Likely he already knew that—it was his job. He probably knew how much I had in the bank, in addition to what I'd set aside for my charitable donations. He never said a thing about that, kissed me on the cheek after buying my lunch at a restaurant frequented by members of congress and went back to his day job.

I was driven to the next function by my assigned driver, after dropping me off at my hotel so I could clean up and change. I was at Bill's elbow that evening while the Ambassador from Afghanistan had dinner with the Vice-President. The interpreter was very good; Bill was satisfied. Before my three-day visit was over, however, we'd targeted the sheik and his interpreter, two ambassadors and one King, all of whom Bill labeled as persons of interest.

Bill saw me to the airport himself when it was time to go, and chastely kissed me on the cheek before letting me walk away. I knew from dropping my shield briefly that he wanted me guarded, but it was because he worried about me. That turned out to be a nice thing and made me feel good. It did worry me as well, as I hoped he wouldn't keep me under surveillance. I wanted to mist home from the San Francisco Airport. I ended up getting a cab instead.

CHAPTER 5

Breanne's Journal

"Hey, Trina." Apparently, she'd been keeping watch from the top of the hill and noticed when my lights came on when I got home. She'd called me immediately after.

"Miss Bree," she said, "I have a really big favor to ask."

"What's that?" I said.

"The uh, boss. He needs a date for a family function."

"He needs you to find dates for him?" I tossed my suitcase and garment bag onto the bed. One of my plans for the following day was to buy a new mattress and foundation for the bed—I didn't like what had come with the furnished house.

"Not usually, but the girl he wanted to take to this one wasn't available. You're the best and most suitable woman I know to fill that void."

"Somebody canceled on your boss? That doesn't sound right." I knew Jayson Rome was Second Vice-President for his father's publishing company, and had offices in a very tall building in downtown San Francisco. Terry told me that much after talking with his sister following my purchase of the house. I didn't really care who Jayson Rome was, but I did like my house.

73

"That's why I really need your help. She canceled just this afternoon, and the party is tomorrow night. His parents' fortieth wedding anniversary."

"Why does he need a date?" I asked. "He should be able to deal with his parents without one."

"He never goes to one of those things with his dad unless he has a woman on his arm. He doesn't like the questions he gets asked."

"About why he isn't married or some nonsense like that?" I asked. I really didn't want to be a woman on any rich man's arm. They usually were too full of themselves and I'd seen too much of that in my past. The exceptions were very few and quite far between.

"That's exactly why," Trina confirmed. "Mom and Dad see he has a girlfriend and drop the subjects of marriage and grandkids. At least temporarily."

"Gotcha. Did you get your car fixed?" I asked.

"Yep. New radiator and everything," she said proudly.

"Good for you. You can always borrow my car, if yours acts up again."

"I don't feel safe driving more than a few feet in yours," she said.

"So I was pushing your safe limit when I drove you up the hill?" I asked with a laugh.

"Exactly. Now, answer my question, Miss Bree. You taking the boss off my shit list for tomorrow or not?"

"He's on your shit list?"

"Oh, yeah. The man ought to be able to find his own replacement date. A secretary somewhere ought to fall over herself at an invitation from the boss, but no, not him. He drops this in my lap at the last minute, and here we are."

"I think you need to rework your employment contract, saying it absolutely does not include finding last minute dates for your boss. I have a good lawyer," I said.

"Come on, it'll be just for a few hours. Smile, shake hands, tell everybody they look good and drink expensive champagne. I'll owe you for another one, too."

"Do you have a good oatmeal cookie recipe?" I asked.

"Yeah, why?"

"Because I love oatmeal cookies."

"I'll bake you six dozen if you'll say yes. You're too scrawny as it is."

"Now, is that any way to treat a friend?" I said, trying to keep the laugh from escaping.

"It is if I'm desperate, and I am for sure desperate."

"Fine. How am I supposed to dress?"

"Cocktail dress is good. He's wearing a black, pinstripe suit. Party is downtown, at a hotel."

"Do I need to meet him there?"

"Oh, hell no. I'll tell him he has to pick you up. You're a lady. Some of his dates are nothin' but trash."

"Does he know you call them that?"

"Sure does. He just laughs."

"At least he has a sense of humor."

"Yeah. He has that, all right. If he didn't, I would've quit a long time ago."

I was dressed and ready to go at seven, when Trina said Jayson Rome would drop by to pick me up. I'd spent the day looking at mattresses and eventually bought one I was comfortable with. I'd skipped lunch —this was my first blind date ever, and I had no idea how it might go. Hank's face kept intruding on my thoughts, too, and I had to mentally shove him aside. Nevertheless, I was vibrating with nerves when a black Mercedes pulled into the driveway.

Did I expect him to be rude and honk his horn instead of coming to the door? No. I would have to lower my standards or consider all men aggravating assholes from now on. I set the alarm and locked the door behind me before walking to the waiting car and opening my own door, thank you very much.

Jayson Rome was handsome, with blond hair and brown eyes. He also wore an expensive suit to go with the expensive car. Tall, too—his seat was pushed much farther back than mine. He didn't bother to introduce himself either, and the first words out of his mouth set the tone for our relationship from that point on.

"I'm not interested in dating or a relationship of any kind," he announced as he placed the car in reverse and backed out of my driveway. "I prefer to date more substantial women."

His last statement was accompanied by a brief glance at my chest. Fury can best describe what I felt instantly. "You know," I snapped, "you won't have to worry about either of those things. Stop the car and I'll get out. Feel free to find one of those women you prefer between here and the hotel. I hear the Tenderloin is full of them." I put my hand on the door handle.

"Wait, wait," he held out a hand. "I said that so you'll know not to expect more from this than there is. While I might prefer something else, my parents will absolutely love you. My mother donates to Mercy Crossings. It's her favorite charity."

"I don't care what your mother prefers," I said. "Stop the car."

"I'll ask my mother to stop donating."

"I don't give a damn. Tell me how much she gives and I'll cover it."

"Damn, you are feisty. Trina said you were."

"I'm not sure why Trina hasn't killed you in your sleep, yet. Stop the car."

His reaction surprised me—he threw back his head and laughed. "Look, we'll get through tonight. I thought you might be mostly empty-headed, with a few language skills to your credit."

"Thanks for the vote of confidence. I still want to get out. I can get myself back home."

"Please, don't let my preferences and rude behavior ruin the evening," he said. "My mother is dying to meet you. She wants to talk about what you do for Mercy Crossings."

"I'm sure she does. Some of those things I'm not allowed to discuss, especially if the mission took place in a sensitive area. We have to sign nondisclosure agreements, and my evening has already been ruined, thank you."

"Understood. Look, I was attempting to protect myself; you have no idea how many women want to wiggle their way into a relationship I don't want. Just let my mother know when you can't talk about some things—she'll understand."

"I don't wiggle my way into a relationship with anybody," I said. "I only did this as a favor to Trina, and I'd still prefer that you stopped the car. I assure you I can get myself home and you'll never be bothered by me again. If Trina ever asks me for another favor, I will politely decline."

"Please, come with me," he sighed. "I'll be in enough trouble as it is with Mom if you don't show up. Trina really will kill me in my sleep if she finds out how badly I insulted you."

"Then why the hell did you do it?" I grumped. "Honestly, I'm surprised those well-endowed women you prefer can even stand to be in the same room with you if you're this rude all the time."

"You know, I think you're starting to grow on me. Maybe we can be friends. I have tickets to the Golden State game next week."

"Oh, sure, play on my love of basketball," I huffed. I did like basketball. It was the only sport I really did like, and occasionally watched the televised games.

"You like basketball? You're kidding, right?" His brown eyes registered surprise.

"Hey, I know what goaltending is, and that ref missed the call in the third quarter two nights ago."

"Yeah. I thought the same thing, and my sports editor took a few letters on the subject."

"He should. Golden State would have won the game if that call had been made." They would have—they'd lost to L.A. by one point.

"Okay, you definitely have to go to the game with me next week. I have two extra tickets."

"Look, a game might be nice, but wouldn't having a female companion prevent you from chatting up any buxom ladies you might find interesting?"

"That's not why I go to games. Trust me, I can find my own ladies. It wouldn't hurt to be seen with a woman now and then."

"Sure. I'm the shill to lead on your adoring public."

"I wouldn't put it that way. Look, I wouldn't mind having a friend who likes basketball. We can talk and yell at the refs, eat popcorn and hotdogs and yell some more."

"I'm vegetarian," I said.

"I'll work around that," he replied with a half grin.

"Great," I muttered.

"Still want me to stop the car?"

"I do, but I get the feeling you're not gonna."

"You're right. I haven't had this good a conversation with a woman in a long time. They're always interested in my money or what I might do for them."

"I have my own money, thanks."

"I realized that when you paid cash for the house."

"How about that?" I said. "And you were still rude."

"If I say I'm sorry about that—because I am—will you be nice to my mom?"

"Why wouldn't I be nice to your mother? She hasn't been rude to me."

"Just expecting my rudeness to color the relationship with the rest of the family," he grimaced. It was the first time I'd really looked at him since he'd made his first offensive statement. "And I'm serious about being friends. Please."

"I'll consider it," I muttered, leaning back in my seat and crossing arms over my (according to him) inadequate chest.

"Mom, this is Breanne Hayworth." Jayson led me straight to his mother when we arrived in the large suite at one of the best hotels in town.

"You're lovely," Kathleen Rome took my hand immediately. "Jayson tells me you work with Mercy Crossings."

"I do, as an interpreter," I nodded. Kathleen had given Jayson his good looks; I saw that immediately. She also had blonde hair, brown eyes and was only a few inches shorter than her son. James Rome, who stood nearby, was taller than Jayson by two inches, at least. He had darker hair and his body language indicated tightly controlled emotions. I deliberately didn't read him.

"Mom, Jamie asked me to talk with him for a little while before the party gets started," Jayson said, referring to his older brother before leaning down to give me an unwelcome peck on the cheek. He really was putting on the act. I'll admit I considered reading him, then thought better of it. I knew all I wanted to know about Mr. Jayson Rome. Jayson disappeared, leaving me alone with his mother, who began asking questions about my work immediately.

I had no idea that Ross Gideon would show up at Kathleen and James Rome's anniversary party. I'd read a couple of old paperback versions of his political biographies—they'd been in the house and I'd avidly read everything I could get my hands on when I was younger, even if I wasn't particularly interested in the subject matter.

"Ross, this is Breanne Hayworth," Kathleen introduced me to the popular author. Ross was in his late fifties, with graying brown hair, fading green eyes and stood perhaps at five-ten with his shoes on. "Breanne works for Mercy Crossings," Kathleen gushed. She'd been pumping me all night about some of my assignments, and I'd given her a vanilla serving of the ones I could openly discuss.

"Ross is working on a biography of Everett Williams," Kathleen said.

"I saw him once," I said without thinking. Everett Williams was a well-respected Senator from the state of Texas. He'd died four years before my reappearance on Earth and people still missed his strength and statesmanship at the nation's capital. I'd admired him— he always stood up for what he thought was right, and the others be damned. He often disagreed with his own party over proposed legislation.

"Really? Do you have any stories for us?" Ross Gideon was immediately interested. "Are you from Texas?"

"Yes, from west Texas," I nodded. "I was working at the time, and I did overhear a story." Everett Williams was famous for his humorous stories.

"Can you recall it? If it's a good one I haven't heard, I'll include it in the book." Worried that I might have gotten myself into something I couldn't easily escape, I drew in a shaky breath. Those days were over for me, but I still didn't like recalling that part of my life.

"Please tell us," Kathleen begged. Well, I liked Kathleen. I might not tell the story for Ross Gideon, but I would for Kathleen Rome, who seemed to be a genuinely nice person. Her son, on the other hand, had disappeared and I hadn't seen him for at least two hours.

"Well, this is what I overheard," I began. "Everett was talking to three state representatives. He was sipping a bourbon and soda at the time. He was waving the glass around, holding a cigar between two fingers of the same hand."

"I have that description from a couple of other people," Ross nodded, as if he were mentally verifying my story.

"Anyway," I said, "he and the others were discussing the sitting President, and none of them apparently liked the man. *He reminds me of a treed toad*, Everett said, waving his glass. *What do you mean?* One of the others asked. *Well*, Everett replied, *while I fail to understand how he got up so high, I intend to help him down just as soon as I can.*"

"That's so funny, and sounds exactly like Everett," Kathleen laughed. It was exactly like Everett Williams. As a vampire, I now had perfect recall. Those words were verbatim.

"I'll write that down," Ross mumbled, pulling out his phone and tapping notes on it. "Thanks. I didn't have that one."

"You're welcome," I said. Ross didn't ask where I'd overheard the story, and I was more than grateful for that.

Four hours passed, guests were departing, and Jayson was still locked in a private meeting with his older brother. I felt increasingly out of place and should have known by Jayson's rudeness at the beginning of the evening that this was how things might end up. Well, just as I'd told him earlier, I could get myself home.

Hunger was gnawing at my insides, too, because there'd only been finger food and champagne, and most of the food wasn't vegetarian. I'd kept the drinks to a minimum, at least.

"Kathleen, it was a pleasure to meet you," I took her hand. "I'll call a cab. Jayson's busy," I added.

"Oh, no. I'm sure they'll break that up in no time," she said, although a frown marred her pretty face.

"No, really. I can get myself home with no trouble." I walked toward coat check and asked for my sweater.

"Well, I really enjoyed talking with you," she said. I think if I'd read her at that moment, I'd likely learn that Jayson Rome was in for a tongue-lashing. I didn't care. He seemed to love his mother, and his treatment of me was going to get him in trouble. I didn't care—he deserved whatever he got. "Happy anniversary," I added, before Kathleen leaned down and gave me a hug.

"Good night," she said softly.

"Thank you for a wonderful evening," I said and walked out of the suite.

The hotel doorman hailed a cab for me when I walked outside, pulling my sweater closer to fend off the chill of the night.

"Where to?" the driver asked as I climbed in the back seat.

"Bogey's Bar and Restaurant. Know where that is?" I asked.

"Yeah. They have good roast beef sandwiches."

"They do," I agreed. It was Hank's favorite. Since it was a Friday night, I wasn't worried about running into him—it was just past midnight and Hank should still be at his club. Twenty minutes later I was dropped off outside Bogey's, I paid the cab driver and walked into the popular bar and restaurant.

Later, I sat in a small booth away from the windows, sipping my third glass of white wine and staring morosely at a half-eaten grilled cheese sandwich. I was considering misting home when a familiar voice interrupted my thoughts.

"Baby, what are you doing here?" I jerked my head up as Hank slid into the opposite side of the booth and blinked at me.

"Getting drunk," I snapped, downing the rest of my wine. "I was just leaving." I gathered my jacket and small purse from the seat beside me.

"No, baby, don't leave. Let me talk to you. I just want to look at you for a while. When I heard what went on in Somalia, I was scared to death you were involved in that."

"I can't discuss that," I said, scooting toward the edge of the booth.

"Bree, please say you weren't in the middle of that."

"I said I can't discuss it."

"Jeezus, Bree, you were in the middle of that." Hank raked fingers through his hair. "Look, I know this looks really bad, but it's not what you think. Me and the club, that is."

"Then what is it, Hank?" I stood up.

"No, sit. I need you to sit here with me." He reached out and took my hand.

"Sure, Hank. Tell me what I saw wasn't really what I saw."

"That part, yes." His eyes turned toward the bar, and just as always, a waitress carried an old fashioned to our table. He nodded his thanks to the waitress and waited for her to walk away, after she'd assured him that his sandwich would be right out. I shook my head at the control he seemed to have. After considering it, however, I realized I shouldn't be surprised.

"Look," he continued, "there's a need for what I do—a need for my involvement in the community. Anybody in the community wants to be in the community, Bree. That's how it works. It's a give-and-take, and what's supplied is needed—by all parties. Everything is agreed upon beforehand—and if it's in a public setting, anything that gets out of hand is stopped."

"And that's you—the one who stops it if necessary?" I sat again and toyed with my empty wineglass. I was feeling the effects of a little too much wine and that, combined with Hank's presence, wasn't mixing well in my stomach.

"For now," he agreed.

"Great."

"Bell? What are you doing with my date?" My head jerked up at Jayson Rome's sudden appearance.

"I'm not your fucking date," I snapped. "You made that clear in your first two sentences earlier," I pointed out. "You two know each other?"

"She knows," Hank sighed. "Sit down, Rome."

"Hank and I met at one of the dungeons in Castro," Jayson said, sliding in beside Hank because I refused to budge from the edge of my seat. "I called Trina—she has you on that stalker app on her phone. She told me where you were."

"Of course she did," I muttered, feeling sicker than I had only minutes earlier. "Now," I said, "how do you two know each other, exactly?"

"I pointed him toward a couple of subs," Hank said.

"The buxom ones you like so much?" I stared at Jayson. "Well, that explains a lot."

"I insulted her earlier," Jayson said.

"Rome, I may kill you," Hank said.

"My housekeeper set her up to go to my parents' anniversary party with me tonight, after Belinda canceled," Jayson explained.

"Which will never happen again," I said.

"What about the basketball game next week?" Jayson whined. "I told Mom I was taking you. She really likes you," he added.

"Go fuck yourself, Jayson Rome," I said as pleasantly as I could. "Maybe you can convince Big-Boob-Belinda to go instead."

"My brother wanted to discuss business. It took up the whole night and my mother let me have it afterward because Breanne got tired of waiting and left without me," Jayson went on.

"Nobody asked you for a play-by-play," I said. "I don't feel good. I'm going home."

"Baby, you're too tipsy to go home by yourself," Hank said.

"Really? Watch me," I rose again. Hank pulled me back down.

"Breanne bought the house down the hill from me," Jayson said, as if someone had asked him to empty his mind of all the information he had on me. "Paid cash."

"Fuck you, Jayson Rome," I repeated. "I'm going home. Feel free to discuss everything you think you know about me after I leave."

"Bree, you don't look good," Hank said.

"I feel like shit," I said. "You can thank asshole Rome for that. I sure as hell won't."

"Bree? Is that your nickname?" Jason asked.

"My nickname is none of your fucking business. I want to throw up. Where's the bathroom?" I staggered to my feet.

"Let me take you," Hank stood and took my hand.

"I don't need your help," I jerked my hand from his. "I can take care of myself. Always have." I stalked away from him, the restroom sign wavering in my vision as I made my way across the bar.

"Go ahead, tell me I fucked up."

"You fucked up. But I fucked up first," Hank mumbled as his sandwich, fries and half-order of onion rings was set before him. "And I still want to kill you. What the hell did you say to her?"

"I told her the truth—that I don't usually date and I prefer big, curvy women."

"That's always an icebreaker," Hank said, lifting his sandwich. "And do I understand correctly that she did this as a favor to you, so you'd have somebody on your arm for your parents' party, and then left her by herself the entire night?"

"I had no idea Jamie wanted a meeting. He didn't email me beforehand."

"And you just dance to his tune, is that it? How rude are you, Rome? Your mother is likely wondering why both her sons weren't at her anniversary party."

"Yeah. I just—yeah. Look, what's Breanne to you?"

"She owns half my club. I didn't tell her what kind of club it was—I was waiting to do that, she got called to fucking Somalia, was somehow mixed up in that mess there, came home exhausted and because the music was vibrating her apartment over the bar, she came down to see me. Walked right in on a flogging. I never want to see that look on her face again." Hank bit into his sandwich and chewed determinedly.

"You're the reason she wanted to buy a house so fast and didn't even dicker on the price."

"Yeah. I guess I am. Half owner of my bar isn't all she is to me, either."

"Planning to bring her into the community?"

"That will never happen. You didn't see the look on her face. Something happened to her somewhere along the way, Rome. She's not cut out for it."

"Hell, she's not big enough to take it, anyway."

"Say that again and I really will kill you."

Normally I wouldn't have misted from the restroom after heaving up the contents of my stomach, but I still felt awful and I wasn't in the mood to face Jayson or Hank again. Let them wonder how the hell I got out of the bar—I'm sure Hank was waiting for me to come out so he could start making excuses again. I made it home—barely, fell face-first on my bed and passed out, fully clothed.

Forcing myself to wake Saturday morning before nine, I made a cup of coffee and then sat at the kitchen island in a stupor while it went completely cold. My new mattress was scheduled to be delivered around ten, and all I could do was feel sorry for myself while a headache pounded through what little brain matter I had left. When the doorbell rang, I heaved myself off the barstool I'd camped on and went to answer the door.

It wasn't the delivery truck. Hank stood on my doorstep, a box in his arms. "Go away," I snapped and attempted to shut the door.

"No you don't," Hank forced his way in, hefting the box (and his shoulders) right past me. "I brought the rest of your stuff from the apartment."

"Throw it out. I don't need it," I said.

"Baby, I brought your stuff. And I'll add your rent you didn't use up to what I owe you."

"No, you won't. I already said we're even, Hank. Take yourself and your kinky ways right out that door again."

"People ask for what I do," he said, setting the box down on my kitchen floor.

"Please stop talking." I rubbed my forehead with shaking fingers. The doorbell rang again.

"Get out. I'm having a new mattress set delivered," I pushed past Hank and went to the door. Trina stood on my porch with a foil-covered plate in her hands.

"Trina, I owe you an ass-kicking," I said as she placed the plate in my hands. I did. I had no idea she'd set up that location app on our phones.

"I'll just pass the ass-kicking to Mr. Jayson Rome," she said. "So make it a good one."

"Look, why don't I cut out the middleman and give it straight to him. I think he needs it," I said.

"You're right about that," Trina agreed. "Who's this?" her eyebrows lifted as she caught sight of Hank, who'd found my coffeepot and coffee. He was busy brewing a cup of coffee for himself. "Hey, handsome," Trina called out. "I could use a cup, and I brought the best oatmeal cookies you'll ever eat with me."

"Sounds good," Hank said, handing the freshly brewed cup to Trina, who settled onto a barstool, grabbed the plate of cookies from me and proceeded to remove the foil. Hank pulled another cup from the cabinet and started brewing more coffee.

"Unbelievable," I sighed, rubbing my forehead again.

"She has a headache," Hank said, grabbing a cookie and biting into it. "These really are the best," he nodded to Trina.

"Told ya," she nodded. "Coffee's good."

"Look, I'm going to the store for ibuprofen," I told my uninvited guests. "If the mattress guys show up, just tell them the master bedroom is down the hall at the end." I waved my hand vaguely in the proper direction and pulled my purse off the kitchen counter.

"Baby, I'll get it for you," Hank stood up.

"No, stay there and be eye candy for Trina. I reckon she's mighty tired of looking at Jayson Rome. I got tired of him in thirty seconds flat last night." I stalked toward the garage.

"Where did that drawl come from?" Trina asked as I walked toward the back door.

"Texas," Hank replied.

When I got back from the nearest pharmacy after buying the biggest bottle of ibuprofen they had, the delivery truck was blocking my driveway. What wasn't already taken up by Jayson's Mercedes, that is. At that point, I was so out of sorts and my head hurt so badly that I was tempted to throw everybody out of my house. As a vampire, I was strong enough—and pissed enough—to accomplish it without much effort.

"What the hell are you doing here?" I snapped at Jayson Rome, who sat at my kitchen island, drinking coffee and eating oatmeal cookies with Hank and Trina as if he belonged there. He didn't answer, so I went to the cupboard next to the sink, grabbed a glass, filled it with water and washed down four ibuprofen, hoping that would be enough to stop the pounding in my head.

"How did you get out of the bar last night without us seeing you?" Jayson demanded.

"You think I'll tell you anything?" I said. "Get out of my house. I paid for it. It doesn't belong to you anymore. Go get some of those women you're so fond of. Do you pay Hank a finder's fee for pointing them in your direction?"

"You really did fuck up, didn't you?" Trina eyed Jayson distastefully as she crunched into another oatmeal cookie. "Is it your job to ruin all my friendships?"

"Mattress and foundation are on the bed," one of two delivery guys shoved a clipboard in my direction for a signature.

"It looks good—I checked," Trina said.

"Fine." I signed and handed the clipboard back. "If you all will excuse me, I'm going to put sheets on my bed and then do a faceplant. Please be gone when I wake up." I walked down the hall toward my bedroom.

"Bree," Hank's weight on my new bed forced my eyes open—I'd been trying to sleep and hadn't had much luck at it. A large hand rubbed my shoulders gently. "Baby, I will never ask you for more than you can give. I promise I'll never hurt you or raise a hand against you. I think I know better than that. I just want you back. Like we were. Go to sleep, now. I can see the pain behind your eyes."

"Bob," Ross Gideon spoke with the private detective he often hired to tail politicians and to do discreet research, "Find out everything you can on someone named Breanne Hayworth. Something about that name bothers me."

"Do you know where she's from? So I can narrow the search?" Bob Sullivan asked.

"Somewhere in west Texas. I heard a story from her last night at a party about Everett Williams and it rings true, I just don't have any idea how she might have come in contact with the Senator before his death. She doesn't look to be more than twenty-two, which would have made her sixteen when he died. We both know he was in poor health and didn't socialize the last two years, so that puts her at fourteen. Too young, I think to be working anywhere near him. Find out what you can and get back to me. Pronto."

"Will do, Mr. Gideon."

"Thanks, Bob."

"Teeg, what are we here for, again?" Stellan asked. "Ferdik was a criminal. Most of the population of Theele knows that. Why are they insisting on a memorial?"

"No idea, but they are, so it's my duty to show up." Teeg San Gerxon gazed out the window at the fading light over the city of Thelik, capital of Theele. A statue and a plaque would be unveiled the following morning and Teeg, as Founder of the Campiaan Alliance, was expected to say a few words. Teeg, who'd once been Gavril Montegue, already had a short speech prepared. It had to be short—President Ferdik's tenure in the highest office on Theele had also been short and filled with graft and corruption.

All four Starr brothers were with Teeg, to guard him while he was away from Campiaa. Teeg had only asked Astralan and Stellan to come with him, and intended to leave Galaxsan and Celestan with Dee, to guard the old vampire who was Teeg's assistant as well as his foster-sire. Astralan argued that Theele might be considered unfriendly territory, since Ferdik had been murdered while visiting Campiaa. Some Theeli still held Teeg responsible for Ferdik's death, although Ferdik hadn't been a stellar politician in anybody's eyes and Teeg hadn't been anywhere near Ferdik when he'd died.

Nall Seak had never been captured, and he was the one responsible for Ferdik's death. Teeg still had a bounty on Seak's head, but he hadn't been seen since his escape after plotting Ferdik's demise.

"We'll be out of here right after the luncheon with President Houx tomorrow," Teeg sighed. "I promise."

"Good. Because I don't like staying on Theele one tick longer than necessary," Astralan walked into the room.

"Look, I know all of you are antsy, I feel that way, too," Teeg offered.

"Antsy?"

"One of my mother's idioms."

"She has a lot of those. Did she give them to you for a birthday or something?" Astralan grinned.

"Don't be an ass," Teeg growled.

~

Breanne's Journal

I woke up after midnight and found only four cookies left on the plate Trina brought me. She, Hank and Jayson had consumed the rest. Pouring out a glass of milk, I settled on a barstool to have a cookie or two. They really were good, and I was on my third one when prescience kicked in.

I wouldn't have saved Teeg San Gerxon. Probably. The one I would save, however, even if he didn't remember me, was Stellan. While the freak sandstorm razed Thelik, I was screaming mentally and hauling Teeg, Stellan and his brothers away in my mist.

CHAPTER 6

reanne's Journal
"Breanne, I'm asking you nicely to please reconsider. Mom and Dad are coming to the game. They have a suite reserved and Mom is expecting you." Jayson almost sounded as if he were begging. I wasn't buying it.

"Take Belinda or one of those other women," I huffed. "I don't do much in the leather department. I'm a vegetarian, remember?"

"Mom loves that about you."

"I'm sure she does. Her son, however, finds me grossly inadequate and walks away whenever he gets a chance. As much as I like your mother, I don't feel good about stringing her along. I'm just a front for you—admit it."

"Bree, I'll invite Hank to come, too. I promise one of us will be with you."

"Sure. That sounds so comfortable," I said. "Your mother will wonder what the hell is going on when Hank pays more attention than you do. Frankly, I don't want anything from either of you."

Jayson was still trying to convince me to go to the basketball game the following evening, and he'd shown up at my front door to do it. I'd been grumpy ever since I'd come back after saving Teeg San Gerxon's ass. Sure, it would put the Campiaan Alliance in chaos, but for a blink, or maybe half a blink—I'd considered saving Stellan and his brothers and leaving Teeg behind to be flayed and swallowed by a sandstorm that had destroyed most of Thelik.

"What can I possible do to convince you to come? Donate to Mercy Crossings or some other charity? What?" He'd arrived at my front door as if he'd been invited. I made him stand at the door instead of inviting him in.

"Give Trina a raise. That car she's driving really needs to be retired."

"What?" Jayson almost shouted.

"Okay, the price just went up. Buy her a new car." Did I realize he'd take the bait? No.

"All right. I agree, that piece of crap needs to go to the salvage yard. I'll buy her a new car."

"A good one. She doesn't want a TinyCar, I know that much."

"You think I'd let anybody out of the driveway in one of those things? I saw yours and almost gagged."

"But since I'm nobody important to you, I can drive whatever the hell I want," I pointed out. "Besides, I got my car from a vending machine. Put in a dollar and it dropped out. It was too bad, too—I wanted a soda."

The corners of Jayson's mouth threatened to turn up. Schooling his face, he said, "I never pegged you for an extortionist," instead.

"I never pegged you for an asshole, either, but disappointment abounds. Sell that Mercedes you have and buy four decent cars with the proceeds. See? Everybody's happy."

"That's a Mercedes McLaren," Jayson howled.

"Then buy eight decent cars."

"If you weren't so smart and my mother didn't like you so much," Jayson threatened.

"You'd what? Have one of those bigger, taller, better-endowed women beat me up? Jayson Rome, feel free to bring anybody you want against me. They won't last ten seconds."

"You'll come to the game? I still plan to invite Hank. I usually sit courtside, but since Dad's coming and bringing Mom," Jayson didn't finish.

"Just don't make an ass out of yourself this time." I shut the door in his face before he could sputter a reply.

~

Lissa's Journal

"Mom, I don't know why we're still alive. Everybody in a click radius died behind us. Somebody misted us away from there—Astralan and Stellan both say their power died when the winds first reached us, and I couldn't even turn to mist. I thought it might have been you." Teeg watched my face carefully—he'd asked me to meet him at his office in Campiaa City.

"Honey, it wasn't me," I said. Worry almost made my voice shake. I hadn't even known he was in danger, and that shouldn't be. Just like the sandstorms I'd witnessed with Merrill, Kiarra and Adam in the Dark Realm, I'd had no warning of this one, either, even with my son's life in danger. After the destruction of Yigga Prison and the resulting deaths around it, I'd hoped for no more sandstorms. Instead, things were ramping up in the Light worlds. Thelik served to spook the population in both Alliances, and I couldn't say I blamed them. I was spooked, too.

"What's the problem?" Gavin and Merrill both appeared inside Teeg's office. At least Merrill's radar still worked, and he'd likely hauled Gavin along with him.

"I'm still trying to get used to this," Gavril waved an arm in Merrill's direction.

"It should have always been," Merrill growled. "And would have been, without your grandfather's interference."

"Look, this isn't the time for a family fight," I pointed out judiciously. "We have to figure out who's causing these sandstorms, and devise a way to save the cities and the people they're destroying."

"I have no idea how to do that—we were barely able to fold away before," Merrill agreed, sitting beside me on Gavril's guest sofa.

Gavin, arms crossed tightly over his chest, chose to remain standing.

Gavin was still angry that I hadn't remained in contact with him, and he was angry with himself (although he wouldn't admit it) because he'd fallen victim to a mind cloud and didn't realize it. He still wouldn't discuss Breanne with me. It shamed him, and he knew he'd damaged any relationship I might have with my half-sister.

Kiarra had placed Gavin on probation, so any wrong move on his part in the next three years would see him kicked out of the Spawn Hunters. I hadn't taken Gavin's side in this, and he understood from that just how pissed I was over his behavior.

Gavril, too, had mistreated his aunt, and he skirted the topic, just as his father did. It made me sigh—I hadn't even gotten to talk with her before she disappeared. When I'd asked Erland to arrange a meeting with my father in Rylend's private study, I'd informed Griffin then that he'd fathered a second daughter. That meeting hadn't gone well and he'd disappeared.

Later, he'd asked Erland to arrange a second meeting on Karathia. He wanted to ask questions about Breanne, but I had very little information to offer. She'd gotten away from Le-Ath Veronis as quickly as she could, and I couldn't blame her in the slightest.

"I've talked with my father, and he's understandably upset that we didn't recognize her. She was Karathian after all—enough to be the Q'elindi Erland suspected," my father muttered, turning away from me. "Where is she now?"

"I have no idea," I'd told him. "You know the Larentii say she's the Vhanaraszh, too." His shoulders drooped and he'd sighed heavily before disappearing again. That was Griffin—never taking responsibility for his actions until long after the fact. I'd ended up tossing a hand in the air in resignation and folding back to Le-Ath Veronis.

At least Ry was asking his warlocks to keep an eye out for her—he liked Breanne. He and Erland, both. Tory hadn't ever met her, and if things continued as they were, he might never meet her.

Cheedas, on the other hand, barely spoke to me on the best of days. I was still attempting to sort that out. He supervised the kitchen and rarely made an appearance at the table, although he had a standing invitation.

At first he hadn't recalled Breanne, but others around him did and they talked about her—and the fact that they hadn't realized she was my sister—incessantly now. Cheedas was brought up to speed after the fact, almost, and it embarrassed him terribly.

I didn't push him on the subject—it was no secret that he'd withheld meals and refused to allow the palace staff to serve Breanne or clean my bedroom while she stayed there. She'd had to do those things herself or go without. I'd seen him in my study shortly after he'd staked me and I'd tried to have a conversation about the mind cloud, but he'd barely responded to my words.

Deeply ashamed best described what he felt, and he wasn't comfortable coming anywhere near me. My sister could *Change What Was* with Cheedas if she were so inclined, but after the way she'd suffered at his hand, that would likely never happen. Had Cheedas not been a modified vampire, I imagine that he might have made his way to *The Line*.

Kiarra, too, said that Pheligar was tight-lipped on the subject of Breanne, but somehow she'd gotten the idea from him that at least one Larentii had been affected by the mind cloud. Since she didn't know much, including the name of the Larentii in question, she and I had let it go. We had other, larger difficulties to deal with.

It was a pleasure to work with her, though. She and I often thought alike, and there'd been more than one time when Merrill had sat between us, called us his girls and had an arm around both our shoulders. I didn't mind those times one bit.

"Honey, I don't know how to figure this out," I eventually said to Gavril. "I'm just glad that whoever came did come to get you and your warlocks. There's no telling where the Campiaan Alliance might be if you'd gone down." I didn't add that I'd have gone down, too. That was my son, after all, and it would kill me (and Garwin Wyatt) to lose him.

"Did we ever learn everything that Breanne is capable of doing?" Merrill asked. "She is your sister, after all."

"No, because she wasn't watched closely, unless she was in a Council meeting or with Gavril," I muttered angrily. Gavin hadn't even bothered to teach her the lessons she needed as a vampire. Grant and Heathe said she'd learned the rules from a comp-vid.

If he hadn't been affected by the mind cloud, I would have kicked Gavin myself over that. It was no secret, too, that Gavril had asked Nall Seak to hit her. Erland had supplied that information. He'd seen her face afterward, and his jaw always tightened when he talked about it. My Karathian warlock seldom showed anger, but he did over that.

"I'm never going to see my sister, am I?" I glanced at Merrill. He, Gavin and Gavril stared—I'd been lost in thought and spoke my thoughts aloud.

"Mom, I'm sorry about that." Gavril stood and stared out the window of his study. It overlooked the grounds at the front of San Gerxon Palace.

"How's Reah?" I quickly changed the subject.

"Pregnant," he muttered. I already knew that from Ry. Tory would be a father again, and he'd already told Jayd to stay away or neither he nor Garde would ever see the baby. Garde had backed away immediately. Jayd was still fuming—he wanted to find a tentative mate for the baby, if it turned out to be a girl like all of Tory's others. He and Glinda had all of Reah's daughters already, and Glinda still hadn't gotten pregnant again.

The last time Kifirin had shown up asking for forgiveness, I'd ended up yelling at him, asking him why he hadn't interfered with Jayd and Glinda, making her pregnant instead of Reah. He'd blown clouds of smoke, told me he was having difficulties with his overlord and disappeared. His disappearance was probably a good thing—I still wanted to kick his ass more often than not.

"Can anybody get close enough to these sandstorms to determine what's causing them? It can't be a warlock or any average power wielder, can it?" Gavril asked, turning back to me. "I had all four warlocks with me, and they were powerless against this."

"Anybody who's gotten close enough didn't live over it," I pointed out. I didn't tell him what else I knew about them—it would only serve to terrify everybody.

"What about the inmates from Yigga Prison?" Merrill asked. "Have we seen any of them after they disappeared?"

"No. Norian and Ildevar have everybody looking, including the ASD, RAA and anybody else they can commandeer in law enforcement. There's no sign of them."

"But we know the bodies disappeared," Gavin growled. "The other bodies were left behind to rot. Theirs weren't."

"Have you asked Trevor to keep an eye open—not just for them but for Breanne?"

"I haven't spoken to him about Breanne," Gavin ducked his head. "He has information on the prisoners." That's when I knew there was something he hadn't told me. I was prepared to wait patiently to see what that might be.

❧

Breanne's Journal

Kathleen Rome wasn't interested in the game. She wanted to chat while Jayson, Hank and James Rome, Sr., cheered three-pointers, drank expensive beer and ate snacks provided to a private box.

"Jayson's magazine is printing an excerpt from Ross's book about Everett Williams," Kathleen gushed at halftime. "Just to create buzz around the book. We intend to release it in three months—it's almost finished."

"It ought to be a bestseller," I said. "Everett was loved and respected by just about everybody."

"James knew Everett—that's why he commissioned the book. Met with him several times—Everett always consulted James on media-related matters."

"I can see why he might do that," I nodded. James Sr.'s name was well-known across the country. He'd been in the newspaper and publishing business all his life, after inheriting the company from his father, John Rome.

"I wish Everett was still alive. He was only sixty-four when he died and those people who claim to be politicians in Washington now are nothing more than a bunch of posturing idiots," Kathleen huffed.

While I might agree with her on the state of most politicians, who seemed better prepared to disagree with the opposing party rather than work out a compromise much of the time, I settled for nodding instead of expressing myself verbally. Some—a few, anyway—actually had good intentions; they just didn't have loud enough voices. A few, too, had enough crazy to fill a psych ward, and those seemed to get all the airtime.

"Ready to go?" Jayson asked, taking my elbow when the game was over. I didn't even know who'd won—Kathleen had monopolized my time. I got the idea she didn't get to talk with many women who shared common interests often. I purposely didn't read her again—I had no desire to see endless dinners and functions where she appeared as a hostess, most likely engaging in idle and purposeless chatter until everybody went home for the evening. Kathleen was intelligent, it was easy enough to see, but her husband ruled the house as well as the business and that was that.

Discreetly, I pulled my arm away from Jayson's grasp—he'd ignored his mother and me in favor of a basketball game. I wanted to tell him he had a wonderful mother and he should cherish her. I didn't. That might open the floor to questions I had no desire to answer.

I thought about Lissa, too, and the fact that we'd never talked. Well, Gavin and Gavril would likely ensure that it remained that way. Cheedas would probably poison my tea if I showed up on Le-Ath Veronis again. Yes, it was undoubtedly a good thing that I intended to stay away from all of them.

～

"Did you ever find the reason Erithia Cordan's casino exploded?" Kooper settled into a chair beside Trevor's desk.

"Forensics found nothing. No bombs or traces of any type of

98

explosives anywhere. If Lissa had been here, I'd have said maybe she caused it. Since she wasn't, I don't have a clue, and neither do the experts who work for your bunch."

"Norian didn't tell me he had a team working on it." Kooper frowned at Trevor.

"Anything like that gets near the palace and he's a crazed tyrant. I'm not surprised he didn't tell you. He's too busy trying to get Lissa back."

"So, she's upset over Skel Hawer, still?"

"I get that idea," Trevor nodded. "Haven't heard what happened to the girl he attacked. Probably back with her sire. Heinrich's a recluse, so that's no surprise. I did hear that Lissa set aside the engagement to Casimir, since he and the girl were never introduced. Lissa doesn't like that sort of coercion."

"Understood. Want to walk with me? I'd like to take a look at the space left after the explosion." Kooper stood and stretched.

"Most of it's gone, now, since we couldn't find anything. Cordan owed money on it, and the investment company wants to rebuild. Already has a buyer lined up."

"No surprise. It's in a prime location. I'm still amazed that the explosion didn't affect nearby casinos."

"Me, too. Come on, I'll walk with you." Trevor stood and followed Kooper from his office.

"Why?" Kalenegar stared at Graegar and his son, Garegar. "Has any Larentii ever been affected by such as this? I felt it fall away the moment Breanne disappeared."

"And there I'd thought you were taking your anger with your father to an extreme by torturing her," Graegar replied, toying with a dying rose and bringing it back to a tight, fresh bud with the power he held.

"I had no idea what was happening. Surely someone should have known I wouldn't treat an innocent like that."

"I have no idea what you might do; you've been gone so long. I only have tales from the others regarding the long feud with your sire. Breanne certainly suffered until she discovered how to get away from you."

"She will hate me, now, and that is my Vhanaraszh."

"I don't know what to tell you, other than she managed to destroy the locating chip Connegar and Reemagar placed. She cannot be found by any of us."

"Will you send out mindspeech? She didn't find you repulsive," Kal asked softly.

"I won't. I have no desire to upset or offend her by asking her to answer, merely to bring her to you. I imagine that a great length of time might have to pass before she consents to be on the same world as you."

"What are you saying?" Kal demanded.

"Father is saying you're an ass, in humanoid terminology," Garegar spoke for the first time. "Grandfather says worse, and he refused to come with us to meet you. Great-Grandfather actually cursed you when he found out what you'd done."

"Of course he did. Do you think I haven't cursed myself? Do you?" Kalenegar folded away.

"I believe he may be contrite, Father," Garegar turned to Graegar and smiled.

"You may be correct, my child," Graegar agreed.

❧

"Trajan, is this how it'll be from now on? You only speaking to me when there's no other option?" Ashe leaned back in his office chair, studying Trajan with a frown.

"You have the nerve to ask me that?" Trajan growled, turning away.

"Traje, talk to me. Tell me how you feel."

"Really? You want to hear what I have to say? The Mighty Hand wants to know what I think?" Incredulity coated Trajan's words.

"There you are, with what you want, only she won't let you touch her or talk to her. I had what I wanted, and you fucked it up."

"Yeah. I fucked this up," Ashe agreed. "How many times do you want me to say I'm sorry?"

"I don't want an apology. I want Breanne. Go find her for me and I'll call it even."

"That's the trouble, Traje. I can't find her, and I don't know why that is. Ren says that Connegar and Reemagar placed a locating chip, but that either stopped working or disappeared, somehow. Nobody knows where she is."

"Great." Trajan rose and tossed his chair against Ashe's office wall. "Just fucking wonderful." Turning to his wolf, Trajan trotted from Ashe's study.

~

"Kay? Kalia?" Bill coaxed. "You have to eat something." Bill pushed a plate of sliced gishi fruit in front of Kay, who sat uncomfortably at the kitchen island. All the others had eaten already, while Kay had refused her meal.

"Come on, it's gishi fruit," Bill said. "It's really good. See?" He lifted a thin slice and ate it.

Kay blinked at him while a momentary flash of understanding lit bright-blue eyes. With shaking fingers, she reached out and grasped two slices of gishi fruit. They were gone quickly. Bill watched in satisfaction as Kay consumed the entire plate of fruit and licked her fingers afterward.

~

Breanne's Journal

"I don't want to talk or offer you a drink or anything else. Just leave," I said. Hank and Jayson stood inside my kitchen, expecting to be waited on, just as they had been all evening.

"About Trina's car," Jayson began.

"Do not renege on that, Jayson Rome," I fumed, "or I swear I'll stuff your head in the toilet."

"No—I'm offering an upgrade, if you'll sign a release for that story you told Ross Gideon the other night. He wants to include it in the magazine article we're running on the Everett Williams book. Dad told me to ask you."

"Is that all?" My hands were on my hips. "I don't care about that," I flung up a hand. "Do whatever you want, Jayson. Just go home."

"Bree, when will you stop being mad? At both of us?" Hank asked. "I know we hurt you. We're not about to expose you to anything you don't want. Can't we be friends, at least?" His dark eyes were pleading with me, and I had no idea why he was bothering. He could get any woman he wanted, who'd allow him to do whatever he wanted. I was a poor stand-in for any of that. An inexperienced fuck buddy—that's all I'd been to him.

"Hank, I'm nothing to you. Admit it," I said. "I'll have Terry rip up the contract. You're no longer obligated. The club's yours. All yours." I turned away.

"Bree, stop saying that. I want my friend back. I want the teasing, the jokes and all the other stuff. I enjoy it. I've never gotten along better with anybody. Even the best sub I know couldn't compare to you."

"Don't ever compare me to that," I shuddered. I was so close to tears, and crying would be disastrous. For all of us.

"Yeah. I see that." Hank reached out before dropping his hand. I'd stepped away from him. Even the smallest amount of moisture and he'd be sorry he'd ever met me. That's the way it had always been. I'd learned not to weep around others at a very early age.

"Bree, just agree to work with me on this. Try to keep an open mind. Please. I know you're afraid, and I know you won't talk to me about why that is. This is me. Hank. You weren't afraid while we worked on the club together."

I didn't point out that he hadn't been honest with me. I berated myself for not reading him again. It didn't matter. Nothing mattered. Some cosmic comedian had seen to it that I'd be continuously set up for disappointment. Love? That belonged to somebody else. Never to me.

"Will you try? Even Jayson has agreed to lay off for a while. It's not fair to parade you around as his girlfriend, when there's absolutely nothing in it for you."

"You got that right." My shoulders drooped.

"Bree, why don't you meet me at Bogey's for dinner tomorrow night. My assistant manager takes care of the club on Sunday nights, because it's usually a slow night. He has my number if he needs me, and the club isn't far away."

"Hank, you don't get it, do you?"

"Get what?"

"We're the fish and bird," I said. "There's no place where we can coexist."

"I don't believe that," he said.

"Living in the state of denial instead of the state of California?" I asked.

"Bree, just come, have dinner with me and we'll talk. If you want to insult me, go ahead. If you want to insult Jayson, I'll bring him along."

"Leave asshole Rome at home," I said. "I've had enough of him the past week."

"Hey, now," Jayson objected. I have no idea why.

"Jayson will stay away. My work will remain separate from us. I promise."

"So we'll just pretend it doesn't exist? That's ludicrous," I said.

"No, we'll ignore it. Like I'm ignoring what happened in Somalia. If I thought too long about that and how much danger you were probably in, I might have a heart attack."

"Hank, I can take care of myself," I whispered, my arms wrapped tightly around my ribs. They ached from sobs I refused to release. "Go home. What time do you want to meet tomorrow?" I'd agree if it would get him and Jayson out of the house. I wanted to cry and I couldn't do it anywhere near them.

"Be there at seven, baby." Hank turned and pulled Jayson out the door, closing it softly behind him.

⁓

"Two girls, missing from Georgetown University," Bill's assistant laid a folder on Bill's desk. "Looks like that campus killer in San Francisco moved to D.C."

"Not good," Bill opened the folder and stared at the top photograph of a nineteen-year-old college student.

"FBI is asking for our help," his assistant added as Bill examined the second photograph of a twenty-year-old.

⁓

Breanne's Journal

I felt cold and an overwhelming weariness enveloped me as I stood outside Bogey's for fifteen minutes, warring with my emotions. A part of me wanted to walk away forever, but that wouldn't be easy. Hank knew where I lived—Jayson had seen to that, the asshole. Another part of me wanted to tell Hank off and then walk away forever. Another, wounded part of me wanted Hank. That's all—just him. The smarter, logical part of my brain was busy beating up the hurt portion, when it was already bloodied. Hank was what he was, and I could never compete or come to terms with that. The best I could do was call some sort of truce and let him go.

"Baby, come inside. You're shaking." Hank grasped my icy hand in his and led me inside the bar.

"Bring a glass of Riesling," Hank told our waiter as he led me to his regular booth.

In minutes, I had a glass of Riesling and he had his usual old fashioned set in front of us.

"Baby, I want you to tell me what's wrong," Hank began. His dark eyes were searching my face for clues, but there wasn't any way I'd give those secrets to anyone.

"No." I had my reasons, and one of them was that it was too painful to think about my past.

"I realize you think I can't separate what happens at the club with what we have," he changed tactics, his dark eyes begging me to understand.

"I don't expect you to. I'm just a convenience. You can find plenty of women who'll do anything you want them to. Who'll let you do anything you want to them. Remember the girl from Singapore?" I wanted my hands to stop shaking as I sipped my wine.

"I should never have said that to you," he muttered, frowning.

"Well, you did. Call her up. Give her a job. Make her your fuck buddy." I was very close to tears again, after spending much of the night before either crying, shaking or both. I'd gotten very little sleep, I knew that much.

"Bree, baby, it's this way," Hank began. "People who want to be in the community are in the community—I told you that. The community is close-knit and what they do is almost religious in its essence, at times. It's consensual, never forget that. It isn't oppression, like so many think—it's just people who want to play and experience each other in a different way. It comes down to choice and consent. I told you what I wanted the first time we had sex. You agreed. You also said you didn't want pain. Baby, you'll never get that from me. Sure, I might try to talk you into something different now and then, but if you say no, then that's the end of it. Part of my job is to listen carefully to my partner and not upset her or make her uncomfortable. If you're worried about abusers—in the community, we sort of police ourselves and those wannabes who only want to dabble or injure somebody, well, we usually find them quickly. I know it doesn't sound logical, but there's trust, respect and often affection or love between the dominants and their submissives. Hell, some of them are married and have kids. The dominants don't have a desire to harm, abuse, or generally treat the sub as something less, like you might think. The subs want or need what they receive. Everything is discussed ahead of time and agreed to."

"Hank, a part of me sort of understands that. Or at least I want to understand it," I wiped a hand over my face. Part of my waking hours the night before had involved searching the Internet and reading books, although most of them left me shaking and tearful again.

How happy was I that I hadn't read the girl who was getting flogged? I could have read her and then my past, which interpreted what she was receiving as pain, would war with what I'd actually be reading from her, which was likely pleasure. I felt my brain might be ready to explode, just from my own personal paradox. All I knew, and would always know, is that Hank's lifestyle could never be for me. I would likely lose my mind over it, if I tried. Therefore, Hank and I had no future. He'd played his hand, but the cards I held were from a different game.

"I hear we're called vanilla," I muttered, refusing to look at him.

"You can't take that as derogatory."

"How should I take it?" My hand still shook as I lifted my wineglass and drank.

"As what it should be—somebody's way of differentiating. Perhaps not the best choice of labels, but it's far better than calling it normal, and calling the community not normal or unnatural—it's neither. The community *is* normal, for a small percentage of the population."

"Hank, I'm trying to understand that. It's just that I can't be part of that percentage. Believe me, it's not really a choice on my part. I have reasons, and those reasons I will never discuss with anyone." I wasn't looking at him again—I was afraid to. "How many women do you think are in it because they want love from the other party?" I had to know. "Do they ever get that? Love, that is? Do they ever get gentleness or consideration? Hugs or kisses, even?" The fact that he'd never kissed me still stung. I understood it better, now, but that didn't take the hurt away.

"Quite a lot do, although some dominants or Masters refuse to fall in love with their subs or slaves. It interferes with the relationship, in their opinion." Well, there it was. The reason for everything. A refusal to fall in love. That was my cue to make an exit. I rose unsteadily. "Good-bye, Hank," I said, pulling my purse strap over a shoulder with trembling hands. "Have a nice life."

He didn't try to stop me, and I went to mist the moment I reached the door. Thankfully, a foggy, San Francisco night covered my exit nicely.

~

"Where the fuck did she go?" Hank knocked on Jayson's car window. Jayson had parked on the street; Hank said Bree would try to run. Jayson's assignment was to distract her long enough for Hank to show up—he had to pay the tab, after all.

"She never came out the door. Not that I saw," Jayson climbed out of the car and raked fingers through thick, blond hair.

"First the bathroom, now this," Hank growled. "How the hell is she getting away?"

"This is fucked up," Jayson huffed. "You know she has to go home eventually, though. This running away thing has got to stop. Look, I can drive you to her house—get in."

Hank slid onto Jayson's passenger seat while Jayson slipped behind the wheel and started the Mercedes.

~

"You've never met your mother," Rabis observed as Ashe sat on the bench beside his grandfather. "She's on Le-Ath Veronis, with the others."

"I know. Lissa is taking care of them for now."

"She's aging."

"I know that, Grandfather."

"Will you not meet with her, at least?"

"Grandfather, I have parents. Granted they're not speaking at the moment, but they have plenty of time to rectify that."

"I know. Your vampire father should have been truthful about the compulsion from the beginning. Things are worse, now, since your mother found out years later and recalled that she'd almost become engaged to a virtual stranger as a result," Rabis sighed.

"I can't talk sense into either of them," Ashe shook his head. "Do you have any idea how long it will be before Kalia comes back to herself?"

"None," Rabis shifted uncomfortably. "I know what you're going to ask next," he added.

"Who was he—my biological father?"

"A strong shapeshifter. Powerful. Royalty. He and your mother—she was never the same after his death."

"She was Queen, wasn't she—before Friesianna took over?"

"Yes. Friesianna had Diamond and his brothers kill your father. They almost killed your mother, too."

"Then I no longer regret any part of their deaths," Ashe drew his sleeve back and examined the square gold medallions circling his left arm. When he'd killed Friesianna's jewel sentinels and the Dark King's destroyers, their power talismans had come to him, unwanted and unbidden.

Resting above those medallions lay the Bright Queen's crown, as if fused to his skin. On the right upper arm lay the Dark King's crown. If they were ever away from him, they could destroy planets if they touched. Only one of the Mighty might hold their power at bay so closely together.

"When you rebuild the race, Grandchild, you will need help. The Mighty who holds the power to *Change What Was* must rejoin those crowns and make them one again."

"The shining woman," Ashe leaned his head against the side of Rabis' small cottage. Rabis' bench sat right outside his front door, in a small clearing of fruit trees. "Grandfather?" Ashe's eyes were closed, his face turned toward the afternoon sunlight filtering through the leaves of gishi fruit trees.

"What is it, child?"

"If I bring my biological mother here, you'll need a bigger house."

Rabis chuckled.

~

Breanne's Journal

"I thought Mr. Rome wasn't coming." I'd barely made it home before they arrived—I'd made a stop at a liquor store. Jayson and

Hank had ensured that I was drinking more than I ever had in my life. It hadn't improved matters, either, but I didn't know of any other way to get to sleep. Too much crowded my mind, lately, and Hank Bell was at the center of that constantly whirling vortex.

I'd barely misted inside the kitchen when Jayson, using a key he apparently kept to my house, let himself in the door. Both stood in my kitchen, staring at me.

"Bree, I just wanted to make sure you were safe," Hank's brows drew together in a frown as he watched me pour a glass of wine.

"Sure you did. So you asked asshat Rome to break into my house to do it." I gulped wine and almost choked.

"Baby, if you'd tell me what's wrong," he began, his dark eyes troubled and his mouth tugging into a worried grimace.

"Everything is wrong," I snapped back. "Every fucking thing is wrong." I flung my glass of wine against the kitchen wall, shattering the fragile crystal. "I should have known something was off. Fuck buddy? Really, Hank? Have Jayson drive you back to your club and find one of those women who wants what you offer. Hell, find one for him, too. Make sure she has giant boobs, 'cause that's what he wants." I lifted the wine bottle. It joined the wineglass, splintering against the wall and splashing wine and shards of glass everywhere. "Every fucking time I find somebody I like, something happens." I whirled on both of them. "Get out. Get out now, or I swear to God I won't be responsible for what happens next."

Jayson stared at Hank in alarm when my cellphone rang. I jerked it from my purse and answered.

"Breanne?" Bill Jennings was on the line.

"What do you need?" I began walking toward the door. Hank was behind me—I could hear his footsteps.

"Bree, we've got problems here with missing girls. I don't know whether you heard anything about those girls who were killed in San Francisco, but it looks like the killer moved here. I could use that special talent you have, I think."

"When?" I was ready to go—just to get away from Hank and Jayson.

"As soon as you can pack a bag. I have an agent on the ground there, waiting at the airport. He'll escort you."

"I can get there in forty minutes," I said.

"He'll be waiting. Seems our cellphones don't work in the sewer systems here, for some reason," Bill added. He wanted my mindspeech. Well, he could have it and just about anything else he wanted. It was likely the same Sirenali had set off this killer, and I couldn't tell Bill that I'd already killed one murdering vampire in San Francisco. I ended the call the moment Hank's hands gripped my shoulders.

"I have to go," I moved away from Hank's grasp.

"Mercy Crossings?" Hank's dark eyes were unreadable when I turned to face him.

"Something like that." I shoved the cellphone back in my purse. "Somebody's waiting at the airport. I have to fly to D.C. tonight."

"Baby, I think you're too upset to go anywhere," Hank pointed out.

"I'm no longer willing to listen to you," I said. "I have to pack a bag. Please leave."

"What if we don't let you go?" Jayson drew a pair of handcuffs from his pocket. If he'd known, maybe he wouldn't have done it. Maybe. Well, other women might let him do that, and maybe it was because he'd let them go if they used a safe word. No safe word had ever been provided for me, and therein lay the difference.

I didn't want to mist away in front of them, so I did the next-best thing. Turning and snatching my purse off the kitchen counter, I ran like hell for the door. There's no way any human can catch a running vampire. I had the door slammed in their faces before they could think about reacting.

CHAPTER 7

"What the hell just happened?" Jayson dangled the handcuffs from his fingers as he stared at the closed front door.

"Rome, show up at the gym tomorrow," Hank growled. "I'm going to teach you a lesson you'll never forget."

"Willem, I have an errand for you," Ildevar Wyyld stared through the window of his study. He knew, just as well as Willem did, that Gaelar N'Seith lay in that direction. Ildevar had only met briefly with Kaldill Schaff a handful of times, yet Kaldill had offered the services of his best seer—Willem Drifft.

"What is it, Deonus?" Willem lifted an eyebrow in curiosity.

"Willem, it is time for us to admit that neither of us knows what tomorrow may bring. I know you've understood who your mates are —for a very long time. You have merely refused to meet with them out of loyalty to me. I ask that you go to them. Let them make you happy—even if it is for a short while."

"Deonus, I do not wish to leave you unguarded," Willem began.

"Willem," Ildevar turned to the elf, "You saw what came to save my worthless skin last time. That was neither requested nor deserved. Had I a lover waiting, I would certainly take the opportunity to go to her. You must take what is offered now, before it is too late."

"But I may be gone for weeks, getting to know them," Willem's forehead creased with worry.

"Then take weeks. You can fold in and out of NorthStar, can you not? I trust you can still read the Telling Winds at times."

"They are not completely unreliable," Willem studied the boots he wore. "Deonus, I am not comfortable with this."

"Then I order you to go to them. The Elf King told you to obey me, did he not?"

"Yes." Willem's voice was so soft Ildevar almost didn't hear it. "He also told me to keep you as safe as I could."

"I will be safe or not. Go. Meet your intendeds. I wish to see you happy."

"Yes, Deonus." Willem bowed deeply to Ildevar Wyyld and folded away.

Breanne's Journal

Bill looked tired. Actually, he was exhausted; I'd lowered my shield to check. Still, he was waiting at the airport when the military jet I'd been transported on arrived in D.C.

"Bill, you should be in bed," I said softly as he settled beside me in the back of a government-owned limo.

"I'll go just as soon as I get you to a hotel. You'll have a guard assigned, too."

"I should be fine," I pointed out.

"I want to make sure," Bill covered a yawn.

"See, you could be asleep right now and somebody else could have picked me up."

"Breanne, I can't explain it, but I want you to be safe."

"I think that's the nicest thing any man has ever said to me," I leaned my head against the back of my seat and closed my eyes. I'd just walked away from Hank—for good. Tears threatened again and I forced them back. I'd never wanted to cry so much in so short a time in all my life.

~

Hank knew Jayson's Krav Maga instructor was silently watching as he handed Jayson a beating. Hank was an expert in Krav Maga, as well as most other fighting disciplines. Jayson had interfered with Breanne while Hank was attempting to approach her, and he knew better.

Hank realized that he should have remembered Jayson's penchant for always having handcuffs nearby—either on his person, in his car or at his office. He liked his subs to come to his office after hours at times—the playtime helped him wind down. For six months, Hank had been training Jayson to be a Master, after Jayson approached him about it.

"I think you cracked a rib," Jayson snapped, throwing a series of vicious jabs at Hank. Hank blocked them easily.

"Think you don't deserve it?" Hank landed a blow to Jayson's stomach, sending him to his knees, the wind knocked out of him. Hank stepped back.

"Try calling her?" Jayson wheezed before coughing.

"Six times. Her phone's turned off."

"I know I'll get another cracked rib, but why don't you just find somebody else?"

"Because I don't want somebody else."

"She's never gonna be a willing sub or slave," Jayson struggled to his feet.

"I don't want that from her."

"Man, half the time I don't understand you," Jayson complained, frowning at Hank.

"That's not true," Hank grumbled, pulling a towel from a nearby pile provided by the gym and wiping his face with it. "You don't understand me at all."

~

Breanne's Journal

"We're having coffee with the boss," my inscrutable guard announced after knocking on my door at eight, Eastern Standard. Three hours in time difference and a sleepless night made me feel like an incontestable train wreck. Sadly, according to the mirror, anyway, I didn't look much better than that, either.

Bill's office was located in Arlington, not far from my hotel. Even with traffic, it took less than fifteen minutes to get there, so I didn't have time to close my eyes and hope for a rejuvenating miracle to visit my face.

"Breanne, didn't you sleep well?" Bill leaned in to whisper when I was ushered into his office. He'd risen like a gentleman and taken my hand when I walked in. My guard closed the door behind us, and I was grateful.

"It happens sometimes," I brushed off his concern.

"Sit down, somebody will bring coffee," he sighed and walked around the desk to slide onto his chair. I sat on one of his guest chairs and took in the room. The office was spacious enough, but Bill didn't have many personal things inside it.

"We found two bodies after a hard rain washed them out of a drain that empties into the Anacostia River," Bill sighed, pushing a photograph in my direction. "We think there may be more, but we haven't searched the whole section," he added.

I learned from Bill that if enough rain fell, the combined sewer overflow would be funneled into the Anacostia River, the Potomac River, Rock Creek or other, tributary waters. If it were another vampire, he may not have counted on the weather washing bodies over a dam built into the sewer, which held typical sanitary waste water back.

If the water levels rose high enough, they washed over that dam to flow into a river or other outlet. It kept area basements, streets and businesses from flooding, although it presented a hazard in that untreated water went right into the area creeks and rivers. Parts of D.C.'s sewer system were definitely outdated.

"We're going to the outfall today, where the bodies showed up," Bill said as an assistant set a cup of coffee on his desk. A second cup, followed by a small bowl filled with sugar and sweetener packets plus small containers of cream and stir sticks was placed on Bill's desk within my reach.

Dumping cream and sugar into my cup, I listened while Bill explained that a victim's clothing had snagged on a fallen branch outside the outfall, and that's where she'd been found. The other body had washed on through and was discovered a quarter mile away.

"You think there was only one stash of bodies, like San Francisco?" I asked, sipping my coffee.

"I hope so. I don't want to dig through the entire sewer system, searching for a separate cache."

"How much time has he had to dispose of bodies, you think?" I looked at Bill over my coffee cup. I'd killed the San Francisco vampire before going to Somalia. If his death triggered this rash of murders, then a second vampire had weeks to kill.

"We have at least twenty missing women reported, since the disappearances in San Francisco stopped," Bill lowered his eyes and studied the dark brown liquid in his cup. He took it black. Plain—just like his office.

"These bodies were found south and west of the Eleventh Street Bridge," he pushed a map toward me, showing outfall points along the Anacostia River. The outfall circled on the map wasn't far from the Anacostia Riverwalk Trail, so I assumed the bodies had been found by someone walking past.

"A jogger spotted the body near the outfall," Bill confirmed my guess.

Twenty minutes later, we were in a car with dark-tinted windows, driving toward the Eleventh Street Bridge. After parking, we were led to a spot where a boat waited, and Bill and I climbed aboard the small craft. The boat's driver maneuvered us toward the outfall entrance where the first body had been spotted. A warning sign was posted near the square, concrete opening, declaring it a combined sewer overflow discharge point, and stating that pollution might occur during rainfall.

"We've checked all the other outfalls, and there weren't any bodies, plus we've had boats out, looking for more. It may be just a fluke that the two we found washed over the dam inside the combined sewer." Bill looked troubled, his brown eyes raking my face before turning to study the water outside the outfall. It hadn't rained in the past two days, so no water came through.

"Can we get closer?" I asked.

"Are you sure?" Bill asked. "It's far from clean." He studied my clothing and shoes. I wasn't really dressed to go traipsing into a sewer. I was prepared to do it anyway.

"Let's go," I jerked my head toward the entrance.

We ended up hunkered over and wading through shallow water, and I knew the shoes and jeans I wore would be thrown away afterward. Bill, before we scrambled inside the sewer, called someone and asked for extra clothing to be brought for us.

"It doesn't smell good," I mumbled once we got inside. Bill had to duck farther than I did to fit into the drain, but both of us saw the concrete dam that stood about half the height of the combined sewer section.

During dry periods, the water stayed below the level of that dam and nothing flowed over it into the river outside. Rising waters in the sewer from heavy rainfall would cause the water to pour over the dam and wash toward the outfall.

Discreetly I sniffed through the combined outfall and even walked in to peer over the dam. The water level behind it was far below the flood range. No bodies were near, and hadn't been, in my estimation. The two girls had been swept from another part of the sewer.

"How far have you searched into the sewer from here?" I asked, turning toward Bill.

"Pretty far, and we didn't find anything," he replied, toying with his phone. "See—absolutely no signal, and we're barely inside the pipe." The phone was held up for me to see.

"That's odd," I shook my head. "Is something jamming it?"

"No idea. I'll ask for a sweep of the area, though."

"Are there any places above ground—an opening or something, where bodies can just be dropped in?" I asked.

"Not an official opening," Bill hunched his shoulders. "There are several locations where something might be dug, but then a hole would have to be punched into the roof of the sewer to drop bodies inside."

"I think that's what we're looking for," I said. After all, the San Francisco vampire had gotten past the police to drop his last victim; therefore, it only made sense that he had a private entrance somewhere. All the other entrances were staked out, watching for his return. "Ready to go?" I asked.

"More than ready," Bill agreed.

∾

At least I was clean again and smelled infinitely better when Bill took me to lunch near his office. He was eating vegetarian at a specialty restaurant, which only served vegetarian and vegan items. He even said he enjoyed his tomato soup and veggie burger lunch. I smiled foolishly at Director Bill and accepted his lie as I ate the same thing.

"We've got a lot of ground to cover if we're looking for a hole where bodies can be dropped into the sewer," Bill sighed as we left the restaurant. "It could be covered when it isn't used, making it more difficult to locate."

I nodded as Bill buttoned his coat against the chill—D.C. was downright cold in December and snow was threatening later. Christmas was only three weeks away and I could tell Bill wanted this out of the way before the holidays.

"Bill," I sighed, hunching my shoulders, "what do you know about vampires?"

∾

"You found something?" Ross Gideon leaned back in his leather chair, making it creak softly as he spoke to Bob Sullivan, his private detective.

"I have a lead," Bob acknowledged over the phone. "If it pans out, I think you're really gonna like it. How close are you to finishing that bio on Everett Williams?"

"It's almost done. Most of the chapters have gone to the editors," Ross replied. "Only need to tweak the last chapter and approve the photographs. Why?"

"Because we may have a juicier fish on the line," Bob chuckled. "If this is what I think it might be, you'll like it for sure, but old man Rome will absolutely love it. He may have to grease some palms to get the best stuff, but it's looking awful good right now."

"Who?" Ross straightened up in his chair, his booted feet hitting the floor of his office with a thump.

"Joyce Christian," Bob said.

"Are you shitting me?" Ross was on his feet in a blink. "Rome will pay whatever it takes to get dirt on her."

"I think we may be able to accommodate him," Bob laughed.

Breanne's Journal

"That's your theory—that vampires are doing this?" Bill didn't know what to think, I could tell. He didn't deny their existence though, and that was a good thing. At least I trusted him to keep the information to himself—if the vamps learned I knew about vamps, they'd probably send somebody to place compulsion. Or, if Bill trusted me enough to introduce me to vamps, they'd either scent me as one, or, if I shielded myself, would be mighty concerned that they couldn't get a scent off me, likely resulting in the same thing. If they ever learned that compulsion didn't work, well, I envisioned a rather protracted fight with the vamps.

"I think—yeah. Bill, I really think it's vampires." I was afraid to tell him it was vampires with an obsession—I was treading unsteady ground as it was.

"I can assign teams to track open ground over the sewer system, but that'll take a lot of people and possibly a long time on top of that," Bill shook his head. "I have limited resources in the country at the moment, and most of those are dealing with other problems."

"I can help," I said. I could, and I'd smell vampire before any humans would, that was a given. "I just need a map of the sewer leading away from the outfall we looked at earlier. I can do this without any help."

"Bree, there's no way I'd send you out there by yourself," Bill protested. "I have one person I might pair you with, but I warn you, she is really tough and not so talkative."

"That's okay. I'm usually not a chatterbox either."

"I know. It's just that she scares most of the men she's been on assignment with. If you go out with Opal and she upsets you, then I expect you to tell me immediately. I'll put her with somebody else."

"Sounds fine," I shrugged. I didn't tell him that I could place compulsion just like any self-respecting vampire could, and we could have cooperation, one way or another. "I've always liked the name Opal," I added. "It's pretty."

Forcing myself not to stare rudely, I read Opal Tadewi as quickly as possible. Bill didn't have a clue that not only was she Native American, she was also a very rare shapeshifter. He knew she was a shapeshifter, but not how rare she was. Opal didn't know that Bill knew (sort of) what she was. Bill thought it was funny and never called her out on it. Currently, I stared at a four-hundred-year-old shapeshifting velociraptor.

Opal had the uncanny, unblinking dark eyes of her alter ego as she sized me up. I'd already thrown up a shield—she was getting no scent from me and that puzzled her greatly. I knew, too, that velociraptors, when they roamed the Earth, were only three feet tall or less. Opal, like many shapeshifters (especially werewolves) was much larger than that. While the normal velociraptors resembled big chickens, Opal was bigger and scarier than that—I could read it in her easily.

❧

"I found three," Q'Ind Ribalo nodded to Hordace Cayetes. "Three pretty little girls. Two six turns old, the other five. They'll be ready in three years."

"Good. That's when the ones we have will turn fourteen," Hordace thumbed through his comp-vid. "Completely trained when we get them, as usual?"

"Yes."

"Perfect. What's your brother up to?"

"He's looking at information on Keef. Says he may be able to use intelligence he's gathered to track him. Keef might not be one of your primary targets, but he's still a big fish."

"Good enough. My sources say Keef is Wyyld's heir. That ought to be enough to unbalance the Reth Alliance founder. Maybe we can get to him if we kill his successor."

"Sounds good—my brother is especially motivated on this one."

"What about Kalia? Any news on that little bitch?"

"Not yet. Even the information we've intercepted from Keef indicates he can't get to her. I have no idea what that means," Q'Ind held up a hand to hold off further questions from Hordace. "I hear she's on Avendor somewhere, but that's where the trail ends."

"I should have killed her when I killed the others her age. It's just that," Hordace sighed.

"She could sing like the angels," Q'Ind agreed. "Nobody could resist that."

"If I'd known that Iversti was paying Cull for her services after Cull married her," Hordace growled. "I told my idiot cousin that she had to stay with him."

"He tricked you into giving her to him. She should still be here with us. Iversti could have had her anytime."

"Cull knew he could sell her, and that's exactly what he did. Iversti had to pay top credit for her."

"Iversti made sure his marks were on her when he sent her back to Cull the first time," Q'Ind observed. "Cull realized his mistake—nobody else would touch what Iversti claimed for himself."

"Too bad Iversti died when he did," Hordace pointed out. "I was ready to send him after Cull. Cull was a liability by that time, and Iversti would have brought Kalia back here."

"Rezil is prepared to go anytime if we find out where she is," Q'Ind snorted. "He knows she was there when Iversti went down. He wants to ask her how his brother died before he kills her."

"Killing her is the easiest way," Hordace muttered. "Although I would like to hear her sing again."

"Too much trouble for us if she lives," Q'Ind agreed.

~

Lissa's Journal

I hadn't sat on top of the palace dome in a long time. That's where I'd settled to get away from everything for a while. More and more I considered sending mindspeech to my sister up and down the timeline—I'd looked forward to meeting her—talking to her. Asking about her life and sharing stories. I worried that she'd been bullied so badly by Gavin, Gavril and the palace staff that she'd never come back. I'd found her, only to lose her before we'd had a chance to connect.

"Beloved," Belen settled beside me in a muted flash of light.

"Belen?" I looked up at him—he'd dimmed his light greatly so he wouldn't appear as a beacon to those who wandered below us.

"I believe your sister killed the Sirenali who placed obsession on Cheedas, but I cannot determine how the obsession was eliminated in your Chief Cook. A Sirenali's obsession outlives the Sirenali, if it is not removed by the one who placed it before their death."

"That's not scary or anything," I mumbled, hugging myself. Did it frighten me that my body had died after Cheedas staked me in the chest? More than a little. I often woke from sleep with that memory

—my heart pounding and my breaths fast and trembling. Several times Karzac had been summoned at the most inopportune moments, just to deal with my panic attacks. "Trevor, Norian and Kooper are still attempting to discover how the Comet's Tail exploded, too."

"I believe the two are connected, but I will not speculate."

"Then I won't spread that rumor. Norian can find out for himself," I grumped. I'd sent him packing—straight back to his suite and his office on Wyyld. I didn't care if the ASD remained headquartered on Le-Ath Veronis—I liked Kooper well enough, and he was in charge here more often than not, since Lendill had taken to spending most of his free time away from Reah with his father, Kaldill Schaff.

Time moves differently for those in Gaelar N'Seith, and I had no idea how long it might take Kaldill to hand the rule of the Elven lands to Lendill. I didn't ask Lendill, either, what he might be learning from his father to prepare him for the Kingship.

"Belen, I'll admit that I'm scared to death over these sandstorms. I thought they might be over when things happened as they did with the Dark Worlds. Now it looks as if they were just toying with us. That they want us to know they can destroy everything, and we have nothing in our arsenal to stop it."

"Yes. I found myself trapped by that same power, and it took someone with great strength to allow my escape."

"You don't think it was—you know?" I didn't want to say Ashe or the Mighty Hand aloud. Who knew whether someone was listening? Nexus Echo was much too common among the powerful.

"No. Certainly not that one," Belen employed his knowledge of humanoid gestures and shook his head.

"So," I sighed. It could have been my sister—it could have been. I wanted to ask Belen if he thought she knew what she was. Certainly, the power she'd employed a time or two indicated it, but did she even know about the Mighty? Something in me—a feeling, perhaps—said she didn't. That frightened me. I wanted her beside me so I could tell her. Not only what she was, but to be wary. Someone or something hunted her, as it did all of them, and anything with enough power might destroy them if they weren't careful enough or watchful enough. I sighed a second time.

"So much hinges on their safety," Belen rumbled. He'd picked up my thoughts.

"Yeah. I wish there was something I could do."

"I as well. So far, I have only managed to be captured as bait."

"Not good," I frowned. "I worry that my sister won't ever come back."

"I know." Belen rubbed my back with gentle fingers. "Had I not been captured, I might have done something. As it was," he didn't finish.

"I know. So many people slink out of my way, now, because they know they screwed up. At least Skel Hawer didn't survive."

"One of the few things that went the proper way," Belen agreed. "I hear he provided a meal for Plovel."

"Good for Plovel."

～

"According to Trina's stalker app, she's still in D.C." Jayson handed his phone to Hank, who sat at his favorite booth in Bogey's.

"I should have set up the same thing," Hank mumbled. "I never thought to rape her cellphone in that way."

"You're calling it rape?"

"What would you call it? Trina didn't ask."

"I don't know. Molest, maybe?" Jayson settled on the other side of the booth. It was after midnight, Hank had left the club in his assistant's hands and left to get a sandwich.

"Either way, her cellphone was fucked," Hank muttered his thanks to the waiter, who set a sandwich and a fresh old fashioned in front of him. Jayson gave his order and waited for their server to walk away before continuing the conversation.

"I need to get an email to her; the old man wants to run that excerpt in the magazine about Everett Williams. He wants to use the story Bree told Gideon, and he needs a release signed. Mom asked me to run a story on Mercy Crossings in the magazine and put Bree's photograph on the cover."

"I don't know whether Breanne will agree to be on the cover," Hank said, pointing the two thin, red straws from his drink in Jayson's direction. "Although you'd sell plenty of copies, just for her photograph."

"I know. Plenty of people would love that—I know what my preferences are, but she's beautiful, there's no doubt about that. If she's not on the cover, then she needs to be on the first page of the article so we can run ads," Jayson breathed a frustrated sigh. "Mom never asks for something like this, and I owe her for fucking up the anniversary party. She says Bree is the prettiest woman I've ever dated."

"Then email the stupid form. See if Bree will sign it—for your mother. And you're not dating her, remember? You're just using her."

"Look, I realize that. Maybe I will try emailing the release form," Jayson leaned back as his sandwich was placed before him. "I don't know what she's doing in D.C. Mercy Crossings works outside the country."

"I get the feeling this is something else," Hank said.

"Another volunteer job?" Jayson lifted an eyebrow at Hank.

"Maybe. I'd ask, except she's not answering my calls," Hank pushed Trina's phone toward Jayson. "Don't fuck with Bree. Mess this up for me and I may strangle you. Really."

"What—the detached and objective Hank Bell gets emotional?" Jayson bit into his sandwich.

"Fuck off, Rome."

I wanted to throw my cellphone at the wall. I had six email requests from Jayson, all of them with a release form attached. Opal was scheduled to come by the hotel and pick me up at nine, and I'd been awake since five, fidgeting.

Bree, the first message read, *Mom wants me to commission an article on Mercy Crossings. We already have permission from the Director, and he also wants your photograph on the first page. Dad wants an excerpt from Ross Gideon's book in the magazine, too, which includes the story you gave Ross. Both those things require a signed release. Please sign a hard copy and mail it to my office. Please.*

Five other messages, relaying roughly the same request, followed that one. If he thought he'd wear me down by sheer numbers, he was right. I was sick of getting his crap already. I'd already called the front desk downstairs—there was a charge for printing, but I could print the damn release form, sign it and then pay a little more to have it mailed to Jayson's office. If I didn't, he'd just keep hounding me until I did. Sighing, I jammed the phone into a pocket of my jeans and headed for my hotel room door.

It's been mailed. Don't bother me again, I texted Jayson after sealing the envelope addressed to his office, the requested release form inside. *Tell Trina to take me off that stalker app, too,* I added before sending the message.

No can do, came almost immediately. *Mom wants an interview done with you for the Mercy Crossings article. Don't worry, I'll have one of my staff writers contact you by email. You can answer his questions that way.*

If he's as much of an asshole as you are, you may get nothing. Jerk.

Did you just call me a jerk?

I called you a jerk, jerk. And an asshole. Because you're both.

If Mom didn't like you so much, he left the sentence hanging.

If I didn't like your mother, I'd file a restraining order, I snapped back.

Does this mean you won't come to my birthday dinner next week? Mom wants you to come. Really.

If it were her *birthday.*

Hank said he wants to come if you do.

Really? I may throw up. Go find some of those women you both like. Take them. They'll be euphoric. Obedient. All that stuff.

Hank says he explained to you that it's an exchange of power. They want to give, we want to receive.

Sounds like the coin toss at a football game.

Your vanilla-ness is showing.

Really? You're the one who dragged out handcuffs, Rome. Don't ever show me that shit again.

Why?

I have legitimate reasons, I assure you. Plus, you'd have to use something a lot stronger than handcuffs if you want to restrain me, nowadays. Besides, I have merinthophobia. Know what that means, asshat?

I know what that means. No wonder you ran away like the devil was after you.

Honey, I've met the devil. The most you can ever hope for is to be the devil's lesser minion.

You have such a high opinion of me.

Your own doing, remember? Look, my ride's here. I have work to do.

"Here are the messages," Jayson handed his cellphone to Hank over lunch at Bogey's. "I should have guessed about the merinthophobia."

"We never thought to ask her about those things. We should have." Hank scrolled through Breanne's messages quickly, and then went back to read them again more slowly. "Probably has claustrophobia, too."

"Did she mean you when she said she's met the devil?" Jayson watched as Hank read Breanne's texts.

"No," Hank sighed. "I think the devil came along years before I did."

Breanne's Journal

Opal had a handheld detector of some sort, and I followed her as she watched the screen and placed careful steps to track the sewer lines beneath our feet. We'd been out all day, hadn't found anything and both of us were tired and hungry. It was also dark, but neither of us had trouble seeing in the dark.

She hadn't spoken much—she was still puzzled as to why she couldn't scent me and that bothered her, I could tell.

With her dark hair pulled into a long braid down her back, she was dressed in black jeans, boots and a leather jacket. "Opal," I said as dead grass crunched softly beneath her feet.

"Huh?" She didn't bother to turn around.

"You don't have to worry about me. The shield is for my protection," I said.

Opal stopped in her tracks and turned to stare at me with her nearly unblinking dark eyes.

"I know you protect yourself, too," I added. She blinked at me then, unsure how to deal with my words—and me. She didn't want anyone to know about her and felt endangered because somehow I'd guessed something about her. We had a temporary standoff while she contemplated her next move. Both of us heard the noise. Opal's head jerked toward the sound—it was behind her; I was facing it. The scent reached both of us, then—the combined scent of vampire and dead human.

Do it, my voice whispered in her mind. She was considering going to her animal, and I wanted her to do it. I could mist faster than she could run, and if our luck held, we might trap the vampire between us. I sent a vision to her of what I wanted, and without a sound, her clothing was destroyed and the velociraptor was running. I didn't have time to give her the awe her form demanded; I turned to mist and blazed toward the vampire.

CHAPTER 8

Gus Fulton was dying. He knew it, too. Lung cancer was eating away at him and the doctor had already said to get his affairs in order. With an optimistic estimate of six months, Gus knew he had things to take care of, and that included a daughter and grandchildren he hadn't seen in nearly a decade. He wanted to leave them something, but all he had was an old house in Pecos, Texas. He'd spent the last ten years of his life drinking and smoking way too much. If the lung cancer didn't take him, then the cirrhosis eventually would.

He'd been forced to retire, too, although he'd worked until he'd turned sixty-eight. He would have been reelected as sheriff of Pecos County if he hadn't been forced out by health issues. He had a reputation as a hard-nosed, no-nonsense officer of the law, but he'd buried some bodies during his time. Some deaths he'd been responsible for, some bodies he'd buried for someone else; all of it done discreetly, of course.

As it was, the only person who could cause trouble for him was dead, but that wasn't what gnawed away at him—his conscience—as well as his addictions did.

"If I'd never met you, Joyce, I might not be in this predicament, now," Gus muttered. Fifty thousand dollars was on the line—money he could leave to his grandkids who only thought of him as a distant, angry old man. All Gus had to do was hand a few photographs and a diary he'd kept through the years to a private investigator, and the money would be his. The orphanage in question had been shut down fifteen years earlier—the church stopped funding it because they hadn't kept appropriate records.

"Good thing, too," Gus sighed and stuffed the journal and photographs in a manila envelope. The investigator's name was Sullivan—Bob Sullivan, from California. Gus snorted as he sealed the envelope. Folks from that end of the country generally had more money than sense, in his opinion.

The money would be given to him in cash—Gus wasn't about to let go of the information until he saw it for himself. He still owned several guns, and nobody would get any of this for free. It belonged to his grandkids, and maybe it would redeem him a little in their eyes. Either way, he'd be gone before the story could be published, and any charges that might be leveled against him would be futile. Joyce had gotten away with murder—well, he would, too.

~

Ashe's Journal

It was something I'd never suspected. Trajan, on an off-day when he wasn't listening to old country and western music, liked to listen to the occasional classical piece. He loved *the Duettino-Sull'aria* from *The Marriage of Figero*, mostly because it was featured in one of his favorite films, *The Shawshank Redemption*.

After setting up the music while working on a comp-vid at the kitchen island, Trajan wrote out a communication to one of our buyers when Kay walked in. I think Bill dropped a dish in the sink when Kay began singing with the two women. It wasn't any amateur performance, either. This would have brought anybody to tears it was so beautiful, and since I was afraid of terrifying her any more than I already did; I misted in and settled on Trajan's shoulder as the bumblebee bat so I could listen.

Kay has the voice of an angel, and no matter how hard Bill has coaxed since then, we can't get her to sing again. I did ask Bill to pull all the classical music he can gather and give it to Kay on a comp-vid, but she hasn't done anything except retreat into herself again. It makes me wonder what it was that convinced her to come out of her shell for such a short amount of time, but it gives me hope that someday, she'll sing for us once more.

Breanne's Journal

Opal can run like the wind—her last name was accurate. I misted ahead of the vampire, who had difficulty getting away from a large velociraptor. It was comical, almost—he'd turned to look back at the creature chasing him, knowing it should have been extinct. He'd already dropped the dead girl he carried in favor of effecting his escape, and he almost ran into me before turning around.

Materializing in front of him, I pulled my claws out and waited barely a blink until he was in front of me. I neatly sliced the head from his shoulders as I stepped aside, and he didn't have time to register shock before his head rolled away while his body slid for yards.

"What the hell?" Opal transformed, stood next to me completely naked and stared at the vampire's head, which was decomposing nearby. The body, after rolling to a stop, was turning to ash.

"Vampire," I wiggled my claws in her direction. "But that's between you and me, okay?"

"Absolutely," she nodded at my foot-long claws. "But I want to ask why you can walk in daylight. Bill's vamps all have to sleep during the day."

"I'm sort of special, and I want to stay away from those guys," I pulled my claws back in with a sigh. "You might say I wasn't sanctioned by the Council, and their reaction to what they consider a rogue can best be described as unpredictable."

"Look, I'm not about to tell," Opal muttered. "The vamps I've met sort of have an uneasy truce with me. They know I'm a shifter, as do the wolves, but nobody has outed me yet."

"I sure as hell won't out you," I said, pulling off my coat and handing it to her. "Let's call Bill and let him know where the latest victim is."

"Yeah." Opal shrugged into my coat and buttoned it around her.

"Look, I can get some clothes for you if you want to stay with the body. It won't take long," I promised.

"I'll accept your offer," she nodded as we walked toward the victim.

Bill walked beside me as I led him toward the vampire ash. I knew what he was thinking—that vampire ash or blood could kill a human if introduced into the bloodstream. I reached out and rubbed his back as we walked. Bill stopped still and pulled me into his arms.

"Breanne, if I weren't such an old man," he muttered against my hair.

"I don't care how old you are," I mumbled against his chest.

"I do," he pulled away. "Come on; let's look at this pile of ash."

I showed him where the head and torso had landed. "I know you and Opal might do this together, but I don't like it," Bill shook his head as he crouched and used a flashlight to examine the vampire's disintegrated body.

"I hope you don't upset Opal with what you know," I sighed. Bill knew. One of his vampires had told Bill she was a shapeshifter. Bill didn't care—Opal was a very effective agent and he appreciated that about her. He hadn't brought any vamps with him, either—he knew their presence tended to upset Opal. Seems too many shifters had died from vampire attacks, and most of them didn't have any defense against them.

"I wouldn't," Bill nodded, standing up again and turning off the flashlight. The rest of his crew plus a few detectives from the D.C. Police Department were gathered around the victim's body, gathering evidence before moving her. Opal watched them from a distance so she could file a report for Bill later.

"Bill," I said as he began walking back toward the others, "this vampire wasn't the same one from San Francisco."

"How the hell do you know that?" He'd stopped at my words and stared at me.

"Because I killed the one in San Francisco," I said.

"Breanne, I've only met one other person who might do the kinds of things you do," he muttered. "And you do it without being vampire." I blinked at him for a few seconds before letting that go. Let him think I wasn't vampire. It was so much easier that way, and didn't put me in danger with the vamps he had in his department.

"I'm surprised you remember Lissa. She's my sister," I said. Bill stopped in his tracks again.

Bree, baby, call or text me back. Hank sighed as he sent the message before nodding to John, who walked through the club's door. They'd gotten everything cleaned up after closing, with help from two employees. Hank always made sure they got away safely before going home. Business was better than he'd hoped, and he could begin making payments to Breanne in a few weeks. He wanted her to know he intended to honor the loan, even if she claimed she wanted none of it.

Hank watched as John walked toward his import parked two blocks away. He didn't climb into his truck until John drove away.

Breanne's Journal

"Look, I don't want to know how the fucker died, I'm just glad we got rid of him," Bill said, sitting wearily on the chair behind his desk. Opal and I sat in his guest chairs, bottles of water in our hands. The forensics team had taken forever to gather the evidence and Opal and I were exhausted and hungry. Sixteen dead and decomposing young women had been found in the sewer not far from where Opal and I chased the vampire. Those bodies were still being processed. Bill explained that to us, and asked us if we had anything to add to the official report.

Opal lifted an eyebrow at me. I shrugged back at her. Who knew that killing a vampire together would form a friendship? Bill and I didn't talk about how I'd killed the vampire in San Francisco—he remembered Lissa and that was enough for him.

"You girls want dinner?" Bill asked when we didn't have anything else to say.

"I think you said the magic words," I sighed.

"Breanne," Bill said as he walked me to my hotel room later.

"Bill?" I replied.

"I just," he raked fingers through his hair. "I hate to send you home, but the investigation's over."

"I know," I nodded. "But you know where I am. All you have to do is call."

"I'll do that. Definitely," he agreed. "Did you know Lissa before she died?"

"Bill, someday we'll talk about that. Not now, okay?"

"All right. I just wish I could let William Winkler know." I had to hold back the snort. Nearly four hundred years in the future, Winkler got to sleep with Lissa on a regular basis. The last time I'd seen him, he'd been howling out his grief beside her body. He'd been the first to shout his happiness, too, when I brought her back.

Gavin, the unemotional asshole, had merely pulled her tighter against him. Hell, I'd even gotten rid of the blood for them. No cleanup and instant resurrection, courtesy of yours truly. Likely, Gavin only appreciated my absence afterward.

"Bree, where did you go just then?" Bill pushed a lock of hair away from my face. He was such a good man, and I knew he had no whips or handcuffs at his modest home.

"Thinking about Winkler and Lissa," I said. I didn't explain; he took my key card to open my door and saw me inside.

"I'll call in the morning after I get a flight set up for you," he said, then handed the key card back and shut the door behind him.

"Bill, someday, you'll be in a much, much better place," I sighed as his steps retreated.

~

"Two obsessions have been triggered. Both vampires have been dispatched. I am curious whether the others will be triggered as well," the lieutenant bowed his head before his master.

"Two I might consider luck. If three and four die, we will reevaluate. Have you gathered information as to how those deaths occurred?"

"The first left no evidence. The second might be attributed to a shapeshifter, but I cannot verify that."

"Are you tracking the shapeshifter?"

"As of now."

"Good. Destroy him if possible."

"It's female."

"Ah. Then destroy her if possible."

"With pleasure."

~

"Honored One?" Bill greeted Wlodek in the traditional, acceptable way over the phone.

"Director Jennings, what do you have for me?" Wlodek's voice was smooth and unemotional.

"It seems vampires were behind the killings in San Francisco and D.C.," Bill replied.

"How many vampires?"

"Two that I know of. Both are dead, now. I don't have ID on the first one, but the driver's license and credit-card information found in the ash of the second lists the name Hugh Spenser."

"Hugh," Wlodek sighed. "Barely two hundred turns, if I remember correctly. I'll have Charles pull his records and update the file. Tell me, how was he taken down?"

"Caught in the act by two of my agents—found with a victim, which he was prepared to add to the other sixteen he'd already dumped in a section of the local sewer. Taken down by a talented shapeshifter."

"Ah. Very well. If you learn the identity of the one from San Francisco, will you let Charles know?"

"Of course, Honored One."

Wlodek hung up without another word.

∿

Breanne's Journal

Opal and Bill saw me off at the airport. Bill winked at me, Opal smiled. I wasn't sure I'd seen her smile before, but we'd talked with Bill during dinner the night before, and she'd concocted a story that we'd caught the vampire off guard and managed to cut him well enough that he'd flaked. That was Opal's term—*flaked*. I liked it. It was so much easier than saying he'd turned to ash. At least she had clearance to know about the vamps—a lot of Bill's people didn't. Bill nodded to keep Opal happy—he knew I'd taken care of the vampire.

Wishing I could fold space instead, I took my seat on the plane and settled in. Bill had gotten me a first-class ticket at least, and I had plenty of room and no seatmate to make polite conversation. If I didn't hate flying so much, I might have enjoyed the luxury of it.

∿

"She's on her way home—the app showed her at the airport in D.C.

this morning," Jayson informed Hank over the phone. "Trina's pissed because I made her get another cellphone."

"I'd be pissed, too. I figure Breanne would like to kill you, Rome." Hank growled.

"I thought you'd be glad she's on her way back."

"I am. I just don't like that you're tracking her like that."

"We have to talk her into going to my birthday party. Mom wants her to come really bad."

"If she goes, I go. You can't keep living this lie, Rome. Tell your parents—about all of it."

"Look, this is how I turned out. Why tell them now?"

"It might help them understand the rest of it—about the dates who really aren't dates. That sort of thing."

"How do you know Dad won't send me packing? I like my job. I'm good at it."

"I can't say that for certain," Hank muttered. "If you're not going to tell them, at least stop teasing your mother by waving Bree beneath her nose. She wants a daughter-in-law and grandkids. Bree doesn't want to lie for you. Either way, I'm coming to the party if Breanne agrees to go."

"I understood that when you said it the first time."

"Since you're invading her privacy, any idea when she might get in?"

"No, but I can have my assistant search all the flights leaving D.C. this morning."

"No, skip that. I may be waiting at her house, though."

"Stalk much?"

"I'm learning that from you."

Breanne's Journal

The pilot announced that the temperature was forty-seven degrees when we landed. Somehow, it felt colder than the twenty-eight I'd left behind in D.C. I didn't bother fighting the crowd for a cab, either; I misted to my house. Should I have been surprised that Hank was waiting in his ancient truck outside my house? Probably not. That meant I had to go back down the hill, call a cab and arrive in a more conventional manner, which added forty-five minutes onto my arrival time.

"Hank, please go home," I stood outside his truck window, which he'd rolled down the minute the cab pulled into my driveway. I'd given the driver a twenty for a ten-dollar fare and sent him on his way.

"Bree, I don't want to leave right now. I want to hug my girl." Hank leaned a muscular arm on the truck's door and squinted at me in the uncommon sunlight shining on us.

"I'm not your girl." I started to walk away.

"Baby, to me that's what you are." The truck's door creaked painfully as he opened it and climbed out.

"Hank, it won't work. Go home." I pulled keys from my purse and walked up the steps leading to the front door, dragging my small suitcase behind me. Hank took the suitcase from my hand while I unlocked the front door. I was tired, hungry and Hank wanted to invite himself in.

"Just leave it there," I pointed to a corner of my kitchen when Hank asked where I wanted the bag. Dropping my purse on the kitchen counter, I opened the fridge and pulled out the bottle of orange juice. Hank settled on a stool at the island.

"I guess you want lunch," I said after pouring a small glass of juice and drinking all of it.

"I wouldn't say no."

"It'll be grilled cheese and tomato soup."

"I like both those things."

Ten minutes later, I set a bowl of tomato soup and a grilled cheese in front of Hank, along with the requested glass of milk. I settled onto a stool two down from him to eat my lunch.

"Baby, you could sit beside me," Hank lifted half his grilled cheese.

"Nope." I crunched into my sandwich and chewed. Did I tell him his nearness made me queasy with nerves? No.

"Bree, I'm not going to hurt you."

"I don't know that."

"You ought to. You'll only get what you want from me."

"Uh-huh. What about all those fuck buddy calls I answered for you, when I didn't ask in return?" I shoved my plate away and covered my face with both hands.

"Baby, all you have to do is ask me. I'll be right there, I promise." How was he behind me so fast? How? His arms moved around my shoulders and I was pulled against his chest. "Shhh, I won't hurt you. I don't mean to scare you, baby," Hank soothed. I forced myself not to cry.

~

"Ashe?" Bill knocked softly on Ashe's study door.

"Bill? Is Kay all right?" Ashe stood the moment he saw the concerned expression on Bill's face.

"Kay's fine—she's sleeping," Bill sighed, raking fingers through his hair. "Ashe, I have memories I didn't have before."

"What?" Ashe motioned for Bill to take a seat. Bill settled on a chair and watched as Ashe sat again.

"I met Breanne in the past. I remember that now."

"That's not frightening," Ashe muttered. "How? When?"

"In D.C. There are other memories, too, of things that didn't happen before. A sandstorm wiped out an entire village in Somalia. If I hadn't been rescued, I would have died there."

"Damn," Ashe sighed. "This means the attacks are moving up and down the timeline. How were you rescued?"

"I can't remember," Bill rubbed his forehead, as if he had a headache.

"Somebody may be setting traps," Ashe said. "That's possible—and highly dangerous."

"What might happen?" Bill blinked at Ashe in confusion.

"Either of the others may not know what they are and fall victim,"

Ashe replied. "Damn, this worries me." Ashe rose to pace behind his desk.

"You think it worries you? I'm scared to death for Breanne."

"Her name keeps cropping up," Ashe stopped and turned toward Bill. "Fuck," he sighed and disappeared.

~

Lissa's Journal

To say I was behind on comesuli requests would be putting the situation in much milder terms than it was. Thanks to Breanne's intervention, there was more money to distribute; I just didn't have enough time or help to distribute it. She'd seen right through the requests somehow, and knew exactly which ones to approve and which to deny. I hadn't found anyone else I might trust to do the same, and now I was thumbing through requests on what should have been an off-day.

"Lissa?" Ashe appeared in my study and took a chair, crossing one long leg over the other and tapping a knee with well-shaped, impatient fingers.

"Ashe?" He and I were related, but it felt weird calling him Great-uncle so I used his proper name.

"Tell me about Breanne. Everything you know."

"She's the Mighty Heart," I blurted, first thing. When one of the Mighty asks a question, they have a way of getting exactly what they want immediately. "She's also the Vhanaraszh and a Q'elindi."

"Damn. Damn, damn, damn," Ashe rose, holding his head in his hands. "Fuck," he added as an afterthought. "Does she know?"

"I don't think so. She knows about the Vhanaraszh. Probably the Q'elindi. Not about the other. Most likely, she thinks everything she can do is because she's the Vhanaraszh. I hear she can read Larentii, and nobody does that."

"Nobody below the Al'Riyu can read the Larentii. That's how they were made."

"I'm not even going to ask why," I muttered, lowering my eyes to the comp-vid in my hand.

"I don't remember much from before," Ashe sighed and took his seat again. "I don't think we're supposed to. It's separate and inaccessible."

"Like previous lives, for the most part?" I studied my great-uncle wearily. "I worry that Breanne won't ever talk to me, even after she discovers what she is."

"She won't talk to me, that's certain," Ashe nodded.

"What did you do?" I narrowed my eyes at the Mighty Hand.

"Yelled. Chased her off. Trajan brought her to SouthStar, I had a fit because Grandfather said Kalia—Kay—was close and she didn't trust women. I didn't want another woman in the house when Kay arrived. I scared Breanne half to death and Trajan barely speaks to me now because I made him take her away."

"I heard something from Karzac about Kevis' new patient," I said.

"You should have heard it from that asshole mate of yours, Norian Keef."

"I chased Norian back to Wyyld."

"A good place for him. Truthfully, I'd like to kick his ass. He and that fucked up shrink from the ASD scared Kay so bad she attempted suicide. Now she won't talk to anybody."

"That's not good. I'll remember that if and when I see Norian again. Honestly, he has OCD, and not in a good way."

"This whole mess is screwed up," Ashe observed. "I can't touch Kay—it scares her."

"You need to explain that, then."

"How much time do you have?"

"As much as it takes." I turned the comp-vid over, determined to ignore it for now.

"Before we get into that," Ashe said, "I need to talk to you about the Elemaiya here on Le-Ath Veronis."

"What about them?" I was very curious, now.

"I want to take them home with me."

"Is that all? Feel free," I waved an arm. "They're yours if you want them."

"Thank you."

~

Breanne's Journal

As usual, Hank left the minute he was done fucking. I listened while his truck roared to life after several tries. Why was I putty in Hank's hands? Why? *You love him and you're a slut where he's concerned,* my conscience informed me. My cellphone rang, so I reached out with a bare arm to pull it off the nightstand beside my bed. Trina's face appeared on the phone as it continued to ring.

"Trina?" I really wasn't in the mood to talk, but convinced myself it might get Hank out of my head.

"It's Jayson," his voice snapped.

"Great. Why do you have Trina's phone and what do you want now? Didn't you get that release?"

"I bought Trina another phone, I got the release and it's already on file in our legal department. Mom wants the staff writer to talk to you at my birthday party. She wants to listen in while you answer questions."

"Jayson, you are so damned mean," I muttered.

"I'm not mean. I only have sex with the women who want what I do. I'm not mean to them, either. They ask for what they get from me."

"I think we're using different dictionaries and we're certainly not talking about the same thing. That's not what I meant and you know it. I'm talking about the blackmail where your mother is concerned. When and where is the fucking party? And what am I supposed to buy you, as the girlfriend du jour, sans large breasts?"

"Next Wednesday at my house, and you can buy me a book or something equally as useful. I don't need anything."

"Except a real girlfriend," I huffed.

"I don't want a girlfriend. I told you that the night we met."

"I don't even want to ask what you consider me," I muttered angrily. "Besides a convenience and a lie you tell your mother."

"I think of you as a friend. A really, really, hostile friend."

"I thought people in the community only wanted friends who were also in the community."

"Bree, I know all kinds of people. I'm friends with some of them. My older brother is as vanilla as they come and I love him."

"So he doesn't know, either?"

"No, and I don't intend to tell him."

"Don't you ever get tired of the double-life, Jayson?"

"Sometimes, but it is what it is. Be here at six, Mom wants to see you before things start at seven."

"Of course she does."

"She loves you."

"She doesn't even know me."

"She sees you as the woman she wants on my arm."

"And you're willing to give her that, no matter what it costs both of us in the long term," I huffed.

"Look, I want things to work out. I'll owe you. Just name your price."

"You have nothing I want, Jayson Rome."

"I can pay off the loan Hank owes you."

"No. I told Hank he owes me nothing. The club is his, free and clear. He can do whatever the hell he wants with it."

"You're impossible," Jayson muttered.

"Yeah. That's why you ought to take somebody you're willing to have sex with to your party. Not somebody you only want the public to see."

"I bought Trina a car. I can buy you a car."

"I have a car."

"That's not a car."

"Perspective is everything. I see it as a car, therefore, it's a car. I don't drive much, anyway."

"Mom will freak if she sees it."

"I'll walk to that behemoth you call a home, then."

"No. Hank can pick you up."

"Tell Hank I can get myself where I need to go. I don't need a ride, either in his or your vehicle." I was already ashamed enough that I'd hopped right back in bed with Hank. I knew I should just write him off, but if I saw him, that's usually all it took.

"Look, I have to go, there's an appointment waiting."

"You called me, remember?"

"I did. Now I'm hanging up." He did. I was glad.

"You're sure of this?" Bob Sullivan was back, waving more money at Gus Fulton for additional information. "My boss says an extra hundred grand for more information. We don't have photographs of the other two, you know, and you didn't give names."

"A hundred grand?"

"Fifty grand for each name," Bob coaxed the old man.

"All right," Gus sighed. "I've got the records from the sheriff's department, when they tried to run away," he added. "Got some pictures, too."

"I'm sure you do." Bob smiled.

"You can barbecue Joyce Christian with the information we're getting," Ross Gideon accepted a glass of bourbon from James Rome Sr.'s assistant. "Too bad she's dead; I'd love to sit in on this trial."

"That'll be all, Stacy," James nodded, sending his assistant out the door. "What do you have?" he asked when his office door closed softly.

"Proof that Joyce Christian committed murder, theft, corruption, you name it," Ross chuckled. "There's more coming, too."

"I always knew there was something about that bitch," James growled. "Show me what you have so far."

"I already have ten chapters written. Not outlined—written. I've been collecting information on her for years, at your request," Ross nodded at James. "All the stuff she did at the state level is already there, I just have to copy and paste a lot of it. Adding this into the mix, well, this is gonna blow everybody away. I've got correlations on legislation while she was doing this other shit. Some of it, you're not gonna believe. I was almost sick, seeing it." Ross pushed a manila envelope across James' desk. "These are the originals—I have copies of all of it to work with. You paid for it—it's yours."

"I would have paid a lot more," James unfastened the clasp and pulled the journal and photographs out. The first photograph made him draw in a shocked breath.

"Thought that one would make you sit up and take notice. The way I see it, that's the book's cover. If you'll give me a staff writer or two, we can have this thing done in three weeks or less." Ross emptied his glass in two swallows.

"Do it," James Rome's eyes were hard as he lifted his gaze to Ross'. "I'll shove everything else aside and print this as soon as it's ready."

"Has our little surprise been prepared?"
"It's ready."
"Then release it."
"Done."

CHAPTER 9

Ashe hadn't been gone an hour. We'd talked for quite a while before he left, too. This, though, sent me screaming through the palace. Gedes, the capital city of Wyyld, was under attack by the former inmates of Yigga Prison.

All of them were armed with the worst imaginable, including Ranos rifles, launchers and cannons. Aryn was ready immediately, while Rigo shouted, "Take me with you," when I sent images of the attack to all my mates. Those connected to the Saa Thalarr were prevented from interfering, but anyone else wasn't held to that. Another stepped forward to volunteer when I landed in the palace kitchen—*Cheedas.*

This was his way of ending his grief, but I wasn't about to allow it. "Stay here," I snapped at him. Norian was already on Wyyld, and Lendill, using every bit of power he possessed, fought beside Norian. Ildevar placed a shield around the palace, but that wasn't the problem —the people of Gedes were getting slaughtered.

I'll meet you there, Erland sent. He was on Karathia, but at least I'd have a power wielder with me. Roff, too, had come, and although I worried for him, he was vampire and didn't have a death wish.

145

I folded Roff, Aryn and Rigo to Wyyld, and surprisingly, Garde had come. He was already turned to Thifilathi and swept humanoid attackers aside with huge arms. They were burning if they came in contact with his black scales and the stench was terrible.

Breanne's Journal

I was in the shower when it hit me. I knew Lissa, Aryn, Rigo and Roff were in danger. Somebody was gunning for them—that much I could tell from my prescient reading. Throwing on clothing, I bent time to arrive at the proper moment.

Hank didn't feel good about pulling Breanne into bed, but he couldn't help himself. He knew she wanted lovemaking, too, and he couldn't do that. Not without kissing her—that was too much temptation. If he kissed her, he'd strip away every bit of information she was hiding from him. He could do it—someone as powerful as he could do it easily when connected to another like that. He felt it was unethical, but he wouldn't be able to hold back.

"Why can't I read you, baby?" Hank muttered as he walked through the club's door. "I could find that stuff out the easy way and then kiss you as much as I want."

Lissa's Journal

They were too scattered and too well armed. Yigga Prison was large—big enough to hold ten thousand inmates or more, and all of those inmates were spread throughout Gedes, killing easily. It wouldn't have mattered much even if the population had been armed —these criminals were shielded in some way, so anything fired at them bounced right off. Norian discovered that quickly when he and a makeshift army of palace guards started shooting. Their Ranos weapons had little effect and the energy blasts ricocheted everywhere. The only person having any effect at all was Gardevik Rath, and his power as a High Demon was somehow disarming the shields surrounding the attackers.

The trouble with that, of course, was that we only had one High Demon fighting for our side, and he couldn't be everywhere.

"Beloved, we cannot penetrate the shields," Belen appeared at my side.

"What?" I stared up at him. Why could a High Demon do what I couldn't?

"At the moment, we can only shield against their weapons. I have not received permission to interfere by exerting sufficient power to eliminate their protection."

"I could have waited forever to hear that kind of news," I muttered. Rigo, Aryn, Roff and Erland stood behind me; they'd backed up the moment Belen appeared. I had to shut out the screams around us—people were fleeing for their lives.

~

Breanne's Journal

"Target their weapons." I'd landed near my sister, who stood with Erland, Aryn, Rigo, Roff and someone else I hadn't met. I held my shields up and deliberately didn't read him.

Lissa stared at me in shock. I didn't wait for her to answer; I went ahead and did what I'd suggested, going to mist and turning the weapons former prisoners carried into flying sparks. Their weapons weren't shielded—they couldn't be or they'd be unable to shoot the population of Gedes, which they were doing with abandon. Once their weapon was destroyed, each prisoner stopped in his tracks, blinking in confusion at his hands. That spelled obsession to me— they'd been instructed to kill and they wouldn't stop killing unless they didn't have a weapon.

I was joined by Lissa, and then Erland figured out how to destroy weapons with a spell. Another, a half elf—I learned that and other things from reading him—was folding space and destroying weapons much like Erland. Each disarmed prisoner stopped in his tracks, unsure how to proceed from there. It made me want to laugh—the one who'd instructed them hadn't considered that we'd destroy the weapons; they thought we'd break ourselves attempting to crack the shields and destroy the former prisoners.

The biggest flaw in the designed attack, of course, was in shielding the prisoner and then having to leave the barrel of the weapon unshielded so it could fire. Poor planning, actually, but it was also genius—the shield was devised to allow the barrel of the weapon to move without closing over it. Genius and stupidity, at one and the same time.

∽

Lissa's Journal

Gedes' police force had set up barricades, but it was difficult to guard against an enemy that had been evenly distributed throughout the city. Most of those still armed worked in twos and threes, one armed with a Ranos launcher, the other two with rifles. Homes and buildings were destroyed with launchers first, and if anyone was left alive inside, they were killed with the rifles. It was a well-planned attack, and that frightened me.

A sandstorm had precipitated the release of these prisoners, and in the interim, they'd been armed and instructed by someone before they'd been set down in Gedes and ordered to kill whatever lay in their path. This required a great deal of power, there was no doubt about that, and it terrified me. The sandstorms we had no defense against, and I worried that there would be more—many, many more. Aiming my hand, I employed the Larentii trick of separating particles and destroyed a Ranos launcher first, the rifles after.

∽

Breanne's Journal

I felt my sister on the other side of the city, doing exactly what I was doing—raising her hand and destroying weapons by turning them into rapidly dying sparks. An eighteen-foot High Demon was roaring and destroying the enemy in another part of the city and Erland, the elf and a few others who'd come were creating spells to eliminate weapons. I was more than surprised that we had so few effective members on our side. Where was everybody? Where? This was home to the Founding Member of the Reth Alliance, after all, and people were dying. How thankful was I that the attackers didn't have tanks or planes?

Gardevik Rath, the High Demon, roared in the distance—he'd taken a hit from a Ranos rifle in the shoulder. I blinked as he was joined by another High Demon, who picked up where Garde left off. This one, though, was taller than Garde—by at least four feet. As enormous as he was, his anger was fiercer as he killed the enemy with furious sweeps of long, black-scaled arms. I wasn't about to argue—I still had enemy to disarm.

Eventually, Garde moved behind Lissa, destroying what she'd disarmed while the other High Demon worked behind me. I hoped Garde wasn't injured too badly—he was still killing effectively and I was afraid of what that might cost him. The one behind me was uninjured and terrifyingly efficient.

Lissa's Journal

"What now?" It had taken six hours to destroy weapons, allowing Garde and another High Demon to destroy as many enemy as they could behind me and Breanne. Norian had instructed the local forces to round up the remaining prisoners, who suddenly had no idea what to do.

I couldn't find Breanne, either, and that upset me. She'd just shown up from nowhere, pointed out the obvious and then went to work. I couldn't even see her mist when she turned, and I could see any vampire's mist. Part and parcel of what she was, no doubt. Garde's High Demon helper had also disappeared quickly, and I didn't know what to make of that, either.

"Breah-mul, what are we going to do with these?" Norian stood beside me, with Lendill shadowing him. Norian was fresh—he hadn't expended energy to disarm attackers. Lendill, on the other hand, looked as if he'd gone through a wringer—several times. He and Erland were both spent—I doubted either could light a candle using power at the moment.

These turned out to be around two hundred prisoners—all that was left after Garde and his unknown helper got through with the others.

"We can't take them to Evensun," Rigo pointed out judiciously. "As long as those shields surround them, they can't do anything else."

"They're protected from themselves, too," Roff muttered, staring about us. "I don't think they were meant to live long after this. They can't get food or water through those shields, and I have no idea what's holding them up, anyway."

"They'll starve to death or die from dehydration. Not a pretty way to go," Lendill muttered.

"I can't get past their shields, so there's nothing we can do," I sighed.

"I'll take care of this." Garde arrived in his smaller Thifilathi, weary and bleeding sluggishly from a shoulder wound.

"Garde, honey, you've done enough. Let me call Karzac."

"Call the physician, avilepha, I will welcome the help."

Karzac arrived, and thankfully, he had Jayd with him. I don't know whether Garde called Jayd or if Karzac made Jayd feel guilty, but it didn't matter—Garde became humanoid so Karzac could treat his wound while Jayd destroyed two hundred obsessed prisoners.

"Lissa?" Ildevar appeared at my side as I watched Karzac treat Garde.

"Ildevar." I hunched my shoulders. "Who do you think did this? Never mind, that's a stupid question."

❧

Breanne's Journal

I didn't stay. There was no need, and I had no desire to get caught in Gavin's trap again. At least he hadn't come with Lissa to deal with the former prisoners bent on destroying Ildevar Wyyld's capital city. I had no idea why the founder of the Reth Alliance kept showing up on my radar, but he did. It didn't matter—I wanted to weep for those who'd died at the hands of obsessed monsters. I couldn't *Change What Was* for so many scattered individuals without exhausting myself and waving a flag for Kalenegar to see. I got the idea that somebody else might be watching, too, and I sure didn't want to attract unwanted attention.

My cellphone rang as I was getting ice water from the fridge in my kitchen. It was Hank.

"Hank?" I answered the call when I knew I shouldn't. Weary couldn't begin to describe how I felt, and there wasn't any way I could explain why to Hank Bell.

"Baby, where have you been? I've tried calling you six times."

"Six times since you got what you wanted and took off?"

"Fuck," he sighed. "I was afraid you'd take it that way."

"Look, I ought to be used to it by now. Bye, Hank." I ended the call and tossed the cellphone on the kitchen counter. It rang again immediately. Hank again.

"What?" I said this time.

"I'm coming to pick you up. Take you to dinner."

"No, that's not part of the agreement, remember? No dinner. No flowers. No kissing, hugging, et cetera and so forth," I pointed out. "Take Jayson. I don't think he wants your kisses or hugs. Besides, I've had a tough day." I had—the ride from D.C., Hank, then the conversation with Jayson and a trip to Wyyld to save as much of Gedes as I could, with help from my sister and a few others had worn me out. The trouble was, I was exhausted and wound up at the same time.

"I keep forgetting you flew in from D.C. this morning. I'm on West Coast time."

"Yeah."

"Bree?" His voice had gone soft.

"What?"

"Don't count me out, baby. I swear I'll always be there for you. I promise."

"Sure. Good night, Hank."

≈

"Opal, we may have another problem," Bill passed a folder to his shapeshifter agent. "Two young women, missing from an Austin campus."

"This makes no sense, Director," Opal flipped the folder open and studied two photographs. "Why do you think this age-group is being targeted?"

"No idea. Breanne might help with that, though."

"I'm assuming you'll call her?"

"Yes, but I'll wait until next week. I don't want to wear her out because she's convenient. Besides, this could be a random attack. We don't know for sure it's connected."

"True. And she's certainly that—Breanne is," Opal agreed while reading through information on missing college students. "Convenient, that is. I like her a lot."

"So do I."

≈

Lissa's Journal

"Erland says Breanne showed up." Drew sipped dark Falchani tea next to his brother at the breakfast table. Gavin's head jerked up instantly. I hadn't told him anything—I'd gone straight to bed after getting home the night before. I'd stayed to help Ildevar prepare a statement for the journalists who were converging on Gedes—after the danger was eliminated.

"Breanne did show up," I nodded, refusing to glance Gavin's way again. "If she hadn't been there, we probably would have lost the entire city. Gedes is relatively small because Ildevar likes it that way. There's only half a million living there. Most work in nearby Fendes. Ildevar won't allow manufacturing near the palace, and all of Gedes is included in that."

"Did you talk to her?" Drake's dark eyes studied me over his tea.

"I didn't get the chance. She showed up, told us what we needed to do and then went to work. She disappeared afterward, too. I wish I knew where to find her."

"I feel bad that we got to talk to her and you didn't," Drew sighed.

"That happened a lot, it seems," I said and lifted my cup of coffee.

"Lissa, please stop. You cannot make me feel worse than I do already." Gavin rose and stalked away.

"Was it something we said?" Drew asked innocently.

"Dee, what good would it do?" Gavril sighed. "She's gone. If Mom can't find her, who can? If I take the compulsion off the Starr brothers and the other two, they'll just be pissed at me and still have no Breanne."

"Child, you made a grave mistake. Perhaps it is time to admit that."

"All right—I fucked up. I really, really fucked up. If Mom ever finds out, the fur may fly, too."

"I fail to understand that idiom, nevertheless, I believe I grasp the concept," Dee muttered dryly. "I still believe it would be better to admit your mistake now, rather than waiting to be caught out, as you often say."

"Dee, it was a mistake. I admit that. I'll lose my warlocks over it, too, no matter when I own up to it. I'd prefer to wait, if you don't mind."

"I do mind, but I see you won't budge on this," Dee replied, a touch of acid in his voice. "Here are the reports you requested." He set a comp-vid on Gavril's desk. "I'll be available tomorrow if you wish to discuss the figures included."

"Why tomorrow?"

"Because I am taking the rest of the day off." Dee walked out of Gavril's study without a backward glance.

~

Breanne's Journal

"Jayson, I said to shut off that stupid app." He and Hank found me at a vegetarian café at lunchtime the following day. "Give Trina her phone back while you're at it," I grumped when both of them slid into my booth. Hank took the space next to me while Jayson occupied the opposite side.

Francie's Veggie Café was still busy, although the lunch hour was winding down for downtown San Francisco workers. I loved their hummus sandwich, because they'd make it the way I wanted it—with black olives, tomatoes, lettuce and cheese. "Do you know how aggravating it is not to have any privacy?" I added.

"He only checked because I asked him to," Hank slipped an arm around my shoulders.

"Refer to my previous statement," I muttered. "Never mind, I'll disable it on my end," I pulled out my cellphone and started scrolling through apps.

"No, baby," Hank lifted the cellphone from my hand and turned it off before handing it back. "Keep it. It scares the life out of me if I don't know where you are."

"Hmmph," I grumbled before taking a bite of my hummus sandwich. A part of me still wanted to delete the app. Another part wanted to do exactly what Hank wanted.

"Are you hungry?" I asked after chewing and swallowing. "I can get your lunch here, or do you require dead, cooked animals before satisfaction can be achieved? I think I can have the pizza place next door slap something together and deliver it here. The same person owns both places, so I don't think they'll have a fit."

"Baby, do you know how good you are?" Hank hugged me tighter for a moment before releasing me with a sigh. "I wouldn't say no to a pepperoni and sausage pizza."

"I'd take some of that," Jayson agreed. Pulling out my cellphone again, I placed the order. The employee laughed when I asked to have it delivered next door and said it would be ready in twenty minutes. I gave my credit-card number and hung up.

"There," I lifted my sandwich again. "Get moneybags Rome to buy drinks at the counter, since he's violating my privacy."

"I'll get drinks." Jayson rose and walked toward the counter.

"He knows what you want?" I turned to Hank. God, what a handsome man. His hair was as black as Merrill's, and Hank was probably the most beautiful thing—male or female—I'd ever seen. Did I want to touch him? Yeah. I did. I turned back to my sandwich and swallowed that desire with a bite of bread-covered hummus.

"Come back to my apartment with me after lunch," Hank breathed against my ear. Could he read me that easily? I sighed.

Hank and Jayson ate the whole pizza. Granted the large size was a chain restaurant's medium, but they ate it. Hank had a refill on iced tea, too. I teased him about not having an old fashioned, but he came right back with the fact that they didn't serve alcohol at my favorite veggie café.

"Next time you decide to stalk, let me know ahead of time so I can plan accordingly," I wrinkled my nose at him.

"Baby, I'll stalk you every minute of every day," Hank mumbled against my hair after pulling me into a hug. "Give me your phone," he added after pulling away.

"What?" I frowned at him.

"Come on. Jayson already has you on that fucked up app. I want it, too."

"This isn't where I intended that to go," I turned my head away and stared at the wall. The surface was plaster and painted a pale gray, with white on the chair rail and crown moldings.

"Come on," Hank coaxed gently. "I promise not to overdo it."

"What? You just said you'd stalk every day all day," I huffed.

"Yeah, but I'll keep it to myself," he grinned. Any grin from Hank Bell would make a men's magazine cover.

"Here." I pushed my purse toward Hank. "Help yourself. While you're having your way with my phone, look up behavior modification classes," I said.

"Why?" Dark eyes glinted curiously.

"Because I need to learn how to say no," I replied. Hank laughed.

"I had this designed for the club. We're gonna break it in," Hank grinned after hauling me to his apartment.

"Huh?" I stared at the contraption he seemed so proud to show me. It was a table—sort of.

"Come on, you kneel here," he patted the lower, padded portion that I thought was a narrow seat, "Lean over this part," he patted the upper padded portion, "And we get it on."

"Uh-huh." I blinked at him, a frown plastered on my face.

"Baby, I'm not gonna tie you to it, although that's what it's designed for," he grinned.

"You'd better not tie me to anything," I said.

"I know what merinthophobia means. I taught Jayson the word, baby," Hank sighed.

"You know, I think I'll go home, now." I lifted my purse off Hank's kitchen island and headed toward the door.

"No, baby. Stay with me. I didn't mean to scare you."

"Then what did you mean to do?"

"Give you a climax and let you sleep," he sighed. "You look tired."

"I'd settle for sleep. I haven't gotten much of that lately," I said.

"Come on, then. I'll wear you out and then let you sleep it off."

"Is that your answer for insomnia?" I lifted an eyebrow at Hank.

"It's my answer where you're concerned. Bree, I've walked around with a constant erection since I met you." He grinned wickedly.

"And there I thought at first you had absolutely no reaction where I was concerned."

"You just weren't looking at the proper end of things."

"Is that all it was?"

"Baby, stop wrinkling your nose or I'll have you on the floor."

"Which is less impersonal?" I asked, nodding toward the sex bench.

"Come here." Hank motioned me forward. "I'll show you less impersonal."

The knee bench slid inward and locked in place. Who knew? Hank set me on top of the bench and then proceeded to lift the knit shirt over my head. He then kissed the tops of my breasts before removing my bra. He'd never paid much attention to my breasts before, past the initial intake of breath on seeing them the first time.

"Perfect. Perfect, perfect, perfect," he whispered against them before taking my left nipple between his teeth and biting gently. I had no idea that would cause my nether regions to clench—hard. I reached for his belt buckle.

"No. No, no, no. Not yet, I'm not done here," he moved my hand, placing it flat on the bench beside me. "Keep your hands on the bench, baby, or I'll hold them there," he murmured. I wanted to moan at his words—I'd never gotten to touch his shoulders or run my hands over his ribs—which is what I really wanted to do. Damn Hank Bell and his fucked up fuck buddy rules. Maybe someday I'd bite his ass and give him the vampire version of a climax. The thought made me smile shortly before Hank bit my other nipple, making me squeal and then moan.

"Come back to me, baby, and what I'm doing to you. I'd blindfold you, but that would scare you, I know. Close your eyes and keep them closed unless I do scare you. Okay? I'm not about to hurt you. I promise."

"Let me see your eyes, first," I said.

"What?" He was puzzled, I could tell. Ignoring the urge to read him (again), I waded into the dark depths of his gaze before closing my eyes as he asked.

"That's my baby," he crooned and kissed my neck gently.

Keeping my eyes closed and my hands on the bench became the sweetest torture I could recall enduring. His hands—and his mouth— traced my collarbone, my ribs and my hipbones. Fingers caressed the bend of my knees and then my ankles. He cupped my heels in his hands, his thumbs softly rubbing my anklebones. Was that hot? Hot didn't begin to describe it.

"Don't resist," he murmured against my ear as he lifted my feet up. "Baby, we're gonna take care of this pretty bush one of these days," he sighed and put his mouth on me. I screamed his name thirty seconds later.

~

"Sleep, baby," Hank brushed lips across my cheek before leaving his apartment. He'd left me bonelessly sprawled across his bed, with nothing more in my head than letting sleep claim me. He'd done exactly what he'd set out to do—worn me out and made me want to sleep. Had I gotten a lip lock in all that time? No. He'd kissed everything else, and parts of me had received extended attention, but I still hadn't been kissed by the mind-bending Hank Bell. Someday, I intended to ask him about that. When I was awake.

~

Lissa's Journal

Lifting the coronet off my head, I stared at myself in my dressing table mirror.

"My love?" Thurlow appeared behind me. He didn't visit often or for very long.

"Honey?" I did a half-turn and looked up at him.

"Might I spend a little time in your bed?"

"I think you might."

"Good." He leaned down and drew my lower lip into his mouth before sucking on it.

Something sure had Thurlow turned on—he seldom moved as fast as he was moving now, and he was taking me with him. I closed my eyes and sighed with pleasure.

~

"This the new toy?" John eyed the bench in the back of Hank's truck.

"Yeah. Works great."

"Tried it out already?" John eyed the piece of furniture with interest.

"And cleaned it afterward," Hank grinned. "Come on, get the tailgate down and help me unload this thing."

"Gonna tell me who?"

"That, now and always, will be none of your fucking business," Hank grunted, pulling the bench forward after John lowered the tailgate.

❧

Breanne's Journal

I woke after midnight. Hank was still working and I wanted a shower. I left a note for Hank, telling him I'd gone home, then misted toward my house in San Rafael. Dropping my purse on the kitchen island with a sigh, I headed down the hall toward my bedroom. I felt hungry, too, since I hadn't eaten anything past lunch at Francie's. I wanted a shower before food, however, and went through the walk-in closet to my private bath.

My abdominal muscles were nicely sore as I cleaned off the remnants of sex with Hank. Yes, he still used condoms, and I toyed with the idea of telling him they weren't needed. Discarding the notion, I shampooed my hair and applied conditioner. If I didn't, it curled too much. Lissa and I had that in common, I suppose, it's just that she had beautiful, strawberry-blonde hair and I was a brunette.

Sighing, I pulled on a fleecy robe and made my way to the kitchen for a very late dinner. My cellphone was ringing the moment I turned on the kitchen lights.

"I'm gonna call that fucking app company," Jayson stated without preamble. "One minute you're at Hank's apartment, the next you're home."

"Jayson, just stop, okay? I'm hungry and I don't need your crap right now."

"Hank keep you too busy to eat?" Jayson snickered.

"Jayson, I swear I'm gonna drive over you with my almost-car."

"That ought to raise a bruise," he laughed. "Seriously, though, we may have another problem."

"What's that?"

"Mom wants us to come to L.A. for a visit this weekend."

"Oh, for cripe's sake," I muttered. "You can't do that to me. Or her. You can't. Won't your birthday party be enough?"

"Dad's made plans to be out of town through the weekend on a business trip, and Mom wants us to come."

"Of course she does."

"I already told her you're an old-fashioned girl and will want separate bedrooms. She's made plans to put us in two rooms across from each other. Just in case."

"First off, I don't want to go to L.A. Second off, what will Henry Hank Bell say?"

"Oh, he'll probably beat the hell out of me during my Krav Maga lesson."

"You do Krav Maga?" I'd always been interested in that, for personal reasons.

"Yeah. Lessons for five years." He was proud of that, I could tell. "Hank can still beat my ass and my instructor's ass, though. Probably at the same time."

"Good for Hank. Maybe I'll suggest he do that when you piss me off next time."

"He's already done it once over you."

"Really? Maybe I'll buy him a new car, just for that."

"What?" Jayson sputtered.

"Yeah. What do you think he might want?"

"Look, if you'll go with me to L.A., I'll see that Hank gets a new truck. He does a lot of hauling, so that's what he needs."

"Sure. Go the blackmail route, why don't you?"

"It's not blackmail—I told him I'd give him a loan for a new truck last week." Jayson was proud of himself. "We're going tomorrow to pick it out. Why don't you come? I'll take pictures of us out together and send them to Mom."

"Liar, liar," I muttered.

"Not. I'm going to buy something for myself while we're out, too."

"You already have a garage full of vehicles," I pointed out. He did—Trina told me he had six parked in his overly enormous garage.

"That doesn't include the classics I have in storage."

"I'm getting a headache," I said.

"I want a new Escalade," he said. "I'll trade in the old one."

"The old one that is barely a year old?" I asked.

"Yeah."

"You're impossible."

"You keep saying that. Are we having a spat? I can text Mom and ask for advice. She'll love that."

"You need to keep me out of that," I snapped.

"You know, I'll bet your hair is all fluffed up now, and you're spitting like a kitten," he laughed.

"Something you're not used to, no doubt," I grumped.

"Well, that's true," he agreed. "Mom will like that, too, since the other girls she's met have never disagreed or questioned me once."

"By design?"

"I guess—yeah."

"Jayson, I really, really hope you're happy," I sighed.

"You mean that?"

"I do. Really. I like your mother. A lot. She loves you—a lot. I'm not really sure why sometimes, because I would have kicked your ass over the anniversary party."

"I know." Jayson actually sounded contrite. "I don't know why, but I always feel better after I talk to you, too, and I can't explain that. We disagree over most everything."

"Well, I sure can't say why that is. We're oil and water, Jayson Rome."

"No, maybe oil and fire," he laughed. "But you've never once said I was wrong in my lifestyle or my choices. I made you feel inadequate in five seconds after I met you, and you've never said I was sick or evil. I sort of enjoy our disagreements on everything else, actually."

"Jayson, will you stop?" I sighed. "I've seen evil. You're not it."

"You keep saying that. I wish you'd explain it. Hank probably wouldn't mind knowing, either."

"I'm not telling. Ever. So don't ask. Stop asking. Fuck." I rubbed my forehead.

"You coming with us tomorrow? We can argue about the vehicles I buy."

"Oh, sure," I muttered sarcastically.

"Good. I'll pick you up around ten and we'll go get Hank. I'll buy lunch."

"Hey, I was being sarcas," I didn't get to finish the word, Jayson had already hung up.

CHAPTER 10

*B*reanne's *Journal*

"I was railroaded," I informed Hank as I moved from the front seat of Jayson's year-old Escalade to the back seat so Hank could sit up front. We'd stopped outside Hank's apartment to pick him up before heading to the dealership Jayson preferred, which sold new Escalades. From there, Jayson intended to take us to lunch and then to a Ford dealership to buy Hank a new truck.

"What will you do with your old truck?" I asked Hank as Jayson pulled away from the curb.

"Give it to charity," he leaned around the back of his seat and grinned at me.

"Okay," I shrugged. He was excited to be getting a new vehicle; that was easy enough to see. "I'll be happy when you don't have to beg it to start," I added.

"Come on, that's half the fun of having a classic vehicle," Hank chuckled, settling back in his seat again.

"No, that's most of the worry of having an ancient rattletrap," I said.

"Are you calling Hank's rattletrap a rattletrap?" Jayson pulled to a stop at a red light.

"Yeah. You have no idea how many times I wanted to buy a roadside assistance membership for him."

"I have one already," Hank pointed out.

"Thank God. I had visions of you being abducted by roving bands of sex-crazed women if you broke down on the highway," I retorted.

"You think I'll be attacked by sex-crazed women?"

"I'm surprised it hasn't happened already. If you disappear for days, I imagine that's probably what will be responsible," I said.

"Baby, would you rescue me?" He leaned around his seat again.

"If you wanted or needed to be rescued," I nodded.

"Good."

"Jayson, that's a behemoth." I stared at the largest Escalade available, in a white diamond color with a cocoa leather interior. Jayson grinned as the salesman handed a key to him. We were going for a test drive, looked like.

"I may want to buy a behemoth," Jayson grinned. Hank was checking out the gadgets and gizmos inside, so I resigned myself and climbed into the back seat. That's when it hit me—Jayson was buying his birthday present a day early. Was he buying it for himself or was this the gift from Mom and Dad? That's when I decided to read him briefly. I didn't know how old he was and I'd find that out, too. I didn't want to see anything he did for kinky fun, and I was determined to stop reading him the moment that came.

"Jayson?" I said as he settled on the driver's seat and started the vehicle.

"Huh?" he turned to me. I lowered my shield. Nothing. Not a damned thing happened. I couldn't read fucking Jayson Rome. Was that upsetting? You bet.

"Uh, how old will you be? I probably ought to know that," I covered up my hesitation with a question.

"Thirty."

"Oh. Okay."

"We're going to the party?" Hank asked.

"Looks that way—Bree's gonna do the interview for my staff writer and Mom's gonna watch," Jayson steered away from the dealership. "Then, she's going with me to L.A. Friday afternoon. For the weekend."

"Rome, no." Hank was adamant.

"I already told Mom she was coming."

"I said no."

"Look, why don't you come, too? That way you can protect your territory. It's not like we don't have enough room at the house. Plus, Dad will be gone."

Without replying, Hank hauled out his cellphone and dialed a number. His assistant manager answered on the second ring. "John," Hank said, "I need you and Trey to cover the weekend. I'm going out of town."

❧

Jayson was happy to pay nearly a hundred thousand for his new vehicle. Half that was credited for the trade-in, but we drove his new Escalade off the lot. I chewed my lip and said nothing as he drove toward Sausalito and a restaurant he'd selected. Hank was pissed about the L.A. trip, I didn't want to go in the first place and the temperature inside the new Escalade had dropped to near-freezing.

"You agreed to this?" Hank pulled me against him while Jayson asked for a table for three in an upscale restaurant.

"I really didn't," I tried to pull away. "He keeps badgering me with his mother and her feelings in all this." I wanted to hug myself. Hank was doing it for me. I didn't add that Jayson had thrown Hank's new truck into the mix. "I think I want to go home," I moaned against Hank's chest.

"Shh—it's a disagreement. It'll blow over." Hank rocked me gently before turning me around and pulling me along—the hostess was leading us toward a window table overlooking the bay. I ordered a salad, didn't eat much of it and didn't talk all through lunch.

Hank picked out a blue Ford truck, with extended cab and plenty of hauling space. I watched as he talked with the salesman about everything, including mileage. Jayson stuck his two-cents in occasionally, since he was Mr. Auto Expert. I thought about my TinyCar and shivered in a San Francisco afternoon that had gone cold and gray.

Jayson handed over his credit-card when it came time to pay. I left the office and stood in the showroom, staring, unseeing, at new vehicles. Twice I was approached and asked if I wanted to buy anything. I wouldn't have left if it hadn't been necessary. It was necessary, and in the worst possible way.

Fes Desh had just put pans of ox-roast into the ovens for the dinner menu when his brother rushed into the kitchen.

"Fes, there's a sandstorm blowing outside," Rane shouted over the sudden noise.

Lissa's Journal

"I hate to interrupt, but a sandstorm is sweeping through Targis," Kyler rushed into the Council meeting, her face pale and fearful. Flavio rose immediately and went to her while I stood on shaking legs.

"Gavin," my voice trembled as I gave orders, "gather everybody you can. We'll go as soon as it blows itself out."

That's the one thing we knew about the sandstorms—they didn't last. It didn't take long, actually, for them to destroy what was in their path. Yigga Prison and the surrounding area had been scoured in less than ten minutes, Earth time.

"Lissa," a pregnant Reah was set beside me by a shaking and angry Aurelius. Edward landed right behind them, and he looked grim.

"What?" My heart stuttered into a gallop.

"Fes," Reah wailed and almost dropped to the floor. Aurelius and Edward caught her between them.

~

Breanne's Journal

The sandstorm that wiped away Beledweyne lasted eight minutes. Satellite images confirmed that, and the images of a brown cloud wiping away lives was shown over and over by the media on Earth.

This brown cloud raged below me, and I knew it was worse. Targis was the capital city on Tulgalan, and home to millions. It was also home to Fes Desh, his family and his restaurant. Was I seething as I hovered far above the massacre of innocents? Seething couldn't begin to describe the anger I felt. As I'd arrived after the sandstorm began, I felt obligated to wait it out and then see what I might do to repair damage. Did I feel the power behind the sandstorm? I'd be a fool to say that I didn't.

~

Lissa's Journal

Fifteen of the longest minutes of my life passed while a quarter of Targis was wiped off the map. Comp-vids were in vampire hands all around me, as electronic feeds from space towers relayed images of the impenetrable brown cloud enveloping parts of Tulgalan's capital city. Those with enough talent might have felt the power behind that terrible storm—if they were brave enough to venture their thoughts in that direction. I was too afraid. Afraid that I'd also hear the screams of the dying as sand flayed skin and muscle from their bodies and dust filled their mouths and noses, stealing their last breaths.

"Cara, there is nothing we can do," Gavin pulled my head against his shoulder. I wept.

~

The lieutenant turned in a circle on a clean-swept street. Yes, he and his servants had achieved their goal—a quarter of the city had been razed effectively. Sadly, none had attempted to stop it, and that meant disappointment for his superior. They'd hoped to draw one of the three out and tempt them with stopping the destruction. None had answered the call. His underlings began appearing around him, awaiting further commands.

"Go," the lieutenant barked. "I will follow you swiftly." They disappeared at his command. "The three—they're afraid," he chuckled. "Afraid to challenge us. I will inform my superior of this. We have won, with little effort."

"Really?" The lieutenant had no time to turn and gaze upon his attacker—his corporeal body turned to sparks and disintegrated.

~

Breanne's Journal

He'd seemed so sure of himself. I had no idea what he was talking about—all I knew was that he'd been responsible, at least in part, for four million deaths. I only hesitated long enough to give him a one-word reply before separating his particles.

Sighing and allowing my shoulders to droop, I surveyed the devastation around me. Fes Desh was dead, and he'd been so kind to me. Offered to feed me at his restaurant anytime. Well, I was going to see what I could do about that. Raising my hands, I set about *Changing What Was*.

~

Lissa's Journal

Reah was shrieking again, only this time, it was with joy. My head snapped up immediately and I knew without a doubt that Reah's brothers were now alive. "Gavin, get us to Targis," I shouted. He complied immediately.

~

Breanne's Journal

It took nearly every bit of strength I had. I probably should have done it differently, too, and perhaps someone could forgive me for bringing Fes back first instead of others who might be more deserving. Regardless, they all made their way back, I just didn't have the energy to bring their homes and businesses back as well. Those things might be replaced while lives—as they currently existed, anyway—could not. Sinking onto what was left of the street before Desh's former business address, I dropped my head in my hands and moaned.

"Breanne?" A hand touched my shoulder. I knew who it was. I used up the last of my strength to fold space.

~

Lissa's Journal

If Gavin hadn't touched her, she might have stayed. Norian and Lendill arrived on Tulgalan to find me not speaking to my first vampire mate. If he'd just let me know he'd found her and allowed me to approach, but no—he had to put his hand on her. He'd scared her and used her and exhausted her, and yet he thought he could put his hands on her, as if none of that had happened. I had a headache, now, and four million people in Targis had no homes or businesses left. At least they were alive.

~

"Father, she landed at my feet, unconscious."

"At least she felt safe enough to land at your feet that way." Renegar lifted Breanne from Graegar's arms. Garegar, Graegar's son, stood at his father's shoulder and watched his grandfather touch Breanne's forehead with large, blue, gentle fingers.

"She *Changed What Was* for four million," Garegar whispered in awe. "All five of us must work together to do this for only one or two lives."

"This is the Mighty Heart, what else might you expect?" Renegar asked. "We must bring her strength back. Make her feel welcome and cared for."

"What about Kalenegar?"

"She will not wish to see him. That is why I will send a call to him now, before she wakes. He should give some of his strength to her first, I think."

"What is this?" Kalenegar appeared almost immediately.

"She saved four million on Tulgalan," Renegar offered Breanne's limp body to Kal.

"I know. I felt the power surge—we are connected in that way, at least," Kalenegar, nearly ten feet tall with shoulder-length red hair and a troubled expression on his face, held Breanne carefully. She seemed so small and fragile to him. Why hadn't he seen that before? He hated that he'd mistreated her. He wanted to shout that he'd been affected in some way, but to Breanne, that wouldn't matter. Only his treatment of her mattered.

"You have my apologies, Lara'Kayan," Kal bent his head and kissed Breanne's forehead.

~

"Another missing girl." Bill handed the folder to Opal. "Ready to fly to Austin?"

"Yes. I can do preliminary work on this, and if we're lucky, we won't need to haul in Breanne."

"I hope that's the case," Bill agreed. "Work fast, Opal. We need this shut down quickly."

~

Hank took the keys from the salesman after Jayson signed the last of the paperwork. "I'm driving Bree home," Hank announced once they were outside the office. "Where is she?" He looked around the showroom. Only a salesman stood at the window, watching fog roll in off the bay.

~

Breanne's Journal

I learned after I'd wakened that they'd let me sleep for three days. I woke with a panic attack, too, because I'd left Hank and Jayson in a car dealership without telling them I was leaving. Graegar lifted me off a very comfortable, huge bed, held me gently, used power to regulate my breathing and then informed me that he was more than capable of bending time, if I couldn't do it for myself in a few weeks.

"Weeks?" I squeaked.

"You have emptied yourself. It is time to replenish that strength." He smiled warmly at me, and part of that warmth infused my bones. I sighed and relaxed.

"See? Much, much better," he soothed. "We have many things to teach you, while you are here."

"Stuff I can't read? Never mind, that was rude." I lifted a hand and rubbed my forehead.

"I would prefer that you retained your shields, as Kalenegar inadvertently taught you," he chuckled. "Yes, I have seen him and he is most contrite, I assure you. Somehow, he was affected by a mind cloud, and that is highly irregular in any Larentii."

"Where am I? I only remember focusing on you," I said, snuggling into Graegar's warmth. He was putting out the heat of a nice, spring day and I felt cold. His arms felt like a warm blanket.

"The Larentii homeworld. Not many can get past our boundary," he said. "The Three—perhaps a few others. Certainly only a few. By design."

"I'm one of the few others?" I blinked up at his beautiful, blue face.

"No, dearest. It took a while for us to reach the proper conclusion, but we now have it in our grasp. You are one of the Three."

∾

"Please tell me what the Three mean?" Graegar didn't tell me at first; he insisted that I eat solid food. Garegar had folded away the moment I'd awakened, and brought back a covered tray of food—all vegetarian. He smiled at me and his father as I ate—everything was delicious.

"This will be your home for as long as you want," Graegar led me through an unusual house later. Resembling a Roman villa, it was built of marble, with parts of the roof open to the sky overhead. It made sense—Larentii needed sunlight to feed. This was a Larentii's home.

"It belongs to Lenigar—who still works at times with the mothers who are pregnant with Larentii babies," Graegar informed me. "It has a kitchen that you are welcome to use, and all the food is in stasis and ready to prepare."

"Most Larentii houses don't have kitchens, do they?" I asked.

"They are not needed, dearest. Sit here," he lifted me onto a kitchen counter after we walked into that particular room. "I will also sit." He did, on a wide barstool, which left us on a level and facing each other. "Now," he continued, "I will explain the tale of the Three."

Staring in fascination, Graegar told me of the One. And the Three. "You, I believe, are the Mighty Heart," his smile was nearly blinding in its intensity as he told me that. "They—you, too—were born without knowing who you are. By design. You were born to the created races so you might change certain things. As gods, you may not interfere, but as what you are now, you may do so whenever you feel it is right or just. Already you have made an impact on many, many lives." Graegar rubbed my shoulders gently.

"I couldn't stop myself. What happened on Wyyld and Tulgalan was wrong," I muttered, lowering my eyes.

"We know this. We also worry that you are making yourself a target," Graegar sighed. "You do not realize yet that we are now in the midst of the God Wars, and it will only take the destruction of one of the Three to destroy everything. Not your energy, mind you—they only have to destroy your body. In our archives are the prophecies—that few besides the Wise Ones have ever seen. In your original state, you cannot interfere. As you are now, the rule no longer applies."

I stared at Graegar while my brain struggled to understand his words. So many times I'd come so close to dying, it was a miracle in itself that I was still alive and inhabiting a humanoid body. It was also difficult—more than difficult, to grasp what he'd told me. He said I was a god. I had no idea what that meant. No reference point or comparison. All my life, I'd been treated poorly. Why would a god be treated that way? I hunched my shoulders and chose to sort that out on another day.

"You must proceed with caution," Graegar's voice broke into my thoughts, "and withhold *Changing What Was* unless there is no other way. The enemy will be watching for you to expend that power again." I watched his handsome, blue face—it was clouded with worry. I took his advice and kept my shields up so I couldn't read him.

"This makes no sense to me," I rubbed my forehead—a headache was coming on.

"That is how we know you are not the Mighty Mind," Graegar chuckled. I dropped my hand and stared at him. He hadn't named the other two—yet.

"We know of the Mighty Hand, but he lives inside a shield none might breach unless all else falls."

"And who might he be, since you know who he is?"

"Ashe Evans."

"The Mighty Asshole, you mean?" Of all the people to be one of the Mighty. A rather painful headache pierced my brain.

"Ah. I heard he made a mistake. Also an indicator that he is the Mighty Hand and not the Mighty Mind. I understand that he is contrite over your treatment, and wishes to meet with you. He has a difficulty and may require your assistance."

"Really? I'm not in any mood to listen to him."

"The mistake was grave, I understand that."

"Yes, but you didn't feel his anger, or have to listen to him yell for Trajan to get me the hell out of his house. I imagine he wants to use me. Sort of like other people want to use me. Or have used me, in the past."

"That is so unfortunate," Graegar sighed and turned his head away. "I cannot read you or your past, as I can others. I know of your treatment on Le-Ath Veronis, at least. You will remain a mystery unless you choose to reveal yourself to us."

"That won't happen." I misted off the counter and walked toward an open doorway. Shivering, I stared through the door at an open meadow, which lay just outside. No manicured lawns for Larentii—everything grew with abandon, although I saw very few weeds. Wildflowers bloomed and in the distance, I saw creatures grazing. The word *Falaca* came to me—that's what the animals were and their wool was a source of the natural, woven cloth Larentii used to make their clothing.

"Will you not set aside your differences and at least agree to meet the Mighty Hand?" Graegar stood behind me, a hand on my shoulder.

"Not today," I muttered and folded space.

"Where the hell is she?" Jayson snapped at the showroom salesman. "We lose sight of her for five minutes and she disappears? You saw nothing? Your showroom is empty, man, and this stupid phone stopped working." He'd checked the app; Bree had disappeared completely on it.

"Jayson," Hank warned. Hank was just as worried as Jayson, but held a tighter rein on his fear and anger.

"Find her. Do it now," Jayson hissed.

Breanne's Journal
I landed in the dealership bathroom approximately six minutes

after I'd left. Bending time and folding space had depleted the power I'd gained from visiting the Larentii homeworld. Strangely, I'd dropped my shields and read Graegar for just a moment after I woke, and I saw that Kalenegar had come, held me and fed me energy. That image warred with the last image I had of him sending a power blast into my brain and giving me a headache that only a very powerful healer could fix.

Gazing into the mirror over the bathroom sink, I sighed, fixed my hair a little and walked out into chaos.

Jayson was pissed. Hank was silent and the showroom salesman was more than relieved when Hank grabbed my arm after I let the bathroom door swing shut behind me. I'd been gone less than ten minutes, tops, and they were about to have a meltdown.

"I'll take her home," Hank growled when Jayson suggested I ride with him. The ride was out of Hank's way, but I'd actually rather face his anger than Jayson's.

"We'll both go. I want my say, too," Jayson huffed.

"Huh?" I stood outside the dealership, staring at Jayson and then Hank. Hank didn't reply—he grabbed my hand and dragged me to his new truck. I was dumped on the passenger seat, the seatbelt was buckled around me and then he climbed in on the other side and started the truck. It roared to life, just as a new truck should.

We didn't talk during the drive back to my house, and I was beginning to be really frightened. I wasn't sure, either, whether I'd have enough strength to mist away—I was exhausted and I really didn't want to admit that to myself.

Hank parked the truck in front of my house, didn't look at me and slammed the truck door behind him. I jerked at the noise and the violence of it. With shaking hands, I unbuckled my seatbelt and reached for the door handle. Hank stood by while I shut the truck door and pulled keys from my purse. My breaths were shaky by that time—I knew fear. Had known it for far too long. Fear is debilitating and can make you much weaker than you ever thought you might be. My body ached from repressed shivering as I unlocked the front door and walked into the house. Outside, I heard Jayson's new SUV pull up.

Hank followed me as I walked into the kitchen, clenching my hands to keep the trembling to a minimum.

"What the hell happened? We checked that bathroom twice!" Jayson stormed into the kitchen and his thunder followed immediately.

"Oh, no," I set my purse on the kitchen counter carefully, so I wouldn't reveal how terrified I was.

"This is what you get for doing this to us." Jayson jerked me to him, turned me over his knee and hit me several times—hard—with the flat of his hand. I shrieked in terror.

"Baby," Hank held Breanne's face in his hands. Her eyes were wild and she was trembling so badly he almost couldn't keep her pressed against him. Her breaths, too, were dry sobs and her heart beat so fast it pounded against her ribs. Hank was frightened. "Baby," he whispered, "come back. He didn't hurt you. You're not hurt. You're safe. You're safe. When you're in my arms, you're safe. I don't know where you are right now, but you need to come back to me."

"I've never seen anything like this," Jayson knelt beside Hank, who held Breanne where she'd dropped after Jayson let her go earlier. "Bree, I didn't know. I promise I won't scare you like that again. I promise I won't do it while I'm mad, either," he brushed hair away from Breanne's forehead. "God, her heart is going to thump out of her chest," Jayson placed a hand over it. "Come on, little girl. Do like Hank says and come back to us." His fingers stroked the line of her jaw. "She's so tiny," he muttered. "I didn't hit her that hard. Not even enough to raise a bruise."

"You won't hit her again," Hank snapped.

"Not if this happens," Jayson nodded. "Come on, Bree. Come back or we'll have to take you to the hospital."

Breanne's Journal

The word *hospital* tore me from whatever fear-induced portion of hell I'd visited. Jayson's face was in my immediate line of vision and I shrieked and struggled against what held me. That turned out to be Hank. I couldn't go to a human hospital; I was vampire. The minute they took blood, things would go crazy. I couldn't let that happen, and I was too weak to do anything about it.

"Baby, he's not going to hurt you. He only gave you a few swats to let you know you scared us. Okay? We know not to do that again."

I heard my heart thumping in my chest and the breaths that were shaky, dry sobs as Hank pulled my face toward him. "Bree, it's okay. You're safe. You were safe before. Jayson didn't hurt you. He never meant to hurt you. He just scared you."

My lower lip trembled and I was afraid I might cry.

"I think we got a double scare," Jayson muttered, dropping his hand to cover my heart again. "Come on, slow down, Bree. Take deep breaths. Listen to my voice and take deep breaths."

It took a while. Hank was doing his best to control my shivering body while Jayson told me in a slow, measured voice to take deep breaths. He even breathed with me, convincing my body to match his deeper, regular breathing. "That's it, hold it for a few seconds," Jayson murmured. Hank gathered me closer as my breathing evened out.

"Feel better?" Hank murmured against my ear.

"When I do feel better, I'm gonna show Jayson what it means to be hit," I snapped, my breath going short again.

"Bree, stop upsetting yourself. You ran away and didn't tell us. Now, I'm not gonna ask about it again, since we've all taken a little punishment over that. Just tell us the next time, okay?"

I blinked into Hank's dark eyes before lowering mine with a sigh. I'd saved four million people and I'd gotten swats for it. *Go figure.*

"Huh," I struggled out of Hank's grip. "I can explain it now, jerk. Know what Vhanaraszh means?" They wouldn't know, and the word had just popped out because I was angry. My movements weren't pretty, either, but I scrambled to my feet and stalked away from Hank and Jayson.

"What? What language was that?" Jayson watched Breanne walk unevenly toward her bedroom.

"Fuck," Hank rubbed his forehead with a sigh.

"What does it mean?" Jayson rephrased his question.

"It means we ought to think twice before giving swats again."

"Graegar attempted to set up a meeting. She became upset and folded away from him." Renegar walked beside Ashe, through the southwestern grove at SouthStar.

"After she saved four million people. I have sensors set up in Targis, in case somebody comes sniffing around after that bit of foolish bravery," Ashe grumped. "Does she know that separating the particles of one of the enemy is only going to force his energy to search for another body? They have to be completely destroyed, and I haven't figured out how to do that, yet."

"None know how to do this," Renegar agreed. "I have discussed this at length with the Wise Ones and others of my kind in higher levels. They all agree—there is no known way to destroy one of the powerful ones. Their humanoid bodies may be killed and they might be contained, as Belen was for a time, but that is all that can be done."

"You're saying that I may have to construct a shield around them so they can't escape?"

"That is the only viable solution any of us have been able to produce."

"The shield around SouthStar is difficult enough to maintain continuously," Ashe sighed.

"I know this, and the residents must be protected—the Ir'Indicti is obligated. There is not an easy solution to this, my friend."

"Yeah. I've understood that for a while, now."

Breanne's Journal

A shower was the first thing on my list as soon as I left Hank and Jayson in my kitchen. I was tired, hungry again and in no mood to deal with two assholes who thought a spanking was the answer to being pissed off. They didn't even talk to me first, and that upset me. A lot.

Shrugging out of my clothes, I realized how little energy I had as I stepped into a hot shower. I was shaking again after toweling off, I was so weary. Hank was sitting on the end of my bed when I walked out of the bathroom, wrapped in the towel.

"Baby, I need to go to work," he said.

"Then go. You made your feelings known. As did Jayson. Tell his mother and that fucking reporter they can see me here tomorrow night. I'm not going to asshat Rome's birthday party."

"Bree, you need to tell me why a few swats with an open palm scared the shit out of you."

"No. Go to work, Hank. I'm tired. I want to sleep."

"Baby, come to the party. I'll see that nobody upsets you."

"Sure you will. I'm supposed to be with Jayson, remember? To make his mama happy."

"Bree, someday, I want to make you happy. I didn't do that today."

"Hank, just go to work," I moaned, flopping onto the bed an arm's length away.

"I'll get you in bed first."

I protested, but he hauled back covers, pulled my towel away and laid me gently on the sheets before covering me up. "Baby," he softly stroked my forehead, "I hope you trust me, someday." Then he leaned down and kissed my forehead. "Close your eyes," he whispered. I did. He kissed those, too. I was asleep before he walked out of my bedroom.

CHAPTER 11

reanne's Journal

Noon. That's when I dragged my ass out of bed. At least I felt better and more rested. That's when it hit me—I still didn't have a gift for Jayson's birthday. After checking the Internet for an hour while I had soup for lunch, I forced myself to bend time again.

Hank showed up at a quarter to six. I was ready—barely. Tired, too, but I was used to that by now. After getting Jayson's gift, I'd gone shopping for a dress—I didn't have many of those and it was probably expected by the crowd that would show up at Jayson's house. The dress was turquoise, narrow at the waist and flared just above the knee. I paired it with Larimar jewelry and pulled my hair into a twist.

"Baby, if you didn't look so tired, you'd be even more beautiful," Hank said, running a hand down my back. "Feel any better?"

"Yeah. Some." I did, and at least I wasn't having a breakdown after getting swatted on the ass.

"Maybe later, we can sit and have a talk with Jayson. He only wanted to get your attention yesterday. He likes you more than he lets on, and when we couldn't find you," Hank didn't finish.

"I thought we were dropping that subject. Besides, he called me a hostile friend not long ago. There's not much you can do with that, and then he smacked me."

"He didn't hurt you and he wouldn't hurt you."

"You know, I'm gonna leave that alone and not ask what he likes to do with those girls he handcuffs to—well—whatever."

"He has a deerskin flogger. And some other toys."

"I'm sure he does." I shivered as Hank led me out of the house and locked the door behind us.

"Baby, in case you didn't figure it out yesterday, Jayson is really good at aftercare. That's one of the reasons I agreed to train him."

"Hank, please stop talking." I felt queasy, and that wasn't a good thing. A part of me knew that people wanted the things Jayson and Hank did. It made them happy and complete in some way. The only point of reference I had in all that, however, was remembered pain, extreme terror and intense humiliation. I would never, ever, raise my hand for more of that.

"Not feeling good?" He stopped and pulled me against him, then proceeded to rub my belly. "It's not for you, Bree," he said softly. "Just see those things as what they are—toys to play with. That's what it is most of the time, baby. Play. First, last and always. Some people even get a religious experience from what they do, and their partner or partners help them get there."

"Hank, I really, really want to see it that way, but it gives me panic attacks and makes me feel sick."

"I know. Maybe we can get you past that, someday." I could almost hear him silently add that I needed to tell him what my problem was, because that would help. I just couldn't do that. Ever.

"Come on, Jayson will likely need rescuing from those people his parents invited."

"Who did they invite?"

"There'll be journalists there, socialites, the wealthy, people Jayson has no real desire to hang out with or get to know."

"Sucks being him, doesn't it?"

"Sometimes it does. Bree, you can't judge everybody by how much money they have."

"I know that," I muttered. "It's just that I've met my share of the wealthy, and for the most part, I've been unimpressed."

"You have money," he pointed out.

"And I have a charity set up to give most of that away. I also have investments placed so I can keep giving it away. To people—kids—who need it."

"Terry handles that for you?"

"I tell him which investments to make and he makes them. He's really good at that, and I pay him for his services. You look nice, by the way." He opened the truck door for me and I climbed inside. Just as before, he buckled my seatbelt and shut the door before going to the driver's side and climbing in.

"You think I look good?" Hank pointed a grin in my direction.

"Yeah. Women will want to lick you." Hank did look good. The usual jeans were gone and he was dressed in slacks, a nice knit shirt and a good leather jacket. His boots, too, looked more expensive than those he usually wore.

"I don't want to be licked. By other women." He put the truck in gear and backed out of my driveway.

"You're a single man, remember? Jayson, too. I'm just excess baggage that doesn't really fit in."

"Baby, if it wouldn't scare you, you might get swats for that."

"It's the truth. I don't hang around the people we're going to see tonight because they make me uncomfortable. I don't hang around the people who come into your bar because I feel uncomfortable. Want to have a conversation about fitting in now?"

"You fit in with the people from Mercy Crossings?"

"Not really. They're all doctors or nurses, and they think they're in a different league. They see my resume—somebody who has no college degree and for some unexplainable reason, can speak any and every language. They're not comfortable around me, which makes me uncomfortable in return."

"Why do I get the feeling you could test out of any college course you wanted to?" Hank pulled into Jayson's driveway and parked to the side to allow others to take the prime spots.

"I don't know why you have that feeling. I really don't want to go to the trouble to find out, either," I sighed.

"Ready for the interview?" Hank asked as we climbed out of his truck.

"I never got an email with any questions. How can I be ready for what I don't know is coming?"

"You should let Jayson know the writer didn't follow through. Sounds like a poor work ethic to me."

"I really don't want to do this, and I only want to talk about Mercy Crossings." If I were asked about my earlier life, I certainly wouldn't answer those questions.

"Don't worry; I'll be there with Jayson's mother."

"What will you do if he asks uncomfortable questions—threaten him with Jayson's flogger?"

"There's an idea," Hank grinned. "I can give him the flogging of his life."

"That's not scary or anything," I muttered.

"Breanne, how lovely to see you." Kathleen Rome met us at the door and wrapped me in a tight hug. After a moment, I hugged her back. Jayson was nowhere in sight and I was overcome with guilt that I was playing right along with his game to fool his mother.

"Hank, how are you?" Kathleen was all smiles as Hank leaned in to kiss her cheek.

"I'm fine, Mrs. Rome," Hank replied politely.

"I castigated Jayson for not coming to get you himself," Kathleen turned back to me. "He said he'd already asked Hank to pick you up. Something about an unsafe vehicle?" She lifted an eyebrow at me.

"It's a new car," I grumped. "He doesn't like it because it will fit in the back seat of his new SUV.

"Dear, perhaps you should listen to him and buy something safer."

"I hardly ever drive anywhere, except to the grocery store," I sighed. "I'm okay. Really." I didn't add that I could tell her how many light-years I'd traveled in the past two days. Not including the time bending in all that, and three days on the Larentii homeworld, mostly unconscious. All of that was without my (according to Jayson) unsafe vehicle. Besides, my TinyCar wasn't listed as approved for space travel anyway.

"Bree," Jayson's breath was warm against my temple as he gave an obligatory peck—he'd finally decided to show up. "Come on, the staff writer is waiting, and he brought a photographer with him."

"Jayson, no," I moaned. "I don't want my picture taken."

"You look perfect. Why not?" Jayson grasped my arm and pulled me along. "Besides, Barry Stokes has already sent one for the magazine—from a mission with Mercy Crossings."

"Jayson, I really don't want this." I covered my face with a hand.

"Breanne, it will do so much good for the charity." I'd forgotten about Kathleen Rome—she was right behind us. I wanted to moan. I didn't. My heart rate had definitely jumped, however. "I'm the one who spoke with Barry about the Mercy Crossings photograph," she added. "He was more than happy to oblige, since I donate every year."

I wanted to tell her that I donated, too—my time, my skills and my money. I was getting pressured into this and I was beginning to dislike it more as time passed. Barry had agreed to Kathleen's request without consulting me. Sure, there was an agreement to sign when I volunteered, and one of the stipulations was that volunteers would promote Mercy Crossings in any way they could. I was promoting Mercy Crossings with an interview and my images.

It still pissed me off that I hadn't been contacted—either by Barry Stokes or Jayson's staff writer.

I had to leave Jayson's birthday gift with Hank while I was photographed ad nauseam, with and without the jacket I'd worn over my dress. It matched, but the dress was sleeveless and showed more of me. The photographer seemed to like that better.

"Baby, don't let them upset you," Hank whispered when he handed my jacket back—the photography session had taken place on Jayson's patio, overlooking San Rafael Bay. I was chilled to the bone; the San Francisco area is cool to cold on most days.

At least the staff writer did the interview in Jayson's breakfast nook, next to a huge window.

"Name's Sam," he held out his hand. I took it and refused to read him, just as I'd done with the photographer.

"When did you start working with Mercy Crossings?" he asked as soon as the introduction was over. Jayson, Kathleen and Hank all sat nearby at the kitchen island, while Trina and a few extra helpers worked in the kitchen to finish dinner before guests arrived.

"Two years ago." I almost breathed a relieved sigh when he didn't ask about my background first thing.

"Why did you volunteer?"

"I had something to offer—I read an article in another magazine, sorry—and they said that Mercy Crossings needed interpreters with unusual language skills. I have those skills. I walked into Barry Stokes' office in Los Angeles and volunteered."

"He says the same—I've talked to him the past two days," the writer nodded. "Barry says that at first he was skeptical, but that you turned out to be a godsend."

I wanted to snicker. If what Graegar told me was true, the writer might have hit on a partial truth without knowing it. Did I feel like a god? Hell no. I didn't even feel like a person most of the time—not any normal person, anyway.

"Tell me something you haven't discussed with Barry—or anybody else. Something that happened out in the field that helped the crew you were working with."

I had to think for a moment. "I guess it was when we were in South Sudan about a year ago. Do you know about the fuss Sudan had with South Sudan?" Sam shook his head. "South Sudan accused Sudan of supplying weapons to rebels, who were fighting South Sudanese forces. All of that was supposedly connected to South Sudan's efforts to build an oil pipeline through Ethiopia. They wanted to bypass their current exportation of oil through pipelines in Sudan. Two months after we left, they managed to reach an agreement, but while we were there, rebels in both Sudan and South Sudan were creating havoc in both places."

"What did you do?" Sam asked.

"While we were in the field, we were surrounded by South Sudanese rebels. Scared the crap out of our medical personnel—they're generally not allowed any weapons in sensitive areas and we'd just walked into a volatile situation. The official language in South Sudan is English, but there are tons of local languages, with plenty of borrowed words inserted into the official language, along with just local stuff being spoken. The rebel leader was Dinka, and knew most of the five associated languages connected to the Dinka people. He thought he'd throw a curve at us, telling us in English that they didn't want to harm us, but he spoke with the gun-toters at his back in his native tongue, telling them he planned to sell us back to the U.S. in exchange for better weapons and supplies." I shook my head as I silently recalled how scared I was at that moment. I'd employed compulsion when I called him out, but I wasn't going to tell Sam that.

"What happened?" Sam asked.

"I blasted him with his own language, telling him we were going to have his ribs for dinner if he didn't get the hell away from us. I guess I scared him enough—they climbed into their vehicles and left."

"That's awesome," Sam grinned. "Would you have had his ribs for dinner?"

"Not me, I'm vegetarian," I said. Kathleen Rome laughed.

"See, that wasn't so bad," Jayson grinned at me after the short interview was over.

"I'm just glad we stuck with Mercy Crossings," I mumbled.

"What?" Jayson turned back to me—he was leading me toward the massive formal dining area, where guests were gathering and ordering drinks from a bar set up for the occasion.

"Nothing. Just glad it's over," I said.

"Come on, you have to stay with me while I greet guests. Mom says so."

"Joy," I sighed.

"Bree, I don't like it, either," Jayson whispered, leaning down and pretending to nuzzle my neck. "Hank wants to kill me, I think."

"I'd help him," I muttered in reply.

"Shh, don't be upset." He rubbed my shoulders carefully. "Hank keeps trying to teach me that it's not always about me."

"That new SUV isn't about you?" I pulled back and gazed into brown eyes.

"Well, yeah, that's about me," he offered a lopsided grin. "Interview went great, by the way. Sam is definitely happy."

"Glad to be of service," I lowered my gaze.

"Hey," Jayson tilted my head up with a finger beneath my chin. "This is for Mom." He leaned in to kiss me. I wanted to jerk away. I whimpered into Jayson's mouth instead.

"Little girl, I'm not about to hurt you," Jayson broke the kiss and whispered against my ear. "Hank really would kill me."

"You didn't have to get me anything," Jayson said after the last guest left. His father, still on his business trip, hadn't made the party. I didn't want to read Kathleen Rome and discover how she felt about that. We sat around Jayson's massive kitchen island, sipping wine. I was wedged between Jayson and Hank, while Kathleen and Trina sat on the opposite side.

"I wasn't about to buy you a book—you'd never read it. You have work stuff to read," I pointed out.

"I thought this was a book," Jayson pulled the flat, wrapped package toward him and began to peel away the taped corners.

"Nope."

"I hope she got a fly swatter to smack you with," Trina said. Hank hid a grin. I wanted to dig an elbow into his ribs.

"What is this?" Jayson pulled the framed photograph from the protective sleeve after tearing wrapping paper away. I'd had to bend time twice to get the photograph and then get it signed before the driver's death.

A famous German driver posed with his Grand Prix racing car. He'd been dead for more than thirty years, and I'd had to be creative to get the photograph done by a reputable photographer of the era, bend time to get the photograph from his studio and then bend time again to get the driver to sign it. The provenance was included with the framed photograph—it was also signed on the back by the photographer and included a letter, which verified its authenticity.

"Holy shit," Jayson muttered. "It's the real thing. This is going in my office."

"I know how much you love cars," I shrugged.

"Jayson, I don't know that any of your girlfriends have ever gone to this much trouble for you," Kathleen pointed out. I wasn't about to jump in the middle of that. I really didn't want to know what his other girlfriends might do to please him. I didn't, couldn't and wouldn't ever compete with that.

"Breanne," Kathleen went on, "what plans do you have for Christmas?"

Oh, shit. I forgot that Christmas was only ten days away. I had absolutely no plans—that I knew of. "I don't know, yet. I usually don't plan anything, in case I get a call."

"I suppose that's smart, but surely they let you have a few days off. I know Jayson's bringing you this weekend, but you might consider having dinner with us. Jayson usually flies down the night before, spends the day with us and then flies back on the twenty-sixth."

"I take the week of my birthday off, instead of the week of Christmas. I get more things done that way, including my Christmas shopping," Jayson held up a hand to stave off what Trina was ready to unleash in his direction. I got the idea that his being home for most of that week forced Trina to work for him at the same time. Even without reading her, I knew she didn't appreciate it.

"I have a question," I said, breaking the uneasy silence between employer and employee.

"What's that?" Jayson turned to me.

"Who does your yard work? I think my yard needs stuff done."

"I'll get the number," Trina rose stiffly from her seat and stalked away. Jayson released a held breath.

"I think you'd better give Trina a couple of days off around Christmas," I whispered.

"All right, but I'm messy," Jayson rumbled.

"She'll clean it up when she gets back," I said. "And if I'm home and forced to do so, I'll bring you food so you won't starve." I'll admit, the smile I pointed at Jayson was completely fake. I wasn't lying, though. I would bring him food, if he wasn't smart enough to forage for himself. I wanted to add that he could probably get Belinda to buy, cook and clean for him, but I didn't.

"Here ya go," Trina handed a folded paper to me.

"Thanks." My smile was genuine, this time. Trina probably knew just as well as I did that Jayson was using me to make his mother happy. I promised myself a clean breakup with my pseudo-boyfriend right after Christmas. Stringing Kathleen along was a huge lie and I didn't want to be part of that.

Hank, too, had been curiously silent most of the evening, all while Jayson's invited guests gushed over his *finally getting a steady girlfriend*. I wanted to throw up.

"I'm ready to go home," I announced, standing up. If I drank any more wine, I'd either smack Jayson or fall asleep. Maybe both. "Happy birthday, Jayson." I walked toward the foyer, where my jacket and purse had ended up. If Hank didn't want to take me home, I had my own way of getting around. I was drunk enough to do it in front of everybody, too. I'd been too queasy to eat much during the meal, and the wine had gone straight to my head.

"I'll take you home." Hank's hand settled on the small of my back.

"Thanks." I shrugged into my jacket, with a little help from Hank.

A few minutes later, I was buckled in on the passenger side of Hank's truck. He didn't say anything, but I watched his jaw work for a few seconds before turning away.

"I'm staging the official breakup after Christmas. I can't do this anymore," I said, staring out the truck window. I couldn't look at Hank any longer. He didn't say anything, either, until he herded me into the house.

"I know you don't want to upset Kathleen, and you're a good person for that. Jayson and I will have a conversation during Krav Maga in the morning." Hank pulled my head against his shoulder and held me for several minutes before kissing the top of my head and letting me go. "We're leaving at one on Friday so be ready at noon; Jayson is using the corporate jet to fly us to L.A. Pack your bag, baby. I'll pick you up and take care of you."

"Hank, I can take care of myself. I usually do."

"I think you need a little help, sometimes. That's not meant as a gibe, either. You have a lot of weight on your shoulders, and those are small shoulders. I have to go to work, now. If I didn't, I'd stay the night and Kathleen doesn't need to see my truck in your driveway when her driver takes her to a hotel downtown."

"She's not staying with Jayson?"

"No. I think it's by mutual agreement, somehow. Don't ask me why."

I watched Hank walk out my door, closing it behind him, with no kiss good-bye. I sighed and hugged myself.

Hank did pick me up at noon on Friday, and handed me a hummus sandwich from Francie's.

"I've already had a burger," he informed me.

"Honey, you are awesome," I pulled the sandwich from the bag, set the iced tea he'd gotten for me in the cup holder and started eating.

"I am awesome," Hank gave me a grin before turning onto the highway that would take us over the bridge and eventually to the airport.

"You know, I really can't disagree with that," I sipped iced tea. He'd gotten peach tea, just the way I liked it, and I was finished with my lunch long before we arrived at the airport.

The company jet was more than comfortable, with space to stretch out or sleep if you wanted. Since the trip would only take a little over an hour, I didn't try to sleep. Jayson didn't have any bruises on his face, so maybe Hank hadn't smacked him around too much.

"Bree," Jayson sighed as soon as the jet was in the air, "I swear I'd already made arrangements before Hank and I talked yesterday. I'll be going to train with another Master on fire play Sunday afternoon. Hank doesn't trust anybody, so he's going to make sure I stay out of trouble. I know I shouldn't have done it—this is Mom's time. And since I'm dragging you with me to make Mom happy, well, it ought to be your time, too."

I didn't answer him, but I had to *Look* to see what fire play was. Prescience kicked in and I gasped.

"What?" Hank was pulling me onto his lap. Somehow, he'd gotten the seatbelt unbuckled without me knowing.

"Hank, you need to ask that woman when you go whether she's sprayed herself with suntan lotion recently. She'll go up like exploding fireworks if you don't." I was breathing hard after the vision I'd had of some foolish girl getting barbecued because she'd decided to visit a tanning salon before putting herself on display. Most suntan lotions weren't flammable. A few of the spray kinds were.

"Baby, I'm not gonna ask how you know that," Hank squeezed me to stop the trembling and unsteady breathing. "I'll ask about the girl, I promise."

"What the hell just happened?" Jayson said.

"Rome, shut up," Hank said amiably. "I'm talking with Bree."

It took longer to make the drive to the Rome estate in Hidden Hills than it did to fly from San Francisco to L.A. The estate was more like a compound, with guest cabanas, an indoor pool, tennis court and exercise facility. That didn't include the main house, which was larger than Jayson's in San Rafael.

I was thankful, too, that Hank's bedroom was next to Jayson's, while mine was across the hall. Kathleen and James, Sr.'s room was on the opposite end of the house.

"We're going out to dinner tonight," Kathleen informed us the moment we'd shown up in the family room after dumping luggage in our bedrooms. "It's a nice restaurant; I hope you brought something suitable," she blinked at Jayson.

At the last minute, I'd stuffed a nice dress and short-heeled pumps into my bag and breathed a sigh of relief at Kathleen's announcement. "Tomorrow, we're going shopping," Kathleen continued. I frowned. Shopping wasn't high on my list—I usually needed something (badly) before going anywhere, and then I went straight for what I needed and didn't bother to look at anything else.

Hank lifted an eyebrow at the shopping comment, but didn't say anything. I wanted to rub his back—I didn't. That would destroy Kathleen's illusion that her son had a regular girlfriend.

Dinner was at one of the top restaurants in Beverly Hills, and we were driven there in a limo by Kathleen's driver/bodyguard. Until then, I had no idea Hank owned a suit. He did. Jayson was the rich man in the crowd, but Hank put him to shame.

"You look lovely," Kathleen admired my dress. It was one of those I'd bought in the D.C. area—my driver had known where to take me and I'd spent a fortune on the little, beaded black dress I wore. The dress was tight, too, and Bill had certainly appreciated it at a luncheon I'd attended with him.

"Mrs. Rome, you'll knock everybody's socks off," I returned the compliment. She would—she was beautiful, and her hair and nails were done to perfection. I'd done my own nails, making a few repairs with the power I held. I'd put my hair up, too—I'd gotten lots of experience at that while posing as my sister.

"Sweetheart, call me Kathleen. Please."

"Thank you—I will. That dress is amazing. Is it new?" I smiled at Jayson's mother.

"This old thing?" she smoothed her plum silk skirt. We both laughed at her standard answer.

~

"I like the stockings you're wearing," Hank whispered as Jayson and Kathleen spoke with the maître d. I'd bought black sheer stockings with a seam up the back to go with the dress—at the salesclerk's urging. The dress and stockings were stunning together, and I wasn't used to that—being stunning, that is. The shoes were designer shoes, and they'd cost a fortune as well. After all, one does not simply walk into a reception at the White House wearing any old thing; I was glad to get two occasions out of such an extravagant purchase.

"If we were alone, I'd be showing you how much I like them," Hank added before we were urged forward by an eager waiter.

"Hold that thought," I whispered to Hank as Kathleen Rome was seated first at our table.

I'm not used to anybody pulling a chair out for me. Prior to my arrival in San Francisco, it hadn't happened. I'd never eaten in the Queen's dining room on Le-Ath Veronis—formal or informal. In fact, with Gavin being the tyrant he was, I'd been lucky to get anything to eat. I sighed as Jayson pulled out my chair and scooted me in while Hank sat next to Kathleen.

"I told the waiter you're vegetarian, and the chef is working up a special menu to bring out." Kathleen smiled as if she'd pulled off the coup of the century.

"That's so nice of you," I said. Nobody had ever gone to this much trouble for me. I deliberately didn't look at Jayson, in case he was grumpy over the whole thing. I wanted to sigh, too, since Kathleen wanted to woo me more than her son ever would.

Drinks came first, and I had my usual glass of wine. Hank ordered an old fashioned and Jayson asked for an expensive Scotch with soda. Well, he could afford the real thing, after all. Kathleen asked for wine, too, only hers was a red. After we ordered, Kathleen chatted happily away about this and that—including politics and how the book on Everett Williams was currently being printed and would be released in three weeks.

"Ross is already working on something new, only he said it was a complete surprise. I think your father knows, Jayson, he just won't tell me." Kathleen pouted prettily. She was the loveliest sixty-year-old I'd ever seen. While Kathleen talked, I almost jumped as a sock-covered toe raked my calf. Hank had somehow managed to remove a shoe and now he was stroking my leg with his foot.

"More water, madam?" A waiter brandished his pitcher of water just as Hank put his foot between my legs. I gasped, apologized to the waiter and told him I would like more water. Hank might be wearing said water in seconds, if he didn't stop what he was doing. The sadist turned his head and smiled so Kathleen couldn't see.

Several times during the meal, I wanted to moan and then attack Hank. Whether that attack was sexual in nature remained to be seen. Jayson talked with his mother about the magazine article on Mercy Crossings, and when it might be published. It looked to be one of the headliners in the January edition. It took all my strength to appear interested in the conversation and not collapse in a skillfully manipulated climax.

The ride home (for me) was completely silent. Hank acted as if nothing was going on and he hadn't wound me up past the point of no return. I was also contemplating his murder if he didn't follow through when we reached the Rome compound.

Kathleen retired shortly after we got back, after giving Jayson several pointed looks. She wanted him to make a move, after he'd ignored me all evening. Well, Jayson could go to hell. Hank was the one I wanted to throttle, one way or another. I stalked toward my bedroom, ready to fling off the dress, the heels and the stockings and step into a really, really, cold shower.

I didn't even get the bedroom door shut; Hank barged in and closed the door behind him, then locked it. Had anyone ever stalked me like that before? Hell, no. He looked like a tiger prowling after his prey.

"I was thinking about a cold shower," I huffed, walking away from him. The tiger struck. I was on the bed and he was peeling away the dress swiftly. Then the bra came off before he began to slowly—very slowly, roll down the tops of my stockings. I wanted to grab his hair and let him know how frustrated I was. He wasn't allowing it.

"Hold onto the sheets, baby. We're going for a ride." He placed a fistful of expensive fabric in each of my hands. "Don't let go unless I hurt you or scare you," he added. Three pillows went under my hips. I was still facing him, and frankly, parts of me were nearly in his face. That wasn't the end of it, either. He rolled my stockings down to my knees, positioned my feet over his shoulders—yes, the shoes were still on—and then buried himself inside me. I was so heated by that time I almost screamed.

"Don't. Let. Go of the. Sheet," Hank commanded. I wanted to—I couldn't control what was happening to my body—Hank was doing that. I shrieked as the first climax hit. I screamed twice more before collapsing and passing out from the intensity of it.

CHAPTER 12

reanne's Journal

Hank was gone when I woke. Oh, he'd been there most of the night, and he'd made sure I was awake whenever he wanted me awake. I didn't think a superhero could walk after that, but he obviously had. I was vampire and I had my doubts whether I could do anything other than hobble a few feet before stopping for a rest.

Wobbling to the bathroom, I took stock of my appearance. A few spots looked suspiciously like dark fingerprints where he'd gripped my ribs or my hips. He'd kissed those places, several times, after holding onto me so hard. Still no lip lock, though, and I had difficulty dealing with that disappointment.

"Maybe next time, I'll give your back a clawing you won't forget," I mumbled at my image before turning the water on in the shower.

"You know I have difficulty commanding a fresh body," the lieutenant moaned his excuse.

"Nevertheless, it has been days. Tell me what you know," his superior growled.

"It was one of the Mighty, I have little doubt—the Larentii would not interfere like that," the lieutenant whined.

"What did this one look like? Which one came?" His light had gone darker as he asked the question.

"I don't know. I was attacked from behind, and even my shield was useless. I could not hear the approach, either, and the voice was like the voice of doom."

"Male or female?"

"I cannot tell," the lieutenant wailed. "I cannot tell!"

Breanne's Journal

"I want to take you to all my favorite shops," Kathleen's eyes shone. I had no idea why she was so pleased to take me shopping—she had a daughter-in-law. Jayson's brother was married and lived on the coast in Santa Barbara. It didn't matter, Rodeo Drive was in my near-future.

"How are you?" Hank murmured when Kathleen turned away to speak with her maid.

"I can't walk."

"I'll carry you."

"That won't be awkward or anything," I pointed out. "Just rent a burro."

"You're renting a burro?" Jayson decided to make his presence known.

"In case Bree can't walk," Hank chuckled.

"Hey, you made enough noise to wake people in Arizona," Jayson mumbled.

"Wow, sorry for your lack of sleep," I muttered sarcastically. Unfortunately, Kathleen had returned and heard my last comment.

"You didn't sleep last night?" Kathleen's voice was bright with hope.

"Breanne kept me awake," Jayson huffed. I considered punching him in the stomach. Kathleen Rome was all smiles.

∼

"You don't have enough jewelry," Kathleen Rome pointed out. "I know you don't like to spend money on yourself—Jayson says so. We have to buy a few nice pieces to go with those beautiful dresses I've seen lately."

I saw all kinds of jewelry, from stores that often lent things to the stars for motion picture awards. Prices were astronomical, and all I could think was how much that might provide to a starving village somewhere. I saw earrings I thought were gaudy, selling for twenty-five thousand.

Eventually, I found a pair that didn't look completely ostentatious and I wouldn't mind wearing, for six thousand. They were diamonds in a white gold setting, and were quite elegant. I refused Kathleen's offer to pay. Jayson just stood by, hands in his pockets, as I pulled out a credit-card and spent more money on jewelry than I ever dreamed I would.

Three outfits and more jewelry later, we drove home. Actually, Jayson drove and Kathleen and Hank sat in the back. I had no idea what was going through Jayson's mind, since I couldn't read him. I intended to ask Hank, however. Even though I was still mad at Jayson for swatting me, he'd been almost human for a short while afterward. Now he was worse than ever.

∼

"I told him to get in or get out," Hank sighed when I asked him later.

"I don't understand this," I hugged myself and went to stand by the indoor pool located in a pool house beside the last cabana. Jayson was doing emails, his mother had gone to rest for a while and Hank had pulled me away from the house.

"Bree—he has to make this decision and he knows it. You said you were planning the official breakup after Christmas. I told him that— you shouldn't have to keep covering for him. I don't think you'd have a problem with him doing his thing at times if he decided to stick around. Would you?"

"That doesn't really upset me; I just don't want to see it or hear about it," I said. "I would worry that somebody was getting hurt, when it was likely the opposite. I just don't know if we'd ever be compatible, and I really, well," I hesitated, because I was about to lay my heart open to Hank Bell, "I want you," I sighed.

"I know that about you, baby." Hank stepped up behind me and pulled me against him. "I don't see that as a problem. Are you the jealous type? I'm not."

"No. Not the jealous type. I'm really not Jayson's type, either. Admit it. That doesn't include the insults, the swats and the ignoring."

"His mother is upset about the ignoring."

"Yeah. She had a headache when we were driving home. Jayson doesn't realize how much she loves him, either." I'd never read her, but Kathleen Rome didn't hide her feelings about her son.

"She does. I've seen her more since you came along, but you're right—she really loves him a lot. You deserve better than what you've gotten from him, too. He could have paid for that jewelry today without batting an eye. He didn't."

"Hank, I don't want anything from anybody that they're not willing to give. I want those things only if they want me to have them. Does that make sense? I don't want insincere effort because it's the proper thing to do." I shivered in his arms—the pool house was cold.

"Shh," Hank rocked me. "We'll fix this. I promise."

"Hank, I don't think there's anything to fix. Nothing you can fix, anyway. Give it up. Jayson doesn't want me and never did. I'll walk away after Christmas and it'll be over. He can go back to the women he wants. His mother will have to understand."

"She wants somebody like you on his arm. He's taken a few to family functions, but they're generally not his choice of companion, and it turns out that nobody's happy."

"That puts me in the not his choice of companion, too," I pulled away from Hank. "I don't do anything he wants. What about Belinda? He found her acceptable."

"He doesn't—she's just the closest he could get to vanilla in his public partners, to make his parents happy."

"So he hit the vanilla jackpot with me, huh? Do you know how that makes me feel?"

"Belinda's not his choice, and certainly not his parents' choice. I think the tattoo of a snake crawling through a skull on her upper arm sort of puts them off."

"This is so bizarre," I muttered, shoving hair behind my ears. "Look, I don't know what kind of women you prefer, either, so I don't know how I stack up against that. I'm not Asian, I know that for sure. Maybe we should call it quits, too." I walked toward the pool house door. Hank had rattled me, and that's probably not what he intended to do. I didn't have big boobs and I wasn't the right nationality to compete with Jayson and Hank's fantasies. Right then, I wanted to talk to Bill. He would listen and not make judgments, and I wasn't sure how I knew that about him.

"Bree, I'm looking at what I want." Hank's voice floated behind me. "When you accept that, come back and we'll talk."

"Bye, Hank," I sighed and walked through the door.

Dinner was takeout Chinese, and I could tell Kathleen still wasn't feeling well. I didn't say anything as she forced a conversation with Jayson and Hank. I picked at my vegetable lo mein and listened without contributing.

"Do you have anything planned for tonight?" Kathleen asked as the table was cleared.

"I was going to read," I said and rose to dump my box in the trash.

"Jayson, why don't all of you go for a swim? The pool's heated," Kathleen suggested.

"I'll consider it," Jayson murmured.

"I'm going to bed and watch television," Kathleen sighed. "I'm trying to get rid of this headache."

"Goodnight, Mom." Jayson leaned in to peck Kathleen on the cheek.

"Night, baby," she said and wandered toward her end of the house.

"I'm going to read," I walked away from Hank, who'd been surreptitiously watching me all through the meal.

"Bree?" Hank followed me.

"I have things to sort out," I said, pulling away from his hand on my shoulder.

"At least come talk to us for a little while. Did you bring a swimsuit?"

"I have one," I shrugged.

"Then let's get in warm water and talk."

"Hank," I moaned in protest.

"Come on," he coaxed. "You can call Jayson an unfeeling, calculating bastard if you want."

"Is he good at math?"

"No idea."

"Then leave calculating out of it."

"Thank goodness, Bree's back," Hank tilted his head and grinned.

"Uh-huh," I nodded.

Hank followed me toward our bedrooms, autocratically informed me I had five minutes to change into my swimsuit or he was coming after me, and stood outside my door for at least two minutes before I walked through the door dressed in a dark-yellow bikini.

"No polka dots?" Hank bent his head and kissed a bare shoulder.

"I refuse to buy polka dots."

"This is perfect," he ran a hand over my ribs and rested it on my waist. "If you walked into the club dressed like this, I'd have to order everybody away."

"I'm not going into the club, dressed, half-dressed or any other way," I snapped. "You want to talk or not?" I walked away from him.

"Is it wrong to want to make them jealous?" Hank caught up with me.

"Hank," I moaned, hugging myself.

"All right, I know it would scare you. Really, they wouldn't hurt you. I'd just have to make sure they knew it would scare you into a catatonic state if they suggested anything."

"You just pointed out the perfect reason not to go."

"You own half the place."

"Hank, it's yours, remember? I don't want it. Consider it your Christmas gift. I'll get Terry to draw up the papers—he won't talk me out of it this time."

"Baby, stop saying that."

"Hank, I can't have a business I'm terrified to walk into."

"Look, nobody will bother you if they know you own half the place."

"You're impossible."

"I could say the same thing about you."

"At least I know I'm impossible. You're just delusional."

"You're saying I lack self-awareness, or harbor a persistent psychotic belief?"

"Oooh, fancy words," I waggled fingers at him.

"Come here, you." I was tossed over Hank's shoulder and hauled toward the pool house. Jayson was already there—turns out, he keeps suits in a changing room at the back.

The overhead lamps were turned out, so only the lights in the pool illuminated the building. Ripples in the water cast an eerie, moving glow across the ceiling. Jayson hadn't waited, either—he was already in the pool.

"Water's warm," he said as Hank set me on the edge of the pool.

"Jumping in or am I tossing you in?" Hank grinned.

"Please don't," I muttered, recalling the last time I'd been unwillingly dumped in water.

"How are you getting in, then?" Hank and Jayson laughed when I sat down on the edge of the pool and cautiously dropped in on the shallow end.

"You're an old woman," Jayson snickered. He didn't know that was actually true. I only looked young. Hank hopped in beside me, giving me the drenching I'd hoped to avoid.

"Thanks," I muttered and moved away from him.

"Come on, you have to stand between Jayson and me while we discuss things." Hank grabbed a hand and pulled me back.

"Sure." My sarcasm was waking up. "What are we discussing?"

"I didn't say we. I said Jayson and me. You get to listen."

"Look, I was drier in my bedroom," I huffed, attempting to move wet hair out of my face.

"Come on," Hank forged his way through the water toward Jayson, who leaned against the side of the pool, his elbows casually propped on the flagstones surrounding it.

"Now," Hank settled me between Jayson and himself. Like Jayson, his elbows were propped on the flagstones. I wasn't tall enough to do that, and only my head and the top of my shoulders cleared the water.

"You're right, this is pretty much perfect," Jayson reached out and ran a hand down my bare belly.

"Hey," I brushed his hand away. He ignored me and the hand came back. They'd discussed me? That was just wrong. And embarrassing.

"Jayson's talking to me, remember?"

"I don't remember agreeing to participate at this level," I snapped as Jayson ran fingers over my ribs.

"Shh, we're talking," Hank soothed.

"What do you think? How envious would everybody be if we took her to a club somewhere?" Jayson's hand strayed to my bikini top. His fingers stroked the skin above the fabric. "They'd be begging to play."

"Okay, I'm getting out," I said, attempting to move away. I was getting shaky already.

"Am I scaring you, little girl?" Jayson rumbled. His fingers raked over my breast.

"Yes. I need to go. Really."

"Bree, Hank won't let anybody touch you. *I* won't let anybody touch you. Not unless you wanted them to."

"I can take care of myself." Sadly, hugging myself as I shivered didn't serve to convince anybody.

Jayson pushed strands of wet hair behind my ear. "Come on, Bree. We won't make you do anything you don't want to. You're safe with us."

"I don't know that." I didn't, and I didn't trust anybody completely. It just wasn't in my nature to do so. For most of my life, I'd seen everything about everybody, and too many people around me had either proven faithless or had betrayed me in some way. I couldn't trust after that.

"I hope we can convince you otherwise soon." Hank stroked my cheek. "Do you know how beautiful your skin is, baby?"

I wanted to tell him that not long ago, my skin had been marked by too many scars. He wouldn't have found me beautiful, then. Only vampirism had cured that malady, along with a score of other things. "Why are you doing this?" My voice trembled on the question.

"I think Jayson wants in," Hank said simply.

"You remember what I said earlier? About insincere efforts?" I said.

"If I thought this was insincere, I would have gathered you up and taken you straight back to San Francisco," Hank said.

"I don't know what to do with this," I raised a shaking hand to my forehead.

"Hey." Jayson took my hand in his. "I'm not used to something this fragile," he took my hand and kissed it. He had no idea. None at all.

"Jayson, I'm not trophy girlfriend material. I volunteer my time and sometimes end up wading in mud and muck to do what needs to be done. I don't look polished twenty-four-seven. I saw some of those women at your birthday party. They'd jump all over you, no questions asked." I tried to pull my hand away. If I exerted too much strength, he'd know something was up. "Besides, I was strong enough to help Hank move his safe inside the club. Of course, that's when I still thought it was just a bar."

"Want to talk about that?" Hank asked.

"No. Just like I don't want to talk about the flogging or anything else that happens there." My breaths were getting shaky.

"She wanted that. Asked her dom for it. Some people like the public aspect of things."

"Hank."

"Baby, we know you don't want that. All you have to do is say no, just like anybody else. No, I don't want to go out with you. No, I don't want to play with you. No, that's not my thing."

"Hank, it can't be that simple and you know it."

"Sometimes it isn't, but if Jayson and I back you up, they'll know you mean it."

"You don't have to back me up."

"I know. You can take care of yourself. Until somebody swats you, that is."

"Look, I was tired and that just went wrong."

"We scared the shit out of you. Admit it. You need to work on that, Bree. Psychologists call it immersion—when you're exposed to what you're afraid of while practicing relaxation techniques or when you're with somebody who makes you feel safe, until you build up a tolerance."

"Hank, please stop."

"I'll stop for now, but we'll get back to that sometime, baby. At the least, I want to make you a little better at talking about it."

"We don't want you to be upset when we go tomorrow for the fire play demo. We're worried that you'll just sit here and freak, which will freak Mom out."

"Jayson, you should have left me at home."

"I won't leave you at home from now on—Mom wants you here whenever I come."

"Jayson, no," I moaned. "I can't do this. I feel like I'm lying all the time. We don't have a relationship."

"We can work on that," he said.

"What about Hank? Are we fooling your mom about that?"

"Hank will be available whenever he isn't working. I don't care about that."

"You'll care if somebody catches your supposed girlfriend out with another man."

"You think I haven't learned to fly under the radar?" Jayson grumped. "Besides, it'll just be casual dating, if anybody asks."

"Sure. We just went into complicated territory." In the Reth Alliance, nobody would blink about multiple mates. On Earth, monogamy was the ideal but often not the reality. It didn't keep everybody from pointing fingers, either. Cheating was big business in the journalistic arena; Jayson should know that better than anybody.

"Bree, you worry too much," Hank sighed. "Jayson's been seeing subs for years. San Francisco isn't small town America. He doesn't flaunt it, and as long as he doesn't rub it in anybody's face," Hank didn't finish.

"This is crazy. Jayson, go find somebody else. I don't think I can do this."

"You can."

"I'm getting out." I pulled away from both of them.

"Bree, it'll be platonic until you say you want otherwise," Jayson called after me.

Great. He'd get sex elsewhere. He just wanted a public friend with almost-benefits.

"Rome, you'd best take care of her when I can't," Hank growled and lifted himself out of the water.

"I can do that. Trina keeps an eye on her whenever she's at home as it is."

"Were you telling me the truth when you said you cared about her?"

"Yeah. She pulls at me in some way, and I can't explain that. Wasn't sure I wanted it, either. I like my freedom, and the minute she said she didn't care that I played, well, that's enough for me."

"Don't ever put her in danger, Rome."

"You think I'd do that deliberately? Mom would never let me live that down."

"It should be that you'd never let yourself live that down."

"Look, I'm still sorting that out, all right? This is all new to me."

"Just remember that it's really new to Bree. She has no idea what to do about this, and it's scaring her."

"You going to bed with her?"

"Planning on it, unless she says no."
"She won't."

Kay's Journal

A moment of lucidity. I have no idea how I ended up in the groves —somehow, Kalia must have found a way to slip out of the house. House. It wasn't a house. Hordace Cayetes' palaces couldn't compare to this house. I knew Bill was worried about me. The others were worried, too. The difference was that Bill didn't seem threatening to me—he loved someone else, and I could see that easily. Trajan frightened me for other reasons—he growled at Ashe on the best of days.

In the few moments I had to myself, when Kalia wasn't terrified and taking over both of us, I wondered about that. Ashe frightened Kalia. She knew—so much better than I did—that he wanted sex. It's strange, but Kalia had too much experience with sex, and none of it had involved love. I'd never had sex, and certainly had nothing to compare any of that to. We could find no compromise on this, either. Kalia's last memories of sex had been with torture, at the hands of Iversti Foculis. I'd killed him for her, because he was evil and needed to be stopped.

That was my secret—Kay's secret. I'd only killed twice in my life, and both times had been out of necessity. It looked completely natural, too—the official cause of death, according to medical reports, was massive stroke. I think if Kalia had my gift, so many others might be dead as well.

"Kay, what are you doing out here alone?" Ashe stood before me, a stern look marring his handsome face. Kalia roared to the surface and I was lost.

Breanne's Journal

"Hey," Hank climbed in bed beside me. I curled into a ball. "You took a shower, didn't you? You smell nice."

A shower was the only way to get the scent of pool chlorine out of my hair, so I'd shampooed, too, when I hadn't planned to do that. "Your hair's still damp," Hank scooted in behind me. A hand reached up and stroked my jaw. "Baby, polyamory works better if all parties know and like each other."

"I don't want to know Jason's playmates."

"I know. That was a stupid thing to say. He'll never commit to them, and most of them don't want it, anyway."

"Hank, I am truly confused. Until I met you, I'd never had sex with anybody. Look at me, now. I'm a slut. A lying slut."

"Bree, I want you to take that back. That is a terrible insult, and the worst part is you handed it to yourself."

"What good can come of this, Hank? Really?"

"I know other people involved in polyamory. They get along great. Some even have a group commitment ceremony."

"Oh, lord." I covered my face with a hand.

"It's not legal according to the law, but they have one anyway." Hank rubbed the back of my neck. "I've even rented out the dungeon for that and for collaring ceremonies."

"Hank, hush. Please."

Hank didn't reply, he just kept rubbing my neck. "Hank," I finally sighed.

"What, baby?"

"They really want that? To wear a collar and kneel and all that stuff?"

"Yeah. They'll tell you they want it. They go looking for it. It's not for everybody," he slid a hand down my ribs and over my hipbones. "Just a fraction of the population does, but it makes them happy—they have what they want."

"Maybe we'll talk about this again—when I'm not so freaked," I sighed.

"See—you've come a long way already. I remember your face when you met me at Bogey's after you found out about the club. You were so pale and shaking. Come here. I'm gonna make you come and then let you sleep."

∾

Someday, I want to wake up with Hank still in the bed. That didn't look to happen, though. My thigh and abdominal muscles ached pleasantly—Hank knew how to make that happen.

Kathleen didn't look good when she showed up for brunch served in the breakfast nook, and she didn't eat much. I was beginning to worry. Hank and Jayson left around noon for their extracurricular activity, after Kathleen had pleaded a headache and went back to bed.

Deciding that reading might distract me from worrying about Jayson and Hank, I settled down to read a book on my tablet. An hour later, I almost flung the tablet across my bedroom—two things had happened. One, Hank and Jayson had been held up by traffic and what I'd seen in my vision had come to pass—the girl involved in the demonstration went up like a torch and two, Kathleen Rome was having a heart attack.

∾

"Where do you think she is?" Trajan asked. Ashe had sent mindspeech a few days earlier, telling his Second-in-command that he had some information on Breanne. Trajan finally agreed to come to Ashe for a talk.

"Traje, I don't have the slightest idea. At least I know why that is, now," Ashe combed fingers through his hair with a sigh.

"Why is that, then?" Trajan's deep-brown eyes raked Ashe's face for any clues.

"She's what I am. Well, not exactly what I am. She's the Mighty Heart. Ren and I both worry that she's making a target of herself, although Ren's son, Graegar, warned her to be careful. The enemy has her power signature now, after that bit of foolishness on Tulgalan."

"So you think saving four million is foolish? She's in danger? Remind me again why she's not safe here with me."

"Look, I feel bad enough about that as it is, and to learn that she might be able to help us with Kay? That's a punch in the gut."

"So it's still about you." Trajan rose and walked away.

"Trajan, I'm sorry. Every time we talk about this, I end up with at least one foot in my mouth."

"Well, maybe it's fair, then, that we're both frustrated." Trajan disappeared.

Breanne's Journal

I didn't have time to call an ambulance or try to find Kathleen's driver. I lifted her easily and folded space to the best heart hospital in the area. The receptionist barely blinked before shouting for a gurney, and Kathleen was wheeled into a room quickly.

Discreetly *Pulling* Kathleen's purse to me, I offered her information to the clerk, whose eyebrows rose considerably at Kathleen's ID. She ran from the room, was gone for a few minutes and then returned, looking flustered. I lowered my shields to learn that Clerk Susan was Presbyterian, had three kids and recognized Kathleen Rome as a huge contributor to the hospital.

"Are you family?" Susan asked.

"Yes," I replied, mentally crossing fingers behind my back. What else was I supposed to do? I'd already attempted to call Jayson twice, then texted him. Obviously, he either wasn't answering me or had his phone turned off. I tried Hank's cellphone, too, and got the same results.

"Hello, I'm Doctor Raymond," a surgeon in green scrubs stood before me. "Mrs. Rome will need a bypass—she has severe blockage and we'll do our best to rectify that."

"All right," I nodded.

"Sign the form," Susan pushed a release in my direction. I signed. What else could I do?

"She's going into surgery now. Did she eat lunch?"

"No, and only picked at breakfast around three hours ago," I said. "She really hasn't felt good since yesterday."

"We'll get on this, and I'll have someone update you," the surgeon promised before hurrying away.

I still held Kathleen's designer purse in my arms, so I pulled out her cellphone and went looking for her husband and oldest son's phone number. No surprise, I couldn't reach either of them. I left messages—both verbal and texts, telling them what had happened, where Kathleen was and then went to sit in a nearby waiting room.

"Mr. Rome, we're only questioning witnesses. Can you explain why you were at that demonstration?" The detective lifted an eyebrow at Jayson. The girl had been rushed to the hospital with severe burns covering her body, and Jayson realized she likely wouldn't survive. How had Breanne known? At the time, he'd blown off her worries. He'd seen all of it come true the moment he and Hank walked into the Los Angeles dungeon.

"I run a magazine. This was a tip on a possible article," Jason breathed a worried sigh. "I had no idea this might happen."

"You know how dangerous this can be?" the detective asked, making notes.

"Yes, that's why I wanted to do an article. If it looked viable, I intended to put a staff writer on it."

"I see," the detective nodded. Jayson took in the man's appearance—he was in his forties and looked competent.

"This is my bodyguard," Jayson nodded toward Hank, who stood nearby. "When will we be allowed to leave?"

"After we question the others. Have a seat outside, and keep your cellphone turned off."

"Thank you, detective."

Breanne's Journal

Graegar told me that any power expended to *Change What Was* could alert the enemy to my presence, so I held that in reserve and tried a different tactic. I didn't know I could do it until I was forced to do it, either. I placed Kathleen Rome in a short, temporary stasis too many times to count so the surgeon and his staff could save her life. I had to do it remotely, too, as my physical body sat in a cold waiting room, seemingly anticipating an update on Kathleen's condition. The poor girl who got burned was dying, too. Should I save her if I could? It was her fault she'd been injured, but then people make dumb mistakes all the time.

I learned that I could juggle several balls at once. Between Kathleen's stasis treatment, I bent power similar to that of a Larentii toward a burned girl in another hospital, repairing charred and damaged tissue. I did what I considered the important things first, lessening the injury and giving her a fighting chance before going back to Kathleen and what she needed to survive.

Yes, I'd expended power to save four million people. I was still weary and in need of rest from that. Graegar had said it would take weeks to recuperate; I'd taken only a few days. By the time I knew the burned girl would live and Kathleen would survive and have no lasting damage to her heart, I was worn out. The sun dipped below the horizon when I rose to lean against the window frame and stare out at the Pacific in the distance.

"You can go. You may want to find someone more competent next time, if you really want to do an article on this sort of thing," the detective was back and giving Jayson and Hank permission to leave.

"I'll have them vetted, first, and will likely send a research writer out," Jayson rose to his feet. "Thank you detective. Do you know the status of the victim?"

"I just heard that the doctors are more optimistic now than they were when she was taken to the hospital. Next few days will tell."

"Let's go." Hank walked in front of Jayson toward the front door of the police station. Jayson turned on his phone to call a cab—the car he'd driven was still at the venue.

"What the hell?" Jayson stared at three texts from Breanne. "Holy fuck. No, no, no," Jayson moaned.

"What?" Hank came over to look.

"Mom's in the hospital. She had a heart attack. We have to go."

CHAPTER 13

*B*reanne's Journal

"She'll be out of it for a while, and that's not a bad thing," the doctor assured me. We stood outside Kathleen's room in the coronary care unit. Numbness permeated my body and at times, I wasn't really sure where I was. I was just going through the required motions and listening carefully to what doctors and nurses told me, hoping it would be retained in my memory in case I needed it again.

"The surgery went as well as we could expect, given the severity of the situation," he added.

"Thank you." I remembered my manners, at least.

"You'll be allowed to visit periodically, and there's coffee and a soft drink machine in the lounge," he said. I nodded.

"Bree? Thank God," Jayson was almost running, with Hank right behind him.

"Doctor, this is Jayson Rome, Kathleen's youngest son," I made introductions as Jayson slid to a stop and stared at the physician. "Your mother is fine, now. She's sleeping after the surgery."

I walked toward the wide, double doors leading to the CCU. I almost made it.

~

"She's just tired," Hank waved away the doctor. "She had to take care of all this herself, when she couldn't reach anybody else."

"I would still prefer to have her examined," the physician huffed.

"I'll take care of it," Hank mumbled. "I used to be a paramedic."

"If there are any unusual signs," the doctor began.

"I'll handle it. Take care of Mrs. Rome." Hank carried Breanne into the hall and toward the elevators.

~

Breanne's Journal

"Baby, how do you feel?" Hank's hands were on my forehead and my heart.

"Crappy," I mumbled. I hadn't opened my eyes, after waking from an apparent faint.

"We're in Jayson's car in the parking lot," Hank sighed. "Jayson's with his mother."

"Where he should have been for the past four hours," I tried to sit up—I'd wakened with my head in Hank's lap in the back seat of a new Cadillac.

"Stay down for a little while." Hank kept his hand on my forehead and didn't let me move.

"Is the girl still alive?"

"You know about that?"

"I know lots of things."

"I imagine you do."

"I feel cold."

"Hot chocolate?"

"With whipped cream?"

"My baby wants whipped cream?" I blinked up into a dazzling smile. "I think there's a coffee shop across the street. Want me to carry you?"

"I can wait here."

"You think I'll let you out of my sight after that stunt?"

"That wasn't a stunt. It certainly wasn't planned."

"I know. You think they sell jackets at the coffee shop? You need to be warmer."

"Hank, was it as awful as the vision I got? With that girl?"

He thought for a moment before making a reply. "It was pretty bad. Jayson was really shaken. As a medic, in and out of the military, I've seen people wounded before, so I knew what was happening and how it would look afterward. Jayson doesn't have that experience. It may be a while before he wants to see this again."

"If she'd just used common sense and stayed away from the tanning bed," I sighed. Hank helped me sit up. I felt a little dizzy, but that's it.

"If she'd just washed off the lotion," Hank rumbled. "Come on, I have to get my girl warmed up with hot chocolate."

"Hank?" Jayson's voice sounded over Hank's cellphone.

"What is it, buddy?" Hank asked.

"You across the street at the coffee shop?"

"Yeah."

"Will you order a capp for me?"

"Sure thing. We can bring it up in a minute."

"No, stay there. I finally got hold of Jamie, and he and Laurel are on their way. Mom is still unconscious and doesn't know I'm here. I can't reach Dad anywhere. Maybe I need that stalker app on my family. Jamie was out on a boat trip and didn't have service until he reached land again. I'll be there in a minute." Jayson hung up.

"Jayson's coming," Hank shoved the cellphone in his pocket.

"What does he want?" I asked.

"Cappuccino," Hank replied.

"I'll get it," I shuffled to my feet.

"No, stay put, shortness," he said. "I've got this."

If I weren't so weary, I would have enjoyed the sight of Hank walking away. As it was, I wanted to close my eyes and sleep for a week. I did close my eyes and didn't open them again until Jayson settled on the seat next to mine.

"Bree?" Jayson cupped my face in his hands. "Are you all right?"

"Tired." I closed my eyes again.

"Cappuccino with hazelnut," Hank set a cup in front of Jayson.

"Thanks," Jayson sighed, taking his hands away from my face. "Man, what a fucked up day."

"Agreed," I said, my eyes still closed. I thought about laying my head on the table and sleeping there.

"Little girl, I owe you," Jayson pulled me against him with one hand and lifted the cup to his lips with the other.

"I did it for your mom."

"I know. That doesn't discharge the debt."

"Sure. Find me a place to sleep and we'll call it even."

"Jayson?" James Rome Jr., followed by his wife Laurel, walked into the coffee shop.

"Want coffee?" Jayson stood and hugged his brother, then leaned in to give Laurel a peck.

"Hank?" I handed Hank my credit-card as Jamie and Laurel decided what they wanted.

"How's Mom?" Jamie asked as he got Laurel seated before pulling in another chair for himself.

"She's fine. The doctor says there were a few scary moments during surgery, but he said Mom kept pulling out of them. Looks like a full recovery—the graft went well and he says she'll be back to normal in no time. I can't find Dad," Jayson added.

"I tried, too. Got nothing. I put in a call to Bob, though, and got his voice mail. They may be together."

"Again?" Laurel whined. "At his age he's doing this?"

Now I knew why Kathleen didn't like shopping with Laurel. Judiciously I kept that information to myself.

"You're Breanne?" I realized I'd never really met Jayson's brother. He'd been in a conference with Jayson during the anniversary party, and hadn't shown up for Jayson's birthday. I had three guesses why, and all of them started with the letter L.

"Yes."

"Thanks for the messages."

"You're welcome."

"Where were you, bro, that your girl had to pick up the slack?" Jamie turned to Jayson.

"Researching an article. Bree stayed home with Mom, and it's a good thing she did."

"I hear that," Jamie nodded. "Are you staying for a few days?"

"Looks like it. At least until Wednesday. I have a staff meeting on Thursday, so I'll probably leave Wednesday night."

"I have to get back," Hank pointed out as he set drinks on the table for Jamie and Laurel.

"Hank, we keep missing each other," Jamie said, extending his hand.

"True." Hank smiled politely and shook.

"Bree, are you staying?" Jayson lifted an eyebrow at me.

"Huh?" I hadn't considered it, since Jayson's brother had showed up for moral support. If Bill Jennings hadn't called at that moment, I might have been stuck with Jayson for three more days.

"Bill?" I said when I stood and answered his call.

"Breanne, we need your help in Austin," Bill said. "We've lost six girls already."

"When?" I asked. Hank's eyes clouded with concern as I stepped away from the table.

"Tonight or tomorrow, if you can."

"I'm in L.A. right now," I said.

"I'll find a plane to get you here. I already have a hotel set up."

"Okay. I don't have much in the way of clothing," I said. "I only came down for the weekend."

"Have jeans and boots?"

"Yeah. One set," I said.

"Good enough. Opal knows your size. She can go out and pick stuff up while you're in the air."

"Opal's there?"

"Yeah. Is that a problem?"

"No. I like Opal a lot."

"Good. Be at the airport in two hours, sweetheart. I'll have a ticket waiting."

"Okay." I ended the call and blinked at Hank, who appeared to be simmering with anger, now.

"I have to be at the airport in two hours," I said.

"Why?" Jayson didn't look happy, either.

"I sort of got volunteered to help a few government agencies. Barry Stokes seems to be my pimp," I said. He was—he'd given full permission for Bill to poach my services whenever I wasn't needed for Mercy Crossings.

"You really speak most languages?" Laurel was being Laurel again —her voice revealing her skepticism.

"*Mimi kuzungumza lugha zaidi,*" I replied. "That translates to *I speak more languages.* In Swahili," I said. "I'll get a cab back to the house. I need my bag."

"I'll take you," Hank said and scooted his chair back. *Joy.* I was planning to mist back to the house. Now I'd have Hank grumpy Bell as a companion.

"Hey," Jayson pulled me down to whisper in my ear. "I want to swat you again," his breath was warm. "We'll talk when you get back. Don't be gone long," he added when I leaned away and frowned at him. "Hank, take the car," Jayson tossed keys in Hank's direction. "Jamie will give me a ride home later."

"Oh, don't you worry," I said. "And we *will* talk." If his answer to everything he didn't like was swats, we didn't belong together. I walked out the coffee shop door, Hank right behind me.

"What did he say?" Hank demanded.

"That he wanted to swat me again. I save his mother and he wants to hit me."

"Baby, spanking is generally the way to say we don't necessarily agree with your choices. Sometimes it means we care. With Jayson, it could be either."

"Well, we're done, then, if that's his reaction to everything."

"Do like he says and talk when you get back. Work this out. He's not gonna hurt you."

"It's demeaning."

"I understand. He doesn't see it that way."

"Come on, he doesn't think he's superior in some way?"

"He treats everybody like that. He's a Rome."

"And I'm the Vhanaraszh. Want to see who might come out on top in that contest?"

"Baby, you'll have to explain that to me someday," Hank sighed. "Right now, we have to haul ass if we're gonna make it to the house, get your bag and then get to the airport in two hours."

"I hear that. And is that the ass Jayson wants to swat?"

"Yeah."

"The breakup will commence as planned. I don't need a ride back to the house, Hank."

"Bree," he warned.

"Really, Hank? Tell Jayson he'll have more luck kissing my ass." I disappeared right in front of Hank Bell.

Tears had to be wiped away before I could see to pack my bag. It wouldn't do to show up at the airport crying, either, because that would be disastrous. I'd exhausted myself saving Kathleen Rome and her son wanted to hit me. Fuck him. This would never work and because of that, I'd just revealed myself to Hank Bell. Well, fuck both of them, and not in any nice way. Slamming my bag shut, I zipped it and misted toward the airport.

"Bree, this is stupid. Fuck," Hank hissed as he stood beside the Cadillac. "Rome, as soon as your mother is better, I'll strangle you."

~

"She just picked up her ticket. She'll be here in five hours," Bill said, taking a seat at Opal's table in the hotel restaurant.

"Good. I'm hitting a dead end, and there's no pun intended, there," Opal said.

~

Lissa's Journal

"Daddy says Breanne saved Grey House's ass. He didn't say it exactly like that," Nissa grinned, "but it's the same thing."

"Your father told me," I nodded. Nissa and I were having tea in the arboretum while Toff, Yoff and Trik practiced rusty sword skills with Drake and Drew.

"I can't believe I have an aunt. I wish I'd met her. Daddy says she's pretty, but she has dark hair."

"I know. The only images we have here at the palace are those before she was turned, and that includes the vid from the Skel Hawer beating. Those aren't pretty, but she was disfigured before that. Nobody knows why that is."

"This is so weird," Nissa said. "I tried to talk to Gav about it, but he just refuses to talk. He saw her more than anybody else outside the palace."

"Gavril is in enough trouble, as is his father," I snorted. "They should have realized something was wrong, yet they did nothing about it."

"I don't understand mind clouds," Nissa blew out a breath. "At all. Why did it only affect Gavin, Gavril and Cheedas?"

"No idea."

"Lissa, you'd better come—we're calling an emergency Council meeting," Rigo came to a halt beside our table.

"What happened?" I stood quickly.

"Evensun has been emptied. Not a single prisoner is left, and there's sand everywhere."

"Oh, no."

~

Breanne's Journal

Bill hadn't been able to get a first-class ticket for me this time. He'd barely managed to find a seat for me at all—all the flights were full or nearly so. I sat between a teen girl and a real-estate agent. The agent, after learning I lived in San Francisco, immediately gave her card, explained that her company had a branch office in my area and told me to call if I had any housing needs. Taking the card, I shoved it in my purse and didn't tell her that I'd recently made a purchase, thank you.

The teen girl was busy reading manga on her e-reader. I didn't disturb her. After the real estate agent ran down, I closed my eyes and attempted to sleep. That didn't happen. I'd messed up, leaving Hank like I did. He knew for sure I was weird, now, and I had nobody to blame except myself.

The uneasy feeling that I'd have a multitude of angry emails or texts when I reached Austin didn't help, either. Hank would likely be demanding some kind of explanation and Jayson, if he even bothered to send anything, would probably just be pissed.

There was a stopover in Vegas before going on to Austin, but I didn't change planes. I left my cellphone off, hoping for peace and a cessation of worry while watching both my seatmates leave and getting two new ones for the continuing flight.

~

"Bill," I did my best to smile at him—he'd stayed up late again to pick me up at the airport.

"Breanne," his smile was genuine. Opal stood at his shoulder, and she offered me a grin. I hugged both of them.

Bill and Opal sat with me while I ate a late dinner at the hotel restaurant. Our goal for the following morning was to sniff around

Austin. The bodies found in the city had been spread around—and not in the sewers, this time. This killer was getting creative, which worried me. Generally that's how a Sirenali's obsession worked—that their victims would find new and creative ways to please the one they now saw as their master.

Six bodies of young, college-age women had been found in four locations—a mall parking lot late at night, a hotel basement, the roof of a bookstore and the front steps of a local restaurant. Nobody saw anything, and the bodies were dumped without any security cameras catching the criminal. A vampire could move fast enough if he were motivated.

"I'll show you the footage tomorrow," Bill said. "Get some rest. Both of you," he nodded to Opal and me.

"Thanks, Bill," I nodded to him. "Goodnight."

∾

Bree, the first text from Hank read, *I want to talk to you. Soon.*

Breanne, do you think to walk away with no word?

Breanne, this is ridiculous. That text was from Jayson. *When you get back, we'll discuss this. My comment was merely to catch your attention and let you know we need to work this out.* Jayson was lucky I was so tired and out of sorts, because I wanted to fold space, punch him in the mouth and fold back to Austin.

Breanne, my arms are empty and my heart hurts tonight. Hank's last message made me cry.

"Baby?" Hank answered on the first ring. I was a blubbering mess as I attempted to speak.

"You're tired, baby. Stop crying and go to sleep," Hank soothed when I couldn't get a coherent word past my teeth. Eventually, after much coaxing, I did as he asked, ended the call and went to bed.

∾

Lissa's Journal

These dunes were twice as tall as I was and they were everywhere. Rigo, Gavin, my Falchani twins, Aryn, Flavio and Roff had come with me. The entire planet had been emptied in minutes—no flayed bodies were left behind, just as it had been for Yigga Prison. Those prisoners —ten thousand of them—had attacked Gedes. Evensun held more than half a million. I shuddered to think of the damage that many armed criminals might create.

"I am your god," he announced to the energy clothed in newly acquired, humanoid bodies standing before him. "You will submit to me and to those I designate under my command. Your new body will allow you to interfere in any way you see fit. Bear in mind that if your body dies, you will still live. I will present you with another body quickly, so that you may serve me. In the coming days, you will be taught what you must know to obey me swiftly and without question, in all I command. Follow me faithfully and we will rule all."

Breanne's Journal

Caffeine. Lots of it. And still I looked as if I'd been dragged across most of Texas and then dumped (unhappily) in a pile of prickly pear. It's funny how Texas comes out in you when you're *in* Texas. Poor Opal was curious but determined not to ask what had happened after I'd gone to my room the night before.

"What are we looking for?" I asked. I'd probably asked that already, but forgot that I'd asked. That's what kind of day it was.

"So far, all six girls have been taken from the same campus," Opal slipped a folder in my direction at the breakfast table. Bill was supposed to join us, but I had the feeling he'd been caught up in phone calls or emails. Opal told me which campus while my eyes attempted to lose focus again.

"Sugar, are you sure you only want eggs and fruit?" This waitress couldn't grasp the concept of vegetarianism and figured I just wasn't normal, somehow. I wanted to tell her that being vegetarian was the most normal thing about me.

"Yes, thank you," I replied as politely as I could. She shuffled away to turn in our order.

~

"You ever gonna drive this thing again?" Trace settled on the passenger side of the ancient, red Cadillac and shut the door. Ashe sat in the driver's seat, a wrist draped over the steering wheel and stared at the grove around him. The Cadillac rested beneath a canopy in the middle of SouthStar's groves and was kept in stasis to prevent deterioration.

"I've thought about it," Ashe sighed. "This used to belong to Lissa's human husband. I've thought about giving it to her, but have no idea what her reaction might be. I think she used to tease her husband about getting rid of it."

"How could she do that? It's a classic."

"I know, but not everybody appreciates vintage automobiles. Maybe I'll give it to Winkler, and let him decide."

"I'd miss it if it weren't here," Trace said.

"Yeah. Me too, Trace, me, too."

~

Breanne's Journal

"Coffee?" Bill arrived and so did the waitress.

Bill had a menu in his hand and coffee at his elbow quickly. He looked important—Opal and I were dressed in jeans so we could work and didn't look so important. And we weren't male, another minus in our camp.

"Breanne, if you need something to help you sleep," Bill murmured when the waitress walked away.

"I'll be okay," I said and lifted my fork—I needed the protein in the eggs, otherwise I would have settled for fruit and let it go.

"Then stop working before six tonight and get some sleep," Bill commanded.

~

"She never got back with me," Jayson grumbled. He and Hank were trading blows in a Los Angeles gym before Hank flew home. Most of Hank's punches were connecting. Jayson's weren't.

"Next time, keep your fucking mouth shut," Hank punched Jayson hard, throwing him off guard. "Don't you know the first thing about a relationship, or are you just too damned used to everybody bowing and scraping? If you are, lose that fast around Breanne. One of these days, you'll be sorry if you don't."

"Fine."

"I mean it."

"I said okay."

"We need to talk, too, Rome."

"About what?"

"About Bree getting called in shortly after college girls started disappearing in D.C. and Austin."

"Are you fucking kidding me?" Jayson stopped moving and stared at Hank in surprise.

~

Breanne's Journal

"I got a scent," I muttered as Opal and I sniffed around the rooftop of a local bookstore.

She stood near the markers where the body had been found. There was little blood, so the girl had died elsewhere and was merely left here.

"Murders two days apart, like clockwork," Opal pointed out.

"Do the abductions coincide with the murders?" I asked.

"Hours apart," She nodded, pushing long, dark hair behind an ear and staring at the roof where the body had lain for hours before its discovery.

"So the vamp has to drink every other day," I said. "You think he's getting bagged stuff or drinking from a donor?"

"It ought to be an unwilling donor, at least at first," Opal huffed.

"Agreed. I can't imagine too many women offering blood to a serial killer."

"We've talked to possible witnesses. Nobody remembers anything," Opal said.

"Did you take anybody of the fanged variety to ask?" I lifted an eyebrow in Opal's direction. She'd been staring at the roof beneath our feet, but raised her head to blink at me when I asked the question.

"No—Bill didn't bring anybody—said if we had you, we wouldn't need 'em."

"True. How hard will it be to introduce me to a likely candidate?"

"Not hard. One of the girls had a roommate and she's very upset. Said she'd do anything to help catch the killer. I'll call Bill and ask him to schedule an interview. It may be tomorrow morning before she goes to work—she has a part-time retail job through the holidays."

"That's fine. Maybe I can wake up by then," I sighed. "I probably need more coffee, too."

"Man trouble?"

"I guess."

"Is he worth it?"

"Jury's still out."

"Don't let him hurt you."

I didn't tell her it was too late for that. Much too late. Jayson had effectively removed himself from the running, in my opinion, but his mother was still fragile. I wanted to huddle in a corner and wait for my inner trembling to go away on that score.

I wanted to trust Hank. Really. I just didn't want any more surprises on that front. Yes, there were some things I wasn't telling him but honestly, what could happen if I walked in, sat beside him, told him I wasn't just the Vhanaraszh (after explaining what that was), but also a Q'elindi and possibly a god? I could hear the phone call to the psychiatrist in my head. I could say good-bye to Hank, too, while that was happening.

~

"Here's the manuscript. I took the liberty of having it edited while I wrote the rest," Ross Gideon handed a thick folder to James Rome, Sr. "How's your wife? I heard it was a close call. I've never seen Kathleen go down like that."

"I think she finally had Jayson tailed," the elder Rome grumbled.

"Found out what the boy was into, did she?"

"Probably."

"What about the girl?" Ross tapped the edge of the folder he'd handed to James Rome.

"Just a front, to make his mother happy. She'll disappear soon enough when this book is released. Has it been sent to the press?"

"Yeah. They know to give it top priority. We can have limited release in less than ten days, and my guess is we'll be flooded with orders after the first day. Does it bother you about the girl? She wasn't aware of this project when she signed that release."

"The girl is nothing. Joyce Christian is everything. We're gonna take her reputation down. I don't care if she is dead—too many people still idolize her and are too ready to quote her garbage. Any new leads on the other two kids? The ones who didn't make it?"

"I have my investigator snooping around the property, but he can't get too far in without risking arrest for trespassing."

"Too bad. I'd like to point out graves to the authorities just before the book's release, but if we can't, then they'll go in after the evidence is presented. I have no idea how that information was hidden for so long."

"Joyce had a lot of people under her thumb, and they were afraid to talk. Too bad that sheriff committed suicide two days ago. We might have gotten more information from him."

"I think he realized how fast we were moving on this and decided not to stick around. He was dying anyway, and in a lot of pain."

"I can't believe the girl isn't scarred and crippled from all that."

"Maybe she is. Maybe we just can't see it."

"Mom?" Jayson carried a vase of flowers into Kathleen Rome's hospital room.

"Jayson?" Kathleen was pale and her voice trembled slightly as her youngest approached her bedside and set the vase on a side table. "Where's Breanne? She saved my life. The doctor told me and your father this morning that if she hadn't gotten me here so fast, I might not have made it."

"Bree got called out on assignment." Jayson didn't look happy.

"For Mercy Crossings?"

"No. Looks like Barry Stokes is lending her to the government at times. She's in Austin. Hank and I noticed that some college girls have come up missing there, just like in San Francisco and D.C. We also noticed that Bree was in D.C. when things were happening there."

"She was in Frisco, too, wasn't she? You think she's involved in any of that?"

"Not involved in the crime, no. The crimes in D.C. stopped after she was called in. I have her on that stalker app—I know she wasn't there until after those girls were murdered, and then when Bree went, the murders stopped. I have one of my investigative reporters on that, now. Bree got a call after girls started dying in Austin. She's involved in the investigations somehow, and Hank and I are scared to death."

Kathleen breathed a shaky sigh and brushed a trembling hand over her eyes. "Jayson, you can stop pretending, now," she whispered. "I know where you were on Sunday. I asked Dan to tail you. I know about Hank's business, too—it's public record. Stop pretending you care about that girl. I think it upsets her. I have no idea what you did to make her come to the anniversary party, but in retrospect, I know she didn't want to be there. I'd like to keep her as a friend, so don't be an ass."

"You know?" Jayson hadn't gotten past his mother's admission.

"Baby, I do know. I hoped it was a passing interest, but I see that you're getting more into it. I hope this is what you want, honey, although it worries me."

"Damn," Jayson combed fingers through his hair and turned away to stare out his mother's hospital window. "Mom, I kind of do like Breanne, although she isn't," Jayson didn't finish.

"I don't think she ever will be, hon. People are different. I've had to accept that. Let them be different, Jayson. Don't force them into your mold. I'm having to do that with my own son, after all."

"Yeah." Jayson rubbed the back of his neck uncomfortably.

"You think Breanne's in danger, don't you?"

"Mom, she was in Somalia when that sandstorm hit."

"Are you joking? How did you find that out?"

"Hank."

"How much does he care about her?"

"You know?"

"I see it every time he looks at her. A woman always knows, honey."

"Mom, I like Bree. I do. I don't compare to Hank, though."

"Is he—does he?"

"He won't do a damn thing his partner doesn't want, and I don't know how he has that much control," Jayson muttered.

"Thank God," Kathleen said. "I was worried after I heard what his business was."

"As of now, Breanne owns half of it, although she didn't know what she was investing in at first," Jayson admitted. "She keeps trying to give her interest to Hank so she can walk away. He won't let her."

"He doesn't want to lose her."

"Look, Mom, would it make any difference to you if I said the same thing? No, I won't ever give up some things, but Bree keeps me on my toes and doesn't let me get away with much. It's different. Certainly not what I'm used to."

"She has to have something, to deal with people like she met in South Sudan."

"Yeah. You're right about that. There's vulnerability there, too, and I can't figure that out."

"Jayson, every woman is vulnerable in some way. You just have to discover what it is and make sure you protect her from it."

"Mom, we've never really talked like this."

"Hon, I've never gotten this close to dying before."

CHAPTER 14

Lissa's Journal

"We're waiting for the shoe to drop." Cleo and Kyler sat with me in the arboretum after a tedious day in a Council meeting. Everybody was on edge, ever since Ildevar decided not to keep the information regarding Evensun from the Alliances.

The news services all had a field day at first, blaming everybody and pointing fingers, until it finally hit home. The attack on Gedes. The destruction of a quarter of Targis. The sandstorm that emptied Yigga Prison. Some were even pointing to the anomalies indicating the sandstorms on the Dark Realm worlds.

Everybody was scared, now, and jumping at the slightest noise. Gavin and my Falchani twins had taken precautionary measures, but it was likely to keep the guards and army focused, rather than allow them to dwell on the reality that they held absolutely no power against what might come.

"Meligar says even the Larentii are holding their breath," Kyler sighed. My nieces and I stared through the huge, glass windows of my arboretum at the twinkling city of Lissia below us.

"None of us can *Look* to see anything," Cleo agreed.

"Ildevar says the Telling Winds have gone berserk," I offered.

"That's why *Looking* doesn't work—everything is in flux. Connegar says Conner told him it's as if all the doors to all the timelines have blown open, and no single path is more logical than another."

"They're waiting for something," Kyler nodded carefully. "Some small sign, maybe, before they tip their hand."

"But what about the Three—have they come together?" Cleo leaned forward and held out a hand, palm up.

"Ashe says no," I whispered. "What if that's what everybody thinks, so they're looking to make a widespread attack? If the Three come together for the first time, they may not know which way to go first. Or, if they don't come together, so much could be destroyed we may not survive anyway. It's a preemptive strike, I think."

"How can you battle an enemy you can't find or identify?" Kyler shivered. "I saw those anomaly maps. In the Dark Realm, they followed a pattern, likely to trap somebody."

"They trapped Belen, and he says somebody powerful released him, but either he doesn't know who or he isn't saying. It makes sense that if it's one of the Three, the enemy was looking for them and their power signature. If it's the same one who saved Targis, they really have a power signature now." I hugged myself.

At that moment, I wished Rigo were with me. As an ancient vampire and an accomplished diplomat before that, he always knew how to calm the situation. He was communicating with his spy network instead, asking for reports on unusual activities and such, so he could bring information to me.

Erland and Ry sent a dozen extra warlocks to Campiaa to protect Gavril, too, but they had their own kingdom to guard. I had no idea what more warlocks might do against an enemy we couldn't track the moment they finished an attack—that's what we'd learned after all the sandstorms in the Dark Realm and the one in Yigga. The power disappeared as if it had never been.

"Where is Breanne?" Cleo asked.

"I don't know." Two and a half months had passed since she'd brought me back from death and subsequently there'd been two brief sightings of her. Granted, the one on Tulgalan had been the briefest, but yielded the most dramatic results. That had taken power on a scale I'd never seen before. Yes, I'd moved planets, but *Changing What Was* is a different thing altogether and something I might never fathom.

"I wonder if time might move differently for her or for the Three," Cleo mused.

"If it moves differently for the Three, then it moves differently for my sister," I said softly.

~

"Charles, I believe a rogue may be behind these murders," Wlodek slid a folder across his desk.

"Austin, Texas, in the U.S.?" Charles flipped the folder open.

"Yes. These murders are very similar to those in San Francisco and Washington, D.C. Rogues were certainly behind those killings—we have confirmation. Who might be available to go? I realize Director Jennings has a team on this already, but I wish to get to the bottom of this quickly. You understand why, of course."

"Of course. Radomir is on his way back from France," Charles offered, his hazel eyes taking in Wlodek's dark, unreadable gaze before dropping to the paperwork again.

"Then arrange for a flight to the U.S. for my youngest," Wlodek sighed. "Perhaps he can rest during the trip."

"I will, Honored One."

~

"Mom knows." Jayson phoned Hank the moment he left the hospital.

"I kept telling you to say something."

"I know. She seems more okay with it than I might have guessed. She says I'm pretending with Bree, and she wants to keep Bree as a friend."

"Well?"

"I—look, I don't know about this. Breanne has something that pulls at me, but," Jayson said.

"Get your shit straight, then, before you talk to her again."

"What are you planning to do? Since we've figured out she's involved in these investigations, somehow?"

"No idea. I want to talk to her and get her to tell me what's going on. Maybe I can figure out what to do if she admits the truth."

"It may be one of those situations where she can't tell us."

"Did your dad say where he was when you and your brother couldn't find him?"

"Says he was doing research. Just walked into the hospital and started yelling at doctors and nurses. Everybody ran after that. Sometimes he's a bastard. They saved Mom and he wants to yell like it's all somebody else's fault."

"People handle stress and anger in different ways."

"Yeah. I understand that, all right."

Breanne's Journal

"The good news, I guess, is that most of the kids have gone home for Christmas already," Bill grumped over dinner. "There's not many left on campus, and security is warning all of them," he added.

"Do they not have somewhere else to go?" Opal asked. Bill had taken us to a restaurant about a mile from our hotel for dinner at seven. He'd kept his word, calling us at six and telling Opal and me to stop working.

"Most are grad students writing papers. They're using the free time to get extra work done."

"Even with the threat and dead bodies showing up regularly? I could find another place else to write," Opal snorted.

"I'm with you," I nodded at Opal. "Some people just think they're bullet-proof, I guess. With these killers, I think all they need is a victim and opportunity. There's no real motive, other than making some girl dead." That was true—so far, college girls had been targeted, and it didn't seem to matter what they looked like. The youngest had been eighteen—the oldest, twenty-four.

"What kind of warning are they getting?" Opal asked Bill. "Is it to stay indoors after dark, or just practice caution or some other, worthless jargon?"

"I can find out," Bill shook his head. "It would be a good idea to tell them not to go out at night, but they'll likely interpret that as 'don't go out alone at night,' or something else that they'll rationalize away."

"It won't matter if they go out in a crowd. That won't protect them from a determined vamp," I pointed out. "What about campus bars or hotspots? Is there a regular hangout that gets crowded, no matter what?"

Bill hauled out his cellphone and made a call to campus police. He had the chief on the line pretty quick. Of course I listened in.

"It's called The Beer Barrel," I heard the chief's answer clearly. "Some go there to do homework. They have free Wi-Fi, but there's always music playing and I have no idea how they can even think with that going on."

Bill thanked the chief and hung up before getting an address for Opal and me. Looked like the bar would be on our list of places to visit the following day.

"Baby, what are you doing?" Hank called right after I reached my room. Opal and I had met in her hotel room after dinner, worked out our list of stops for the following day and then I'd left to get an early appointment with my bed. Hank had invaded my thoughts during the day—when I wasn't yawning, anyway.

"Going to bed. Last night was a write-off," I said, pulling the usual duvet down and folding it across the bottom of my bed.

"When were you planning to tell me you're helping with those investigations?" Surprisingly enough, there was only a hint of accusation in Hank's voice.

"Hank, you're ex-military. I hope you understand the sensitivity of the situation," I grumped. Yeah, I knew I hadn't been honest with him. He'd had one big secret. I had lots of them, some big, some small. Again, I found myself wishing I could just pour it all out for him and that he'd understand completely. That wasn't going to happen. I stared at the usual, white sheets covering my bed. At least Bill got us a nice hotel, and the mattress was definitely softer than a two-by-four.

"I want to sit and have a talk when you come home," Hank said. "It bothers me more than I like to admit, when I know you're not safe."

"Hank, that's really nice of you to say. Not many feel that way," I said. "I've taken care of myself until now. That's not likely to change."

"Bree, you're not letting me be the man."

"I didn't know that was up for debate. You appear to have all the right equipment."

"You're misinterpreting this intentionally."

"You're saying you get to be in charge?"

"I'd like to be, where your safety is concerned."

"Hank, nobody can protect someone from everything. You have to admit that."

"I might be a little better at it than you think."

"You know, I get that about you. Up to a point."

"I want to know about your disappearing trick."

Well, there it was. I was waiting for—and dreading—that question.

"It's called misting," I said, deciding on the truth. Really, how else could I explain it, without claiming to be Houdini?

"Misting. Huh."

"Yes. I turn to invisible mist. It's something only a very few people can do, and I only came by the talent recently."

"How recently?"

"For me, a little more than two years."

"We'll talk about that, too, when you get home."

"Hank, some of this stuff—you'll have me committed."

"No, baby. Try me. You may be surprised."

"Uh-huh. Jayson Rome will have me committed, then. He'll be all over that."

"Jayson will behave. I'll see to it."

"Maybe I'll hand him a few swats. See how he likes it," I muttered. Yeah, I was still upset over that.

"I didn't call to upset you, or keep you from sleeping another night."

"I think that's a given," I stifled a yawn anyway. "How is Kathleen? Have you heard anything?"

"Mrs. Rome is doing well. Jayson's father came home and started ordering the hospital staff around. I have a feeling they're all running scared and cursing him behind his back."

"You think that's why Jayson?" I didn't finish my question.

"I do think that, most of the time. People react to all sorts of things in their lives. Jayson likes to be in charge."

"In a big way, by his own admission," I said.

"That bothers you, doesn't it?"

"Yeah. I think he wants to tell me what to do. I don't want somebody ordering me around. I know what needs doing and that's what I do. Frankly, for somebody to come along who thinks he knows better than I do, well, that's just an insult."

"I understand that. On the other hand, you need to listen, too. Nobody's right all the time, nobody's wrong all the time. For the people who care, some of the things you do are downright frightening, baby."

"Hank, I don't think you've seen frightening. I've seen it. Felt it. Lived it. This investigation? This is nothing."

"Breanne, you're doing nothing to calm my fears for you."

"Just settle down, okay? I've made it this far."

"That's not—that's not it, baby. Weird shit is going on, and somehow, there you are, right in the middle of all of it. I don't like it. Not even a little."

"Look, people are dying. I have to do something about it if I can."

"And you may be making a target of yourself. Don't you realize that?"

"Yeah. I've had somebody say that to me already."

"Who?"

"Somebody tall and blue. See—I told you this is weird, unbelievable and you'd have me committed over it."

"Bree, I think you need to come home. Right now."

"So you can admit me to the nearest psych ward?"

"No. So I can protect you. There are plenty of things out there, and they're not nice. They're gunning for you, I feel it. Tell whoever you're working for that you have to leave."

"I can't tell Bill Jennings that—that's ridiculous," I snapped before I thought.

"Bill Jennings. Director Bill Jennings? This is worse than I thought," Hank muttered. Did he think I wouldn't hear?

"Hank, there are things about me you don't know. Lots of things. They sound crazy. I have to deal with this. Really. You have to let this go and allow me to do what I can."

"Baby, Christmas is five days away. Do they have any plans to shut down the investigation, or let you come home for the holiday, at least?"

"I don't think this killer is planning to stop for a holiday," I said. "He's been killing every other day, and we don't have many leads."

"When is the next date?"

"Tonight," I muttered angrily. "And I'm too tired to go do anything about it."

"Where were you—when you went missing at the dealership?"

"Tulgalan. I'll give you a thousand dollars if that makes any sense at all to you," I huffed. "Good night, Hank. I'm going to bed. I'll probably have nightmares about a killer stalking college girls." I hit the end button on my cellphone before he could make a response.

"Honored One, I have arrived at the Austin safe house," Radomir informed Wlodek over his cellphone.

"Good. If the vampire follows his usual pattern, tonight is a killing night. Charles has gone through the records, and no extra orders for blood have arrived from the area. Unless the rogue has built up a supply of frozen blood, he is drinking from the population every other night. Find him for me, child. You know how I hate being indebted to humans or shapeshifters."

"I understand that, Father."

"Good. Do you have the information Charles sent?"

"Yes. I am studying it now."

"Do this quickly."

"I will."

~

Breanne's Journal

Who needs sleep? Hank's call served to ensure hours of sleeplessness, when he likely intended the opposite. It didn't matter now—I was wide awake. Misting out of my hotel room, I headed for The Beer Barrel.

~

"Here, try this."

"What is it?" Willem lifted an eyebrow at Shane. Willem had shown up at NorthStar days earlier. Shane, Tomas and Franklin had taken one look at him, the M'Fiyah asserted itself and now things were going well. Shane had made barbecue for dinner, and Willem, elf that he was, had never heard of it.

"Come on, taste it. Trace loves it."

"Where is he?" Willem cared very much for the tall werewolf, although he'd only seen him a few times.

"Working at SouthStar. It's the off-season, and he and Trajan are doing the pruning, fertilizing and other stuff that has to be done in the groves."

"Where are Galaxsan and Celestan?"

"Guarding Teeg."

"Ah."

"Come on, you're just stalling. Take a bite of this or we'll hold you

240

down," Shane grinned.

"Really?" Willem looked hopefully at Shane.

"You're taking all the fun out of this," Shane chuckled.

~

Breanne's Journal

I smelled vampire the moment I misted inside The Beer Barrel. It wasn't our murderer, though. This vampire I knew—from the future. Radomir had come; the Vampire Council had sent an Enforcer. Radomir had the same idea I did—hit the college hotspot to see if the rogue showed up to pick a target.

The place was nearly full, even with the warnings. Granted, most of the patrons were male, but several were there with girlfriends. Laptops were everywhere, with glasses of beer or other drinks sitting nearby on scarred tables. It looked exactly like I'd always imagined a college hangout would.

Those young men probably thought the same as Hank—that they could protect their women from any murderer. They had no idea what might be stalking their girlfriends, just as Hank had no inkling what might be hunting me.

Honestly, I wasn't sure who was hunting me, either, but I'd seen their handiwork. Destroying four million lives with a sandstorm in Targis, after wiping Beledweyne off the map? That was more than frightening, and I still wasn't recovered enough to repeat my trick if they decided to do that again. I might be able to do a little, but nothing on that scale until I was rested.

Misting behind Radomir, I followed him as his broad shoulders worked their way through a small crowd ordering at the bar. Likely, he wanted to ask the bartender questions. Strangely enough, if Radomir hadn't tried that tactic, I wouldn't have found him. He was human, there was no denying the scent. He also bore compulsion. For the moment, however, he was intent on ordering a beer.

I knew two things about Radomir. One, he would become a member of the Saa Thalarr in the future. Two, he would also protect

Ashe Evan's secrets in the future. For as long as he could, anyway. Compulsion from a sire would always hold precedence, but Radomir was more than honorable.

Radomir, I spoke into his mind. Yes, he had latent talent, but it wasn't reliable. Somewhere in his past, he held a smidgen of Elemaiyan blood.

Is someone there? He wasn't expecting to hear mindspeech, or to be heard when he sent back. I heard him perfectly.

Yes, I replied. *The young man to your left—the one in the red T-shirt holding out a five-dollar bill? He has had compulsion laid.*

"Show yourself," Radomir growled low. Well, I'd started this, and he was right not to believe just anybody.

"I'm right here," I said, touching his shoulder lightly. I lowered my shield so he could smell what I was, too.

"What?" He turned swiftly and stared—an unusual reaction from any vampire older than four hundred, and he was certainly older than that.

"He's had compulsion laid," I nodded toward the young man, who was still waiting for his order to be taken by a very busy bartender.

"You're vampire," Radomir growled.

"Yeah. And your target might be getting away unless you do something."

"You're hunting the killer, too?"

"Oh, yeah," I huffed. "I killed the rogues in San Francisco and D.C. Now I want this fucker, too."

"Bill Jennings," Radomir began.

"I'm working part-time with him. You should keep that quiet, by the way," I added.

"The Council doesn't know you exist," Radomir muttered, beginning to take me seriously.

"I understand that. Right now, that doesn't matter. Lives are at stake, and I want to save them if I can," I pointed out.

"I will retrieve this young man. You will follow me," Radomir placed compulsion. Well, as usual, that didn't work, but I wasn't going to tell him that. I followed him quietly as he ordered the young man to come with us. The human trailed us right out of the bar.

"Tell me who he is," Radomir commanded, his voice dripping with intense compulsion. All three of us sat in the back of a rental van while Radomir questioned our prisoner. Still thinking I was under his compulsion as well (he'd told me to sit quietly while he worked), Radomir proceeded with the interrogation.

I'd already read the young man before Radomir got started. He didn't know the vampire's name—he only had a location. He was supposed to pick up a girl at the bar and lead her in the vampire's direction. Likely, that's what the vampire's usual plan was, and he'd selected other young men to lure away his victims.

This one had been instructed to take the girl to another bar, pick a fight with her and then leave her there. The vampire would arrive, place compulsion, the girl would then leave by herself and meet with the vampire later—for blood drinking and murder. The whole thing chilled me.

What I did get from the young man was a clear picture of the vampire's face. Dithering for a few moments while Radomir received the same information I'd already gathered, I took a chance and inserted the vampire's image into Radomir's mind. He was an Enforcer—perhaps he'd recognize this one.

"Tanner Johns," Radomir growled before jerking his head in my direction. "You are quite talented. I will defend you before my father. Come, we will find this rogue and dispatch him, first."

More compulsion was laid on the young man—to go back to The Beer Barrel and forget he'd seen either of us. He climbed out of the van and wandered away.

We now had an address for another bar, and Radomir entered that on a GPS while driving. I didn't point out how dangerous that was— he was vampire and he hadn't said I could talk again. Let him keep thinking his compulsion worked. Things were much safer for both of us if he believed that.

The Coconut Lounge was a much classier bar than The Beer Barrel. By a long shot. Radomir never knew it, but I shielded both of us as he cleared a path for us inside the bar. He was tall, dark-haired and had a Middle Eastern ancestry, much like his older vampire sibling, Flavio.

Although he never scented us, Tanner Johns obviously recognized Radomir. He'd been sitting alone at a small table in a dark corner, watching everyone who walked into the bar. Radomir scented Tanner immediately. Tanner was up instantly and running for the door, Radomir flying after him.

～

"I have a location for the shapeshifter, my liege. Shall I eliminate?"

"As quickly as possible."

"Thank you, my liege."

～

James Rome, Sr. studied his chief staff attorney. He'd brought a galley of the book to Marshall Earls, because Ross Gideon had made a suggestion. James thought it a good idea, too, and wanted his attorney's opinion before proceeding.

The pale title of the book splashed across the dark photograph used as the book's cover. The photograph still stood out, no matter how you looked at it. And once you looked at it, you couldn't draw your eyes away. It was the horrible accident you couldn't help but stare at, time and again.

"I agree," Marshall shoved the book across his desk toward the elder Rome. "Turn a galley plus all the evidence over to the FBI and let them get started on this. If you wait until the book's published, anybody still out there and involved in this has time to run. Let the authorities start their investigation now. When is the planned publication date?"

"Two weeks."

"That's a head start, at least. I don't have a problem with that. There could be if the major players in this weren't already dead, but since they are," Marshall sighed and shook his head. "I think this may be one of the worst things I've ever seen."

"I can't believe nobody reported it," James snorted.

"Power and money," Marshall observed. "Power and money."

Breanne's Journal

Tanner was fast. Radomir was older as a vampire and catching up, but Tanner still had the lead. The chase ended up on streets and alleyways in a nearly deserted downtown Austin. Tall buildings clustered around us as Radomir raced after our quarry. I went to mist and did my best to get ahead of him, but he kept zigzagging between multistory buildings and other businesses closed for the evening.

A fierce wind had kicked up, too, making it a cold, December night in Austin amid canyons of glass, steel and concrete. I misted through a narrow, back alley, where a few bits of leaves, trash and debris rattled against a steel doorway in a small alcove. A Dumpster lay just outside that doorway, and the brief scent of spoiled food flew past as I continued my pursuit.

That's when it hit me—I could mist straight through a building instead of going around it. *Keep following him*, I sent to Radomir. *I'll try to get in front*. Well, he hadn't said I couldn't send mindspeech. Blasting through the building, which held offices and a restaurant on the lower level, I blazed toward the building's far corner—my quarry would have to get to that point before changing directions again.

With only a blink to spare, my mist cleared the building. Becoming corporeal, I lowered my shoulder right in front of Tanner and caught him in the midsection. Two things happened, then—I was knocked flat on my back and Tanner flipped high into the air from the collision. Radomir, showing absolutely no surprise, arrived and removed Tanner's head as he fell.

Tanner's head rolled next to where I lay gasping for breath, and I stared into eyes going lifeless before the rogue vampire flaked. What I saw before he died terrified me. He wasn't the only vampire rogue in

Austin—two more had come, prepared to take up where he left off, should he be killed.

It was an intelligent move by the one placing obsession, and Tanner had certainly been obsessed. In San Francisco and D.C., there'd only been one vampire loosed on the population. They were hedging their bets, this time.

"Are you all right?" Radomir lifted me off the ground. I was still struggling to breathe normally, and coughed a few times before I could speak again.

"I'm fine. Tanner there," I pointed my head toward the flaking body, "has friends. Two friends, to be exact, and they'll take over the killings as soon as they learn their buddy died."

"You cannot be serious." Radomir's dark eyes bored into mine.

"I can. You have to believe me on this."

"This is untenable," Radomir sighed. "Did you get names? Never mind, that was a foolish question." Well, he didn't know how my curse worked.

"Oscar Forde and Keir Arthur," I muttered. I couldn't read the actual obsession in Tanner's eyes, but his thoughts had turned to his two rogue buddies, who'd exact revenge for his life. He'd also expressed his satisfaction for even more girls dying. It wasn't hard to put it all together.

"I have no idea how you're doing this," Radomir muttered. "Do you know where they are?"

"No. They weren't with him where he stayed, and I have the idea they aren't together where they are, either. Did Tanner have a cellphone?"

Radomir toed the pants Tanner had worn—they now lay on the ground, saturated with Tanner's ash. "Here it is." Radomir rummaged in a pocket, pulling out the phone. At least it had been protected from ash where it was—Radomir didn't even have to dust it off. He pulled Tanner's wallet and keys, too. No need to leave that stuff lying around for somebody to find.

"I expect you to help track these others, as they are also rogues hunted by the Council," Radomir informed me.

"Then let Director Bill know you're here," I countered.

"Very well," Radomir sighed.

"There's something else you should know," I said.

"What is that?"

"I don't fry in daylight, Bill Jennings doesn't know I'm vampire and I really need to get back to the hotel."

~

Radomir insisted on driving me back to the hotel, after I argued with him for a few seconds about its necessity. Both of us knocked on Bill's hotel room door, and it wasn't difficult to see that Bill knew Radomir when he opened the door.

"Radomir, I had no idea you were in the area," Bill invited us inside his room. He was still dressed—and working on his laptop—when we interrupted him.

"Breanne," Bill added, "I thought I told you to go to bed early."

"Best laid plans," I shrugged.

"We only got the first rogue," I informed Bill later after he had drinks sent up by room service. Poor Radomir pretended to sip coffee while I had a tall glass of orange-pineapple juice and Bill had a martini.

"Tanner Johns," Radomir supplied the name of the vampire he'd dispatched. "But Breanne tells me that the other two, Oscar Forde and Keir Arthur, are waiting, should their fellow rogue fall."

"Not good news, and I've learned to trust Breanne," Bill nodded. "This doesn't sound good at all. How soon do you think they might discover that Tanner's dead?"

"I have his cellphone," Radomir pulled the item from a pocket and handed it to Bill. "There are several unidentified numbers on it."

"I'll have a trace run," Bill said. "Bree, go to bed, you're exhausted. Let me talk with Radomir for a while."

"All right," I sighed and rose. "Good night." I walked out and closed Bill's door softly behind me.

~

"That young woman is extremely unusual and very rare," Radomir began as Breanne's footsteps faded.

"You don't have to tell me that," Bill grumped.

"Where did you find her?"

"She volunteers for Mercy Crossings, as an interpreter. There isn't a language she doesn't understand. Somehow, because there are still too many questions and few logical answers, I believe she's responsible for getting me out of Beledweyne alive."

CHAPTER 15

*B*reanne's Journal
  Baby, I hope you slept last night. Hank sent a text—it waited for me after I got out of the shower at seven.

It's 5am there, I texted back. *What the hell are you doing up?*

Late night, plus a few repairs in the bathroom had to be done.

The unisex bathroom/dressing room?

Yeah. Somebody got a little feisty and broke one of the faucets.

OMG. My imagination just ran wild.

Probably not wild enough, Hank texted back.

You know I'm not gonna get that out of my mind now, I tapped.

You just made me laugh. Baby, why aren't you here right now?

Honey, we got the guy last night after I talked to you. Bad news, though, there are two more.

You went out after you talked to me? Breanne Hayworth, I have no words.

Is that a first?

I think my temper is about to explode. It's probably a good thing you're not here. I'll talk with you later, after I cool down.

Well, nothing like being in trouble with Henry Hank Bell, I guess. Tossing my cellphone onto the bed, I went to find something to wear.

249

~

"She said they got one guy, but there are two more," Hank informed Jayson during their morning workout at Jayson's gym.

"How deep was she in all of that?"

"Probably in the middle of it."

"You think she has a death wish?"

"I don't know what she has. She's giving me heart palpitations," Hank grunted, throwing out a punch. "We probably should change the subject."

"I heard from Dad's legal department this morning," Jayson said, ducking Hank's blow. "They're sending a galley of a book that Dad and Ross Gideon are rushing through the process. Didn't tell me what it was, just said they wanted to give me a heads-up and to look at the mailing as soon as I received it."

"Does that happen often?" Hank stepped away from Jayson's punch.

"No. I don't recall ever getting a galley before, unless it's something to do with an article in the magazine. Nobody's said anything about a connection, so I have no idea what it is. Guess I'll find out. It surprised me, though, to hear that they're putting something else in front of Everett Williams' bio."

"How soon will you get it?"

"Said they were mailing it out today."

~

Breanne's Journal

"Here are the photos from Radomir," Bill slid two pictures across the breakfast table toward Opal and me. I let Opal take them—I'd already seen images in the dying eyes of a rogue vampire.

"So you got to work with a vamp last night?" Opal turned unblinking eyes in my direction. Yes, she was asking a silent question for which I had no answer. No good answer, anyway.

"Yeah," I muttered and lifted the obligatory cup of coffee to my lips.

"I'm upset that you went out without telling us," Bill scolded. I could tell he was worried for my safety, but I still hunched my shoulders uncomfortably.

"I know," I mumbled after swallowing a mouthful of hot coffee. "I won't do it again."

"Bree, if something had happened, how would we have known where to start looking?" Bill wasn't done, yet. "Granted it turned out well this time, but what if it hadn't?"

"Bill, I'm sorry," I muttered. "I know what you're thinking, but I've had to fend for myself for a long time." I didn't add that I'd been responsible for others, too—most of my life. That was my past. My future looked much the same. I was in a position to do something; therefore, I felt obligated.

"Look, we'll talk about that later," Bill sighed and went back to his menu.

"What are we doing today, since suspect number one is now flaky?" Opal broke the uncomfortable silence between Bill and me.

"We'll try to track the other two. Didn't get much of a lead from the numbers on the first suspect's phone," Bill said. He hadn't lowered his menu to answer, which meant he wasn't looking at me. I sighed and dumped another sugar packet in my coffee.

"Do we know where the first suspect was staying?" Opal asked.

"Yeah." Bill dropped his menu to stare at me when I made my admission. I'd gotten it in my reading the night before—I'd known the other two weren't staying with Tanner—they'd separated on purpose.

"Well, maybe we ought to go there first," Opal said dryly.

"Breanne," Bill's menu went up again, "We really will talk. Right after breakfast. Opal, find something else to do for half an hour after we eat."

"All right."

Shaky might best describe how I felt as I followed Bill back to his room. He was likely going to yell, so I kept my shields up and tight; I didn't want to read what he intended to say. He opened the door and pointed me inside. I went. The door closed behind us. What happened next I almost can't describe properly.

"Bree," Bill jerked me into his arms and kissed me—hard—"you scare the hell out of me." He kissed me again, just as hard. My face was in his hands, and they were large, nice hands, his face inches from my own. "Your sister died from caring too much. I can't begin to tell you how it will kill me if you're lost, too."

"Bill, I don't intend to be lost," my voice wobbled and I was afraid I might cry. I couldn't hurt Bill like that.

"Sweetheart, you need to tell me when you go out. I could have gone with you. I would have gone with you." He pulled me against him again, tucking my head beneath his chin and rubbing my back with gentle, soothing strokes. My arms stole around his neck and he sighed against my temple.

Tanner Johns' hideaway wasn't much—a metal bunker sunk in the backyard of a two-bedroom house. The house was furnished but empty of occupants, and lights were wired to a timer to turn on and off according to their programming.

The bunker was equipped with a small lamp, a narrow bed, a tiny table and a cube refrigerator. The fridge held no bagged blood, so Tanner had been drinking from the population.

"This is frustrating," Bill sighed. We found very few personal effects inside the bunker—mainly clothing, shoes and a few receipts for the same items. As Bill had Tanner's wallet in his possession, he already had copies of credit-card charges. Obviously, Tanner paid cash for drinks or anything ordered in the bars where he'd placed compulsion on college girls—just in case anybody made a connection.

"None of the phone numbers panned out?" Opal turned dark eyes on Bill.

"Four were for disposable phones, and we have no answers and no locations," Bill shook his head. "We're back to the beginning, and it's anybody's guess when and where the next murder will happen."

"Did any murder happen last night?" I turned to Bill. "Anything we might attribute to Tanner?"

"Do you think that's what his associates will look for—whether a murder occurred?" Bill's brow furrowed as he considered my question.

"You made those calls on Tanner's phone, didn't you?"

"Yes—didn't want to spook anybody."

"Maybe a death is the signal that all is well in rogue vamp land, then," I shrugged.

"Let me check on that. I'll send a team in here, but there's nothing to find," Bill said.

"Where are Joyce Christian's twins now?" James Rome Sr. sat at a table in a Los Angeles restaurant. He'd invited Ross Gideon to the exclusive eatery for lunch.

"They're in a very good private facility, since no relatives were willing to take them in. Been there for two years. They have Down Syndrome," Ross replied.

"I remember. Is there any evidence that they were abused?"

"None that I can see, but I couldn't get into their medical records."

"How old are they?"

"Nearly thirty."

"So Breanne Hayworth took care of them until she disappeared—is that right?"

"Looks that way. Money is donated through her charity to keep the twins where they are now—if she hadn't done that, they'd have gone to a state-run home."

"Where did Hayworth's money come from?"

"Lottery winnings. It's all public record."

"So she's still taking care of Joyce's kids. Do you understand how ironic that is?"

"I haven't failed to see it."

"Is there any information about where the twins are in the book?"

"I didn't put it in—I figure that can be a follow-up for the paper."

"Good idea. Have you written the article, yet?"

"Half done."

Breanne's Journal

Somehow, whenever I attempted to *Look* to find anyone with an obsession, I always drew a blank. I felt something was protecting them; whether it was the Sirenali's talent or something else, I couldn't say.

Opal and I stood inside an ice-cream store, waiting to get a cone. Bill had gone back to the hotel to catch up with the electronic portion of the investigation while Opal and I took a short break. Her cellphone rang as we stepped up to the counter.

I half-listened to Opal's conversation with Bill while I ordered for both of us; Opal liked chocolate chip ice cream—I'd gotten that in a brief reading. "We found a likely candidate we can initially attribute to Tanner," Bill said.

"Is the word going out?" Opal asked as I handed the cone of chocolate chip to her. She gave me a nice smile before going back to her conversation with Bill.

"It's on all the local stations—breaking news," Bill replied.

I handed money to the server after getting my strawberry ice cream and waited for change.

"You think our targets will buy it?" Opal asked. That was our worry—whether Tanner's rogue buddies would believe that Tanner was still alive.

"I'm hoping. The woman was a little older—twenty-seven, but she was a part-time student at the college. Local law enforcement knows who did it and they have the suspect in custody, so it's just a convenient lie for now."

"Thanks, Bill," Opal sighed and ended the call.

"So we may have a day and a half—if they buy it," I sighed as we sat at a small table near a window.

"Yeah. And nothing to go on," Opal agreed. "We can still talk to the roommate like we planned, but chances are it was a different human and all of it leading to our already dead rogue."

"Yeah." I bit into my strawberry ice cream and let it melt on my tongue. Ice cream was still such a treat for me, and I appreciated it every time I got some. "Do you still have those photographs? Of the other two?" I asked.

"In the car."

"Maybe we should ask the roommate if she saw either of them. Just in case."

"Not a bad idea."

"Director Jennings, hold for Director Kelsey, please."

Bill was surprised to be getting a call from the FBI Director. Local agents were working with some of his people, but they'd had limited success at getting any information. Frankly, Breanne and Opal were doing a better job than the army he and the FBI had on the ground in Austin.

"Jennings? Dan Kelsey, here," the FBI Director said.

"Yeah, Dan, what's up? Any new information?"

"Not on your project, no," Dan replied. "What I have is information on one of your special agents—at least that's how she showed up in the database."

"Which one?" Bill hid his worry immediately.

"The new one—Breanne Hayworth?"

"Yes?"

"Don't worry, she's not in trouble, but you need to see information that was just passed to me on a former Texas politician."

"How is Breanne involved in that?" Bill asked.

"A victim. In the worst way you can imagine. It's a book that will go public in less than two weeks—the author came across evidence and wrote a book, releasing all the information he found. The major players are deceased, but we're looking into others who might have been involved. We'll make arrests if that turns out to be the case. I wanted to give you a heads-up—I get the idea that Ms. Hayworth may not be aware of the scope of this material, and you may want to give her a leave of absence to deal with this."

"What? How quickly can you send this to me?" Bill asked. As concerned as he was, his worry just ramped up dramatically.

"Drop by the local office in Austin—I'll have the book and the photographs transmitted electronically. Be prepared, Bill. It's not pretty."

Breanne's Journal

"Have you seen either of these men?" Opal handed the two photographs to a twenty-four-year-old grad student. We'd caught Dana Yarbrough as she was getting ready to go to her temporary job at a local department store.

"This one looks familiar, but I can't remember where," Dana tapped the photograph of Keir Arthur. He was the better looking of the two vampires, with dark-blond hair and deep-blue eyes. Most women would look his way, actually, so I wasn't surprised that Dana might remember him if she'd seen him before. Compulsion notwithstanding, of course.

"Do you ever go to The Beer Barrel?" Opal asked.

"Once or twice a week," Dana shrugged.

"Do you think you might have seen him there?"

"Hmmm, maybe. He sure would have stood out, but every time I've been in there lately, I've been pretty focused on my paper. I usually sit in a corner and study or work on my laptop."

"Is there any other place you may have seen him? Maybe at your job or something?" I asked. Dana turned to me, then, as I asked my question.

"Oh, my gosh—I think that's it. Yeah—I saw him trying on jackets in menswear," she said. "Leather jackets. One in black and one in brown. I just see so many people in there, that it didn't come to me until you said that."

"Do you remember when you saw him?" Opal asked.

"It had to be last week—it was late at night, and I haven't closed since last Thursday."

"You think that's when you saw him, then?"

"Yeah. I think it was. Usually I get off around eight, and this was just before ten."

That's when I decided to lower my shield and read her. Dana was pretty, with thick, dark hair that swept her shoulders in a blunt cut and large, lovely brown eyes. Certainly pretty enough to capture a vampire's eye, and I was shocked by what I read in her—Keir had drunk from her. He'd waited for her in the parking lot when she got off work, placed compulsion and lured her to his car.

He used her as a donor, I sent mindspeech to Opal. *I think we should have her watched.*

"Dana, can you tell us anything else about him?" Opal took the photograph back.

"That's all I remember. Is this Amy's killer?"

"We don't think so, but he may have information," Opal hedged.

"Oh. If I see him again, I'll let you know," Dana offered.

"Good. Call immediately, no matter where or when," Opal said.

"Thanks for talking with us," I said.

"Breanne, I wish I knew how you come by some of your information," Opal started the rental car and put it in gear.

"It's weird," I said. "I can see it in their faces, at times."

"That is weird. And very helpful." Opal backed out of the narrow driveway and headed toward our hotel. We needed to meet with Bill and have agents watching Dana by nightfall.

Bill wasn't at the hotel when we arrived; he said he was doing something at the local FBI office when Opal called. He did say he'd get some agents there to tail Dana and watch for Keir, in case he showed up again. Opal and I decided to stake out The Beer Barrel as soon as night fell. I had a feeling we'd be hearing from Radomir, too, but that wouldn't be until dark as well.

~

"Mr. Rome, hold for Bill Jennings, Director of the Joint NSA and Homeland Security Department," Jayson's assistant informed him.

"What?" Jayson sputtered. He didn't have time to protest; Bill was already on the phone.

"I hear you managed to convince Breanne Hayworth to sign a release for photographs and other information," Bill began immediately.

"What's this about?" Jayson snapped. "We're doing a magazine article on Mercy Crossings."

"That's not all that's going on," Bill accused. "I just saw a copy of a book your father asked Ross Gideon to write on Joyce Christian. When I contacted your legal department in Los Angeles, they informed me that you convinced Breanne to sign the release."

"What book?" Jayson demanded, before going completely still. "What book?" he asked again, worry creasing his forehead.

"A book on Joyce Christian, and how she was buying children from a church-run orphanage to help with her young twins, only she ended up torturing them. She killed two out of three she adopted, that's what book," Bill's voice became aggressive. "Now you're telling me that you lured Breanne into signing that release on the promise of an article on Mercy Crossings? If I learn you've misled her, I'll have you investigated."

"Oh, my God," Jayson's hand scrubbed his face. "That's what the old man's been up to. Look, all I knew about was the article on Mercy Crossings. That's it. Dad wouldn't say what he's been working on lately, but I did get a call from the legal department, saying they were sending a copy of a book that I needed to look at."

"Somehow, that hack procured photographs of Breanne when she was young—maybe fourteen, handcuffed in a dark closet, naked and unconscious. Experts tell me her wrists are broken, her face is battered and the rest of her body is either black with bruises or scarred from previous abuse. The journal entry I saw from the one taking the photograph says a golf club was used to inflict the damage done in that photograph. Other beatings are also described, with whatever Joyce Christian had available. Frankly, I don't know how Breanne is sane or able to walk nowadays."

Jayson rose from his desk and cursed. "Look, I didn't fucking know about that," he said. "I didn't. I was only asked to do the Mercy Crossings article. I had a photographer and a staff writer take pictures and do an interview—only about Mercy Crossings. I had no other agenda than that. Investigate my father if you want, Director Jennings, but I had nothing to do with that."

"You still got her to sign the release. How about I investigate Rome Enterprises as a whole? I can assure you I'll have it gone over with a fine-toothed comb."

"I'll call my father, but I can't say it'll do much good," Jayson muttered, sitting again. He knew his division was clean, but he didn't work with the other publishing branches. "You say she was tortured?"

"Yes. Extensively. As I said, two others—a fifteen-year-old girl and a sixteen-year-old boy, died from the same treatment before Breanne was adopted at the age of ten. Joyce put her to watching her twins, who have Down Syndrome. Whenever something happened in Joyce's life that she didn't like, she had a ready scapegoat—she tortured children who weren't her biological offspring. The whole thing is completely horrible."

"Were the two deaths reported?" Jayson asked.

"No. We have some evidence that the bodies were buried on the Christian Ranch in Western Texas, but they haven't been located, yet. There are photographs of the bodies before burial, however—the one taking the photographs wanted to protect himself in case Joyce ever turned on him."

"Where is he now?"

"Dead. Self-inflicted gunshot wound, but he was dying anyway.

Left a journal and the photographs behind—sold them to Ross Gideon's private investigator, Bob Sullivan."

"Sullivan." Jayson shut his eyes and leaned back wearily in his chair. "The old man was with Bob."

"I'll be asking your father questions, just as soon as he responds to my multiple phone messages," Bill growled. "I'll have my department contact you from now on."

~

"Hank, come to my office." Jayson called Hank the moment Bill Jennings hung up.

"What's going on?" Hank asked over Jayson's cellphone.

"I'm about to have the legal department fax copies of photographs to me. I think we both need to see them," Jayson muttered.

"Photographs? Of?"

"Breanne. Hank, please hurry. I'm not sure I want to see them without you here."

"On my way."

~

"I can assure you she doesn't know," Bill covered copies of photographs with his hand—he couldn't bear to look at them any longer. "I just spoke with the person who convinced her to sign a release—he swore it was for a magazine article on Mercy Crossings, not for this."

"The housekeeper has moved to Ecuador, and the veterinarian is in Venezuela," Dan Kelsey replied. "I hate that the girl will be broadsided by this. Any number of people could have reported this and gotten immunity from the department."

"Politics," Bill huffed. "And money. I'm assuming you read the part where she was siphoning money from her campaigns to pay her personal expenses?"

"Yeah. I'm having her records subpoenaed from her former

attorney's office—he managed the funding for the care of Joyce's twins, only that went dry two years ago. He made sure he got paid, though, and was ready to send Joyce's twins to a state-run facility. Ms. Hayworth has her own attorney paying the private facility where they're staying now."

"I see. Do I understand correctly that the name Hayworth is from Joyce Christian's grandparents?"

"That's correct. She didn't want them to have her last name, so all three adoptees were given the name Hayworth."

"What happens to the estate?"

"In the hands of the attorney and a realtor who's trying to sell it, but taxes are owed on the property. We'll go in to look for those two bodies, so the sale will be held up for a while."

"I don't know how to tell her about this—and I have to tell her. She can't see the headlines in the papers and on the news—it'll destroy her," Bill sighed.

"What's happened to her already should have done that. I don't understand how she's survived. The photograph at the back of the book—in the Mercy Crossings uniform—looks really good."

"She looks better in person. Dan, I need to call you back. I have to plan how to present this to her and make it easier for her, somehow."

"Understood. If you need any help, or if she has information to share on possible collaborators, let me know."

"I will. Thanks for the warning, Dan."

"No trouble."

"This is awful. I've never seen anything like this." Jayson turned the copied photograph over, he couldn't bear to look at it anymore. "They tell me this is the book cover."

"Rome, this will kill her. That bitch failed, but your father might succeed." Hank was furious, his eyes going completely dark.

"Look, I didn't know. Mom didn't know, either. What do you think this will do to her? She just got over a heart attack. Fuck. No wonder

Breanne ran like the devil was after her when she saw my handcuffs. She kept saying she'd met the devil. Here's the evidence." Jayson slammed a fist on the photographs lying on his desk.

"Rome, do you have a number for Director Jennings? I want to talk to him. Somebody needs to approach Breanne carefully with this. I have no idea what she'll do when this is shoved in her face."

"I'll ask my assistant."

~

"Director Jennings, this is Hank Bell."

"You're the one Breanne listed as the person to call in an emergency," Bill replied immediately.

"She did?"

"Yes, when she filled out her paperwork," Bill said. "I'm assuming you spoke with Jayson Rome after I called him earlier."

"You've had her checked out." Hank's voice was flat.

"Completely. It's standard protocol."

"Understood. Look, you can't just shove that in her face—we'll lose her."

"You think I haven't already considered that? The thing is, the longer we hold this back from her, the worse it'll be."

"Agreed. When do you plan to tell her?"

"In an hour or so, when I get back to the hotel."

"Try to hold onto her," Hank sighed. "I just don't see this turning out well, no matter what."

~

"Wait here. The shapeshifter should return to this room shortly," the lieutenant informed his assassins. "Take her head and you will be rewarded."

~

Breanne's Journal

Bill found us in the hotel coffee shop, and I could tell something was wrong the moment he sat.

"Breanne," he began, "I want to speak with you again—in private. I have news, and I'm afraid it isn't good."

"What?" I stared at Bill in alarm. Yes, I probably should have waited to let him break the news as gently as he could, but I was frightened and fear seldom produces rational thought. My shields dropped immediately, and I saw it all. Rome Enterprises, Ross Gideon, the horrible, horrible book and the photographs. In my wildest dreams, I had no idea that Gus Fulton had taken photographs following my last attempt to run away.

I hadn't seen him after that, so there wasn't any way to read that fact in his face. I'd been too crippled to attempt to flee again, and I'd been stuck with the monster who'd bought me from an orphanage for two thousand dollars and no questions asked.

My hand over my mouth, I stood and stared at Bill for a few seconds—I read the pain in him at the knowledge of what he'd seen and read. Yes, he'd skimmed the book, but all those things I knew already. I just thought they'd never come to light—Joyce Christian had hidden her secrets well.

The realization of what this would cost me also invaded my mind —everybody would see the photograph of my tortured body on the cover of a book. Remembered horror made me tremble, and shame and humiliation made me want to weep. I folded space before thinking.

My cellphone rang the moment I landed on a south Texas beach. It was Hank. Well, there was no facing him or anyone else. Likely, Jayson had shown Hank those photographs—I knew from Bill's reading that he'd spoken with Jayson, and Jayson had denied knowing about the book beforehand. I had no idea whether that was actually true or not. Brushing tears away as I stared at the cellphone in my hand, I crumpled the phone in my fingers and flung it as far into the waters of the Gulf as I could.

~

"The location of her phone is in deep water," Bill barked. "I have no idea if she's with it. Send a helicopter. Immediately."

~

"She knows." Hank slapped his cellphone on Jayson's desk.

"Fuck," Jayson laced fingers in his hair and tugged in frustration.

~

"Opal, I don't know what to do." Bill punched the elevator button for his floor. "What if we don't find her? What if she's gone for good?"

"I don't know what to do, and without her, those two rogues are still loose." Opal blinked dark eyes at Bill. "I really like her, and I really like working with her."

"I know. I like her, too."

"Bill, you love her and you know it."

"Yeah. I know it."

~

Removing her keycard from a pocket, Opal inserted it into her hotel room door and turned the handle.

~

Lissa's Journal

"I feel cold." I did—I was shivering, and I had no idea why. It was warm enough inside my suite, and Drake and Drew were with me—more than enough to chase away any chill.

"Come to bed, baby," Drew coaxed, reaching for my hand. Drake was already sitting on the edge of the bed, waiting for me.

"Something's happening," I whispered, suddenly terrified.

~

Breanne's Journal

I could have done nothing. I could have continued to walk a Gulf Coast beach, feeling horribly sorry for myself and leaving Opal dead in her hotel room. I couldn't do that. My past ensured that I had no desire to tolerate injustice.

The moment the knowledge of her death hit me, I was mentally screaming and folding back to Austin. Her two assassins, still quite pleased with themselves, stood over Opal's bloody, headless body. I destroyed them first, then gathered power around me.

Yes, I was still angry—about Opal's death. About my past. About Rome Enterprises blindsiding me, cutting into my life and allowing it to bleed out for a sensationalism-hungry public. There weren't enough tears to heal my past. I had no idea if anything might do that. Holding my hands over Opal's body, I *Changed What Was.*

CHAPTER 16

reanne's Journal

Graegar tried to warn me, and perhaps I should have listened. *Perhaps.* Opal woke and moaned in the floor at my feet when prescience kicked in. Yes, they were waiting. The rogue godlings who'd managed to create sandstorms across universes, killing innocents and destroying everything in their path, had been waiting. Waiting on me to *Change What Was.* Waiting for me to expend that energy. It was a beacon to them, telling them exactly where I was. I had to move quickly or Opal, Bill and everybody else in Austin was in trouble. They wouldn't live over it, either.

"Bree!" Bill's voice sounded as I misted away—he'd burst into Opal's room, his sidearm drawn. I had to think fast or he'd be dead—likely in a matter of minutes from a sandstorm headed toward Texas.

As swiftly as I could, I turned to mist while Bill shouted at me to stay. Then, struggling to form a coherent plan, I folded space to the Moon and sent out a blast of power, just as I could do when *Changing What Was.*

Did I feel them change course, veering away from Austin and heading toward Earth's only satellite? Yes. There was a gathering storm behind me; that was easy enough to tell. I folded to Pluto, the

266

dwarf planet Hank and I had discussed during our first meeting, and sent out another blast of power. I was laying breadcrumbs for them to follow, and I felt their anger swell as their desire for my death increased. They strove to catch up with me.

Desperate, I considered what to do. I wasn't strong enough to take on all of them—I knew that. I blew out another blast of energy, just so they'd know where I was and keep following me. If they knew how badly they might hurt me, and that I'd turn back and take my final stand there with him, they'd have gone straight to San Francisco and attempted to destroy Hank Bell. They didn't know that, though, and I was more than thankful.

Would they follow me if I bent time, too? They were certainly locked on me where I was. I bent time ten years into the future. They followed like hounds on a fresh scent. Fifty years and still they flew behind me. It only made sense that they would do this—I'd given them a trail to follow and they weren't about to lose me now. I'd sealed the fate of everything and everyone, just by *Changing What Was* and giving a friend's life back to her. I worried that I'd run out of energy, too, as I still wasn't fully recovered from Tulgalan.

~

"Wake, Radomir." Radomir blinked—someone sat on the edge of his bed inside the Austin safe house.

"Who?" he began, but his question was cut short by a command.

"You will not recall her or anything about her. The time is not yet right for that." Radomir gazed into dark-gray eyes and watched as stars fell through their depths.

~

Breanne's Journal

I didn't know there was a limit on how far into the future I might go. Perhaps it had something to do with my present circumstances—the universes had come to a crossroads of sorts and where it might proceed from there depended upon my actions. I'd arrived in the Reth Alliance barely three months after I'd left Le-Ath Veronis behind. For my sister, little time had passed since my disappearance.

For me, more than two years had gone by, and many things had happened during that time. For a brief moment, I'd been happier than I'd ever been. Ever. And then a seemingly random sandstorm wiped away lives, I'd discovered Hank's secret and things changed.

The book, too, would destroy what was left of that life I'd so carefully built for myself. For two years, nobody knew my past, and I'd enjoyed pain-free days. I was able to shove it aside and not remember much of it. Now, even as mist or energy, it made me ill. I raced through the Reth Alliance, rogue gods on my heels, bent on my destruction.

Graegar had warned me. I carried the lives, good and bad, that inhabited all the universes, with me. How had this happened—that I didn't know this earlier? That someone, somewhere, didn't arrive like they had in all the stories I'd heard, to prepare me for this? It made no sense. None.

I recalled Graegar's words—that my statement to him that this made no sense led him to believe I wasn't the Mighty Mind. Well, where was the Mighty Mind, if he or she were so smart? Why weren't they telling me what to do to take care of the malicious army of powerful beings at my back?

Just like always, I was on my own.

~

"We've lost her. We've fucking lost her," Hank mumbled, his head in his hands.

"How do you know?" Jayson sat beside Hank on the sofa inside his office.

Without a word, Hank handed his cellphone to Jayson. A text from Director Bill Jennings was displayed. It read, *Breanne disappeared. Her cellphone in deep water off Texas Gulf Coast. No idea where she might be.*

"Fuck," Jayson sighed. "Fuck."

~

Breanne's Journal

Passing over Evensun, I saw it was empty. Information came to me, then, as to why it was empty. Rogues had been given bodies so they might create havoc among the created races. Lives would be bent to their will or destroyed. Planets would be overrun. Everything would be corrupted in a stunted, warped version of how it was supposed to be. I cursed those at my back and wished they'd never been made. *Twice*. And then it came to me.

~

Lissa's Journal

"She's in trouble. I know it." I thought my heart would beat its way out of my chest, I was so frightened.

"Baby, we have to wait this out." Drew held me, while Drake stroked hair away from my face.

"But what will we do?" I wailed.

"Hush. We have to wait," Drake soothed.

~

Reah's Journal

"Love, stop fretting. It can't be good for the baby. Your time is close."

"Edward, what will we do?" My tears dripped on Edward's shirt as I wrapped arms around his neck.

"I don't know. Surely it can't end like this. It can't."

~

Ashe's Journal

Even if I hadn't felt the edge of the knife everything balanced upon, Trajan's howling would have warned me. His wolf knew his mate was in danger, and there wasn't anything he might do about it. I wanted to weep. For him. For Breanne, who'd never stood a chance, and for all those whose lives could be changed in less than a blink.

My eyes remained dry as I gazed across miles of trees. Should Breanne fall, SouthStar might become an island in a very dark storm.

Breanne's Journal

What seest thou else, in the dark backward and abysm of time? It was from Shakespeare's *The Tempest*. I was tiring and the rogue army was gaining on me. If I were to make an attempt, I knew it had to be soon. Would it take me, too, if my scheme failed? *It doesn't matter* flitted through my brain. *They'll catch up to you eventually, and they'll take you anyway.* Now it was time to act. Time to see what I was made of. *Time.*

When I'd taken Cheedas from the dungeons in my sister's palace, I'd butted two timelines next to each other so the obsession might be removed from a later Cheedas by an earlier Erithia Cordan. Those two timelines hadn't stretched far from one another—only a matter of hours, actually.

This—this was so much more complicated, and I knew if I took time to think about it, I'd allow my pursuers to catch up and I'd be lost without a fight. I gathered every bit of power I could as I drew to a stop. The enemy would be upon me in less than six seconds. We were down to time. Again.

Li'Neruh Rath stood upon Evensun, watching the skies overhead. He'd sent Kifirin away—he wanted no company now. Things would fall or be saved, and he had no idea which way they might go. Fate was set on the thinnest edge, and he held his breath as everything slowed.

Breanne's Journal

Nearly every bit of strength I had was poured into such a small amount of space. Two timelines were butted together, and as I looked past the one I currently occupied to the other, a brief image of Saturday morning cartoons with Joyce's twins popped into my mind. One animated character would trick another to slam headfirst into a painted tunnel. Shockingly enough, the hapless character fell for it. Every time.

No animated characters chased me now. Murderers were at my back, and they'd arrive at any moment—to kill me. Pulling the last bit of strength I possessed, I sent a final blast through the opening and into the other timeline. Quailing invisibly at the edge, I waited for them to either follow the blast or discover my ruse. Either way, I had no strength left to leave this place. Likely I'd die anyway, but at least it would be my choice.

~

"Koop, do you ever feel as if you've forgotten something? Something important, that you ought to remember? Do you?" Trevor studied Kooper Griff as he sat behind the desk in his Casino City Sheriff's office.

"I was just thinking that, too. What do you suppose it might be?" Kooper watched Trevor's dark eyes as the old vampire's forehead wrinkled in thought.

"No idea. Every time I think I have it, it slips away. I usually forget about it, too, until it shows up again. Maybe I'll remember it sometime."

"Yeah. Maybe."

~

Breanne's Journal

I felt as if I were watching the swiftest race ever run, they flew past me so quickly. How they failed to notice me, huddled as invisible mist beside the portal, I may never know. They'd followed my last blast of power, just as they'd followed all the others, fully expecting to catch up with me after I tired.

Had I been corporeal, perhaps I might have felt the rush of their passing, as they left the current timeline where I was and passed into one where they'd never existed. I watched as their energy winked out once they reached the end of the tunnel I'd constructed.

Like a speeding train attempting to stop once it realized it was necessary, the force of the last few stragglers rushing forward drove all the others through to the other side and oblivion. There may have been half a million of them or more. Too many. All of them perished, once they went farther back than the earliest any of them existed. Yes, where I'd sent them, only the One—and the Three were. Where I'd sent them, they couldn't be. And they weren't.

Once all of them had passed through and their energy winked out, I stared into the tunnel. Briefly, I considered going through as well. There lay peace. Yes, my mist—my corporeal body—would be no more. Perhaps it would no longer matter to me that I'd been tortured, abused or betrayed. It wouldn't matter that a book had been written, and horrible photographs displayed. I wandered past the edge and into the tunnel as I gazed upon the promise of no pain.

Should I have expected it? It was the way my entire life had gone. The agony was blinding as I was struck—so hard I landed against a wall in my sister's palace, cracking my head against marble and losing consciousness as I slid down the wall. My last memory as darkness came was of shouting—shouting for help.

Who was it for?

I had no idea.

The End